CW01657929

The Stoney Collection
volume two

new stories & poems from 24 emerging Dublin writers

PC Studios
A PUBLISHING & MEDIA COMPANY

This is a PC Studios book

First Edition

ISBN 978-1-0687726-1-0

Publisher & EIC: Paul Carreo
Editors: Lorna Keane, Jamie Sampson, Ciara Campbell,
Thomas Waelkens, Emily Flaherty, Jack Kennedy & Ruairí McDonnell
Poetry Editors: Caoilfhionn Duggan & Sylvia Konstantinova

visit www.paulcarreo.com for more
PC Studios, a publishing & media company

For all you quiet storymakers in hiding, stuck indoors or stuck in your heads, we welcome you with open arms.

CONTENTS

Foreword

Writing half-decent stuff is hard. Really hard. Most writers concede it takes a load of inspiration (coupled with thousands of hours staring at a blank page). But that kind of inspiration isn't always found in the most obvious places.

You could spend weeks, months or years trawling through the work of all the greats only to wind up stuck in the same spot, or rehashing what's been done before.

This was one of the biggest reasons I created Stoney Writers Group. I wanted to get inspired by the work we don't always see.

By people who are constantly writing, and those who are barely writing.

By people who are getting published, and those who don't know the first thing about getting published.

By people who are winning awards, and those who aren't bothered about winning awards.

By people who can only write fiction, and those who are constantly experimenting with something new.

By people from different places, generations and cultures, with fresh perspectives, experiences and stories.

Because talent comes in many shapes, from the most unexpected voices – and we too often miss the best of it.

I found heaps of hidden talent like this (and an insane amount of inspiration) in this Dublin-based group of emerging writers. Some published, some not. Some award-winning, some not. Some desperate to perfect their work, others just enjoying the ride. Most seeking a platform to share their work – and a tribe of fellow writers that inspires them to just go ahead and put something out there.

Our first book, The Stoney Collection: Stories & Poems from Twenty-one Debut Dublin-based Writers, published in October 2024, packaged up a portion of this work. We hosted a sold-out launch event. We made it onto some of the most renowned bookshelves in Dublin. We got great reviews. But best of all, we got the platform we were seeking.

Fast-forward a year and here we are again with volume two. The twenty-four stories and poems featured in this year's book are richer, deeper, more personal - previewing a wealth of unseen talent that's been nurtured to a certain point. And that's what it's all about really.

The aim of Stoney Writers Group is to help emerging writers develop their voice in a space that's welcoming, inclusive and safe. A space where they can be bold - experiment with new things and take their work in exciting new directions. Or where they can focus - develop and enhance the stuff they like writing most. It's up to them.

Whether you're looking for inspiration, or just a chance to lose yourself in some bloody good writing, there's something here for you.

So here you go. Another collection of works from a truly treasured community of writers who constantly impress me. To say I'm proud to be counted among them is a total understatement.

Have a browse, take your pick, and sit and read a while.

Lorna Keane
Founder, Stoney Writers Group

Introduction

Cobblestone roads, stoney as they often go, are the thoroughfares that provide. They provide the promise of many forks ahead and they offer occasions of homecoming to tell our tales from afar. We cut a rocky path to come and to go, but it is at the divides where we decide to linger. Moments to sit and observe the moving world. Opportunities to mingle with other comers and goers. A chance to share our news, the dreams of ourselves and of new worlds, and the parables we weave around them. This is how strong communities gather and grow.

And this is how Stoney Writers Group has gathered and grown from a meeting to a mission. The mission is to celebrate independent writing by fostering a community of shared creativity. In that spirit, we welcome you back, dear reader, to our *Volume Two* ramble down the stony roads of storymaking, our book of new stories and poems from debut to emerging writers, all working to uplift each other for the betterment of the craft.

Publishing an anthology of stories from such talented and establishing writers is like hosting a street market along the cobblestone roads of Dublin's lively District 7. Tents pop up from peculiar vendors peddling their mystical arcana, huddled droves gather in wonderment, and celebration illuminates the open square. Before long, it's become a reliable tradition, one that nourishes everyone for the year.

Here the tradition continues, following in the footsteps of The Stoney Collection's first edition from 2024. Our second volume represents a leap forward for this dedicated neighbourhood troupe of writers, with over sixty members who meet regularly in

Stoneybatter and Smithfield, and whose emerging voices have grown stronger in each other's company. From Sunday workshops and monthly sharing sessions to moral support and tough love, we've spent the year honing what we believe to be some of the finest short stories and poems yet.

This year's authors and poets chose to explore a few common themes, from churning seasons of change to the shifting perceptions of self. In writing new stories for this volume, each took special care to give these themes their own unique dimension. Some harvested the colourful senses of fall and nature, others brewed toil and trouble with gothic haunts and dark romance, while a few mulled over spiced hints of fear and tragedy. Together, they stitched a cohesive look at the betrayals of memory and our primal urge to grasp at truth. The flow of the stories complemented each other so well, in fact, when lacing them together, I began to suspect our group had conspired behind closed doors to curate the order without me.

Alas, The Stoney Collection beats with our group's values of inclusivity and the sheer belief that all dreamers have a good story inside us. In keeping with this ethos, you'll see as before, each chapter puts the writer or poet first. Please take some time to get to know the contributors, as it's my privilege to introduce them to you. We've taken special care to order these stories in a way that feels like a natural progression to the themes mentioned earlier. After each writer's introduction, you'll notice a more detailed summary of their contributing work, as well as the common thread each story weaves together.

Regarding the order, the collection threads a needle throughout, beginning with the opening hues of autumn senses, nostalgia and change, before colouring in shades of longing, identity and memory. Aine's *Evening* and Emily's *The Blueberries Taste Great Here* set this stage precisely, complemented by

Angharad's poem (*One Autumn Day*), reflecting over turning seasons and enraptured nature. The blurry misleadings of nostalgia continue with William's *Apple Cider, Pumpkin Pie*, before introducing our gothic historical tales of cultural memory in Stephen's *Green* and Ruairí's *Sidhe.* Underscored by Sylvia's poems of longing and grief (*the cut, Armour*), we delve deeper into supernatural shadows of time and memory with Aayan's *Reflection* and Gabriel's *Persistence.* These illusory shadows of misremberings and fractured identity get a technology upgrade in Lorraine's *Six of Cups* and Jamie's *Good Egg*, balanced against Thomas' time-caper *The Clockmaker's Curse.* We then close out our section of fantastical worlds with the figurative ghosts of the past in Cormac's *Chapelizod* and Joe's high-court identity dispute, *Royal Blood.* Caolifhionn's poetry (*Heart's History, Reashore*) then beckons us back to the modern world while retaining moments of conjured perception and reclamation, while Ciara unsettles our senses and notions of nostalgia with *Daltonist?* and *The Harpist of Grafton Street.* From there, we loop back into blurry worlds of hazy indecision with Neil's *Town Frau, Country Frau*, before confronting feminine and masculine trauma with H.G.'s *When We Were Girls*, Chris' *Taking Inventory*, and Lee's poems (*Green and Blue, Man's Superpower*). Grief and unhealed trauma take on the weight of remorse through the cold crimes in Gary's *Dissonance* and Orlaith's *Old Plains.* And finally, we end where we began, turning back from autumn to summer stories, reflecting both a coming-of-age in Lorna's *Nell Bowen* and a lonely, severed past in Jack's *Uncaring Continent.* And although it's been a privilege to witness such a unified progression, what follows next is yours to explore and unfold.

As is our dedication to uplifting each other, an emphatic 'thank you' cannot be shouted from the high towers enough for all this year's volunteering editors. Thank you to all you inspired caretakers, my steady beating metronomes, my lifelines of sanity for a project of this scope. Returning to our board were Thomas, Ciara, Jamie, Sylvia, Caoilfhionn, and Lorna. We also welcomed Emily, Jack and RuairÍ to the squad, lending fresh eyes & inspired ideas. As you read through these stories, appreciate that a peer-to-peer editorial process is, in fact, the very fulcrum, core to what our group believes we can accomplish together. I know the writers felt the love, and you, the reader, will feel that same warmth come through.

Yes, we believe communities serve to lift each other up so we can share the best bits inside us with the world. Lorna founded this group and set the stage for a warm and inclusive session. The meeting turned into a mission once we put each other ahead of the stories themselves. Looking at the shifts of last year next to this year's anthology offers the shimming hope for more embraced creativity in all our lives. Looking at some of our community veterans, what they've shared in sessions and in the book, shows me how much we've dedicated ourselves to continuous improvement. Looking at the debut work, reminds me what magic awaits silently in us all, emerging in its own time when among trusted peers.

I personally have been made a believer that modern literature doesn't need to be exclusive or pretentious. Everyone has their own diverse voice and a superbly bright burning story waiting to shine. Find your own tribe, one that supports you for your differences, not in spite of them, and you'll find that story bursting out of you joyfully for all the world to enjoy.

Finally, this collection is a polaroid in time: sunfaded in memory, cherished on family bookshelves, and enduring as a precious heirloom linking us to where we began. These are the stories we dreamt of harvesting throughout the year, the pearls we polished as a team, the tiny frozen spaces that linger amidst rushing change. As the days turn, from another summer lost to the hurried holidays ahead, we invite you to press pause with this book and enjoy the fleeting relief of change, neither what was, nor what will be, but simply what is becoming. Turning from page to page, our greatest wish is that you find the same joy in these stories as we did in bringing them out of each other.

Paul Carreo
Publisher, PC Studios

Áine Ní Mhaonaigh

Áine is an established fiction writer with distinctive work rooted in modern Irish life and lyrical tones that evoke the spirit of Patrick Kavanagh. Her influences are wide-ranging, from Irish to Norwegian writers, and she cites Jon Fosse and Per Petterson among her favourites. Her work has appeared in journals including The Stinging Fly, and we are pleased to present her as a debut figure in our community.

We open our collection with signs of a season turning and the autumnal notes of her vignette, 'Evening'. As summer wanes, Cormac wanders through fields and village lanes, quietly bearing witness to the time's procession.

Evening

And it was the end of summer. Inevitably, a drawing close of everything. The mountain ash, blurting its red berries lush and outrageous, some of them already lying in a stained crush on the ground. Cormac always felt the same regret at this time of year, what it was he could not say, but as if, out of a loosely held cup, a golden nectar had been spilt in swift, uncatchable drops. Out in the fields against the August light lying wide and yellow over everything, he had watched the last of the harvest and listened to the sound of machines churning the air while birds made themselves scarce higher into the endless blue that was above and out wide at the tips of the headlands. In his hand, he crushed an ear of grain and felt the sharp compression of the small, close heads. A farmer's son, he was no stranger to the turn of the season, but still a part of him would always want to hold on to the moment. Slowly, he let the ear of grain fall from his hand and might have wished to change places with the old stump next to him, resting where one half of an iron gate used to stand. Later he drove in for the paper. Out in the gardens that led up to the church and the small shop that marked the heart of the village, he could see against the dipping cottage walls, the verbena still on their slow tilting wave, but beginning to purple out now, a darkening begun somewhere under their tiny petals, that admitted helplessly, a simple demise, a teatime of their long, supine lives.

Everyone in, everyone home they were saying, and the angle of the slipping sun was just as it was always at this time of year. Shadows of houses becoming longer and more drawn against the cobblelocked driveways, picking their way, stone by stone, until they reached porches and doorways, drawing them also into the strange florescence of the slow climbing shade. What would it be, Cormac wondered, not to notice all those slight alterations. Behind him suddenly, three children passed on the footpath, one on a bike, and two others running either side, waiting for their turn, attending their opportunity. Voices echoed, brightening for a moment the evening air. Cormac walked on, past low walls, past gardens, past small windows of houses lining the main street, overhung fully now in places with the murmuring branches of mountain ash that, from time to time, stirred a little in the late breeze, pixelating the light into small harmless red dots. Everyone in, everyone home now, sitting at their teatime tables, leaning across into each other.

Emily Flaherty

Emily is a breakout fiction writer and debut contributor to our collection. Her bold work grapples with identity, history, and cultural legacy, shaped in part by her time living and travelling in France. Her literary influences include Tom Stoppard, Donna Tartt, Rebecca Makkai, Alice Zeniter, and Curtis Sittenfeld. Occasionally, she'll even admit to reading Wikipedia summaries of horror films she has 'definitely not watched.'

'The Blackberries Taste Great Here,' continues our sensory narrative with reinterpreted memories and the meaning we craft through storytelling. From her days in France, Emily has believed there's a story we've all been telling from our youth. But what happens when you find that story is not quite true?

The Blackberries Taste Great Here

Then

You are told to retrieve the abandoned riding crop. In other circumstances, maybe you'd protest, but you don't. Antoine, impenetrable; his sunglasses watch you until you comply. Ellen stares at the ground.

Your palm scratches rust as you clamber the gate. When you drop, you nearly slip; the dead leaves, your poor choice of tennis shoes. Your feet make acute angles on the slope.

The enclosure is all slope really. You can only see its edges on the narrow side; lengthways it seems endless.

You are not scared of horses *per se*, but it would be too much to say that you are comfortable. The foals are spindly legged, fluffy maned. The sky above the treetops is very blue; everything smells of pine.

Just as you crouch down, hand outstretched, a sudden piercing shriek, animal or human, and, then beneath your feet, a rumbling, the earth shaking. But when you look up, it is not the ground that is shifting beneath your feet, it is the horses, all of the horses, running down the mountain. And you are just *there*.

Moving bodies, clouds of dust, running, falling, pummelling into each other, inches from you a giant beast caught in its own momentum crashes from one craggy shelf to another, lower, closer to you, cascades of pebbles and small rocks, and you stand there, still standing, caught in the rush of displaced air, dirt on your face somehow –

And it stops –

And it is only when you take a breath that you realise you have stopped breathing.

The forest is perfectly, disquietingly still. Undisturbed, like nothing ever happened. You hear birdsong. You turn then, this is when you turn, to look back at Antoine and Ellen, maybe to check they are ok, maybe to confirm what just happened, and this is when you see that they are gone. No sign that they were there at all.

You march back, stompy, aggrieved, mitigated only by frequent stops to hook down swathes of blackberries with the riding crop. You gorge in anticipation of sweetness, but most taste bitter.

Later, much later, in the bathroom in the tower, you find Ellen, stepping out of the shower in her towel, her face wet.

It is funny, because this is not the part of the story that you will tell people about later.

It is funny because this is the part where you could have died.

Now

You are in a hotel room near Charlottenburg, in what was West Berlin, now is just Berlin, and you yourself have now stepped out of the shower, examining yourself in a fogged-up mirror, smearing the condensation clean with your fingers.

A work trip. In and out; packed only hand luggage, no time to see the city, one free evening; you fly out tomorrow. And you are meeting Patrick. Haven't seen him in – is it fifteen years? Not since.

Anyway, you only messaged him on the off chance, because your friend who told you that you needed to get out there, said he looked cute in photos from years ago and if you weren't going to download an app... You rolled your eyes, but said you might message him anyway, to catch up. She repeated the words 'catch up', but she made air quotes with her fingers.

You told her the whole France story from years ago; she said it sounded wild.

Then

"He told me to sleep in a tent in the woods," Patrick says then, looking into the black, his cheeks dimpling, but he's angry.

This is how it happens; you never hear from Antoine directly. His words are recounted to you by others.

An evening after dinner, Patrick, Ellen, you, on the terrace that overhangs. Patrick is smoking, his hands and his cigarette dangling over the railing. If this were a graphic novel, you wouldn't draw the night that outlines his features – you'd just leave it blank, black, nothing. The valley is the night.

Ellen says that there's room in the tower. Then, separately, she remarks that the internet is down again.

Patrick says the router is in Antoine's bedroom; you wonder how he knows this, then *why* he says this.

You have been doing this for a while now; working on farms in random locales in exchange for bed and board, and maybe the promise of adventure. You have stayed in many odd places; this is not your first 'used-to-be-vaguely-a-castle'. Even by your standards though, the sleeping set-up is odd. You – that is, you and Ellen, the remaining girls, now Beth has left – sleep on the third storey of a three-storey small tower attached to the farmhouse. Patrick has always slept elsewhere. Now, apparently, in the woods.

The first storey, which is not the ground floor, is where the tower joins the rest of the house. Two doors – one to the hallway and one to Antoine's bedroom. Historical reasons relating to the patriarchal practice of maintaining the chastity of the property's daughters. Protection or control? Anyway, the door to Antoine's room is covered by a picnic blanket; you can't see the door, just the blanket, but you touched it once to make sure that it was real, and that it was closed. Technically it's Antoine and his wife's room, but no one has ever met his wife – she is in America. They tell you.

Ellen suggests why doesn't Patrick just sleep in the tower, maybe on the first storey, where Beth used to sleep.

It does not need to be said; none of you will mention this to Antoine.

A cushy number in many ways, what little work you and Ellen do is mostly limited to feeding the horses and goats twice a day. Patrick works digging trenches with an iron crowbar. Other times, he scythes fields. Sometimes he takes his shirt off, and you watch how his shoulder blades contract.

Breakfast and lunch you eat together, just the three of you, leftovers and bread and lots of jam. Dinner, Antoine makes, and you eat it in mostly silence alongside Antoine and his mother, who dresses like a Sicilian Widow, all in black wool even in the heat. They speak in a French that you don't understand; it's the old tongue, you learn, a language not dead but almost; one tongue silenced for another. French, unofficial subjugated for French, official.

With the internet spotty, and no phone signal because of the mountains your free time passes, wholesomely.

From above, from where the house is perched, the valley is seemingly untouched, just forest and rocks and mountains, until the peaks turn blue in the distance, but when you go down into it on hikes that turn vertical, you find traces of long-ago human settlements; stones don't grow in wall formations.

You play cards; you win most games, sometimes Patrick beats you, but Ellen never does. One time, she teaches you a game, and of course you win on your first try, and you can tell she is disappointed. You pretend that winning doesn't matter.

Patrick plays you music on his iPod. One afternoon, the three of you lie out in one of the meadows and you listen to the entire

Rumours album. He tells you that this is *definitive, era-defining, educational.*

You and Ellen are nineteen and twenty; Patrick refuses to tell you how old he is, and this becomes a running joke, but he's older for sure. He instructs you on what spirits you should drink with what mixers (rum and coke, or rum and rye, but never rum and soda). Also, stories of his life, like that time he had sex with a cougar, his word choice, and afterwards, she was gone but she'd left money – like *for* him – and he took it. This was when he first moved from Berlin to Barcelona. He has shoulder length dark hair and long eyelashes.

Ellen asks, so what, you just took her money? Patrick musses her hair and says that she is so cute, adorable. He touches her more than he touches you, but who's counting? He rubs antiseptic into scratches on her knees, but you also have cuts and bruises.

Ellen shows you photos of her friends, her two dogs, her grandparents, floral arrangements, sunsets. The part of Ireland where she is from is pretty but in a boring kind of way, which also you feel describes Ellen. When you return home, several weeks later, and you show you mother photos that Patrick took of the two of you together, you and Ellen, your mother will say immediately, oh she's *much* prettier than you.

But also you are already tired of waif-like delicate females whose vulnerability endears. This one time you tell Ellen that rabbits eat their own progeny, and she actually cries. You're not sure whether you'd prefer this to be some performance of femininity or her actual personality.

Though maybe you're not so immune yourself to the ways and means of self-production; you don't tell them about studying law or when you do, you gloss over it. Because you don't want them to think you're boring or alternatively because you don't want them to see you're ambitious.

But anyway, at the time it irritates you, how much Patrick and Antoine seem to be so protective towards Ellen, or maybe a better word is *attentive*. So, when Antoine asks you to retrieve the riding crop that day, the day with the horses, it's no coincidence that he sends you and not Ellen. And it's no coincidence that when you report later to Patrick that you nearly died, he is also more concerned about Ellen, because she was gone for a while.

You ask Ellen what happened and you don't listen to the answer.

At some point it was found, the green dress that started it, in the pile of clothes left by past seasonal workers, those who came before you, passing through between here and there. Abandoned discards and left-behinds, a pile of denim. And then the dress.

Ellen holding it out against her slim body, her blonde hair static-ing on the silky material.

"Who would bring this to a farm?" she says.

The question is almost too obvious to ask. You debate as to whether it is a ballgown or a cocktail dress; it is long, strappy, glamourous, descriptors completely incongruous to farmwork, mountains and mulch.

"Who would *leave* it?" you quip.

Because as strange as it is that the dress is here, that someone brought it here, it's even stranger that it is left behind.

Patrick says, "Maybe she never left!"

You laugh, Ellen blanches, Patrick smirks.

You say, pushing it a little, "That's why you're digging that trench!"

Patrick says, "I mean we haven't heard from Beth since she left."

Ellen says, "Guys! Stop it, guys!"

Initially it's fairly standard as an in-joke: the girl in the green dress is buried in the flower beds. Her bones are in the meal you feed the horses. Quickly you graduate to the obvious next stage, the obvious implication, though oddly you don't dwell on this, or not verbally – in this joke reality – Antoine murdered the Girl in the Green Dress. Because. Because he's a serial killer. TV tells you there are serial killers everywhere, so why not here? He lures girls here with horses, because girls like horses. Etc.

Patrick likes to scare Ellen; she gets all nervy and he smiles. You notice him watching her; subsequently, you avoid looking.

It doesn't help that you *still* haven't heard from Beth since she left; it doesn't help that before she stepped into Antoine's van, she pressed into your palm a ball of paper with phone numbers of taxi companies in Florac.

It doesn't help that Patrick, for once serious, tells you to watch yourself around Antoine, and when you ask, just says cryptically: "Beth said things."

It doesn't help how isolated you are; Florac is six hours on foot. No phone signal (so much for the list of taxi companies). No internet, and the router is in Antoine's bedroom, a fact frequently mentioned but not discussed.

It doesn't help that Antoine has a habit of appearing, as if from nowhere, wherever you are. It doesn't help that, well, there's no other way of saying this, he's just a *little creepy*. You've never seen his eyes under his dark glasses. His presence arouses tension: Patrick stops joking; Ellen makes herself small; you find yourself watchful, alert.

To get away from the others and that odd tense mood that descends, you find a field of long grass to lie in, and you take in the endless sky and the blue and orange flowers that grow up around you, and you close your eyes in that pleasant sleepy heat that makes your hair hot to touch, and when you open them Antoine stands over you.

You keep making jokes, but it stops being funny. You become more aware of your surroundings; you only make jokes when you aren't in the tower, or when you aren't near open doors, or when you aren't near a patch of woods from which Antoine might emerge.

You have no idea what is happening anywhere in the world, your world has shrunk to this place.

You are unloading damp clothes from the washing machine.

Your back to the door. You hear – nothing. When you turn around, Antoine is regarding you. He has removed his sunglasses; his eyes are very small. A punnet of blackberries.

You nod to each other, and you make some gesture towards the washing machine and your basket as if to say 'ah, laundry', and you think that is going to be it, that he'll be on his way, but he continues to stand there, looking at you, and you don't really know what to do. To continue seems impolite.

He asks you something, but his words don't catch, and you shake your head, and with each repetition he steps closer, and you notice both his physical closeness, and your own instinct to retreat from him, except behind you is the washing machine.

T'avais peur?

He is asking if you are scared.

You feel your adrenaline kick up a notch, your mind is jumping to conclusions before you click that he is asking you if you *were* scared, that's it, *were you scared of the horses that time*, and conversation makes sense, inwardly embarrassed at yourself.

No, you say, and it is a lie, but for some reason, it is important that you do not admit fear.

He looks at you, and you see him look you over, and then he laughs, and you wonder if you should laugh, but you're not sure what the joke is. Is the joke that you were too stupid to be scared? Or is the joke that he knows that you were scared, that he knows you are lying?

He tells you that you like blackberries. He has noticed that your lips are often stained purple. You have that odd feeling you get when you realise that someone has been paying attention to your details.

And then, he reaches into the punnet, and snags one single blackberry and holds it up to your lips for you to open and swallow.

You wonder later if you eroticised the moment. Is it inherently sexual to place food in someone else's mouth? You remember that old film, made by that director who was also a convicted rapist, where the villain fed the victim, who was the quintessential literary victim, strawberries and then later quote unquote ruined her. With sex, obviously. In old books, sex is a bad thing that happens to women.

Anyway, in this moment, it is necessary that you do not permit this. You feel this on a very primal, basic level, maybe from that same instinct that told you to lie about being scared. You reach up and prise the blackberry from his fingers, and then you place it in your own mouth. It never occurs to you to refuse.

Instead, you thank him. Say the blackberries taste great here.

You aren't present for the next bit – so where are you?

Maybe it is immediately after the encounter in the laundry room, and you are hanging your damp clothes on a clothesline, and one of your socks catches in a sudden gust and blows off the edge of a cliff, and you scream into the valley and no one hears you.

Maybe it is another time, when you take your phone, and walk the length of the driveway, the gravel crunching, and when you reach the road, you hold your phone high above your head in different directions, but no signal. On your return, you remember the way the house stands against the valley, blacking out the sun. The chill as you step into its shadow.

Or maybe it is another time, again. A vacuum of time unaccounted for.

Crucially, you aren't there when Antoine discovers that Patrick has been sleeping in the tower, kicks him out, and then calls Ellen a slut for good measure. You enter in the immediate aftermath, when Patrick is shoving his stuff into his backpack, and Ellen's body is all tight, and neither of them can explain.

It crosses your mind: were they hooking up? The thought stills you. But even if, what does it matter? You certainly do not care.

"All I'm going to say is he really doesn't want me in the house, whatever that's about," Patrick spits, as he brushes past you, leaving.

Even at the time, the words strike you.

You wonder absently if Antoine used the word 'salope' or 'pute'. They both mean 'whore', but only one is the one you pay for.

Now

Still pretty, Patrick; the years have been kind. He takes off his sunglasses and hangs them in the 'v' of his t-shirt; glinting back the bar lights.

He asks what you're having, and when you order a cocktail, he calls it a 'woman's drink'. He tells you he loves his kids but not their mother, "Just to be clear I'm not still with her," he affirms, and you don't know what exactly to say to that. His eye contact is just *there*, every time you look at him, he's looking at you, so you consciously regulate your own, dilute the intensity, playing with the straw and the ice-cubes of your 'woman's drink'.

That song from *Rumours*, and you mention it to him, *remember when*. You feel the smile on your face, you see your smile on his face, and for a moment it's that flick switch, connection. Patrick says: "See the problem with modern music –"

And you *are* interested, but he completely dismisses your completely valid points about the Britpop of the nineties, the indie bands of the noughties, breezes past, just keeps talking as if you haven't said anything. He uses the words: *definitive, era-defining.*

You quip: "Educational?" There's a joke there, but he doesn't get it, he says, he literally says, with a particular tone you can't identify: "I can still educate you."

In that moment, you don't respond immediately, a quiet ebb in the bar's surround sound, his words hang there, and maybe it's the silence that makes it awkward, rather than the words themselves. But then he says: "You're not going to be offended now, are you?" before segueing into how everyone is always offended these days, no offense or anything. He drinks his gender-appropriate beer darkly.

You decide you are not having that conversation.

"So, the Antoine thing." A pivot. You half-laugh for a semblance of lightness, "An overreaction, surely?"

Then

A hand on your mouth. Eyes open to blackness. From sleep to screaming consciousness –

Ellen's voice, the way it splinters – *downstairs, someone.*

Listening to the darkness –

Buildings drum their own noises, truly, pipes and floorboards and fridges, they creak and pitter-patter and drone, you remember this from when you were a small child and the radiator frightened you, *something* you hear is not *someone here* – your ears catch sound, sounds; multiple, unmistakable, arhythmical, *here*, seconds later, *there*, this is not the static of stationary objects, this *is* –

A reasonable explanation, surely, scenarios in your head, in the film he slit her windpipe, she made that awful sound that wasn't a scream –

Light would alert, feeling your way, the mattress, the floorboards, slow, careful, *quiet*, Ellen whispers, protests, the opening in the floor, dark, terrifying, until you close in close, still dark, but brighter than expected, eyes catch some surface gleaming reflected light. From downstairs. Someone has – someone *is* –

Somehow lowering yourself onto the ladder, the rung is *not* there, all of you jittering, you –

"Hello?"

Patrick's voice.

Another rung and you see him. Curled in a sleeping bag, illuminated by his tablet.

Relief hits you like a stomach-ache. Downstairs, you push your feet into the floor to stop shaking. Ellen talking rapidly; Patrick explaining.

"We just thought –" You feel stupid.

Ellen says: "We need to leave."

Hissing, whispering, still in shadow, how much time has passed, a conversation that goes round.

"Tomorrow," Patrick says, "He's driving me anyway, I'll be with you the whole time."

But she is shaking her head. "Now," she repeats.

Patrick asks if you'll stay; you're asking yourself the same question.

"I'd prefer not to leave you here with him," he says, and you like that.

The conversation flips; you, increasingly less convinced about staying on alone, Ellen and Patrick insisting, persuading.

"Ok, I'll go with you!" you say, and it feels right.

Patrick and you agree; wait till tomorrow, the lift.

Ellen says: "You think he'll let us all leave?"

Narrow corridors, tight corners, squeaking hinges and floorboards, this door is locked, but maybe the one in the kitchen. Consider smashing glass; Patrick manages to unstick a door. Warm night air and cicadas, and gravel, crunching and unsteadying, is that a light, Ellen says, and you run then, that is when you run, all of you, not looking back even once and you are so incredibly loud.

Picture this: a road through the mountains on a moonless night. Or try to, anyway – because you can't *see*. No streetlights, no aforementioned moon: only the circles cast by phones.

Sometimes, the road dips and flattens, the silence muffles, and the air is fresh with pine, you think: *trees*. You know the forest is there, or it should be there, you hope it's there, even if it does mean that yes, you are walking through a deep dark forest in the middle of the night, except the alternative is the edge of the mountain, the precipice.

Absence of smell, air that feels colder, steepness and sharp bends – you cannot see the precipice, even if you point your phone all around. You just know it's there. Sometimes.

Belatedly, when Patrick puts half a foot on nothing, and then crouching on the road, confirms, yes, that's the edge, yes, we nearly walked off it, you are hit with the dangerous stupidity of your decision.

You are three dots of light in the night and Ellen's phone is dying; you are the people who did not bring a single bottle of water between them for a six hour hike through the mountains; you are all of your body parts that hurt; you have absurdly only beef jerky and blackberry jam; the jerky makes you thirst, the jam you eventually consume despite having decided not to because you don't have any spoons, passing around the jar, scooping it into you with your fingers, sticky; you fear any number of things: mostly the precipice, death or permanent injury, also Antoine, car beams, the noise that you hear around you that starts, stops and starts again; you are two dots of light in the night; the terror of being a single dot; you are a rucksack and a wheeled suitcase that you swear is dislocating your shoulder, and also you are blisters, bleeding; when you stop to eat the jam, Patrick says that it was still the right call, and the term 'pussywhipped' jumps into your mind; after he nearly walks off the side of the mountain he uses an umbrella to confirm the ground is there; you think: at least he's going first.

The sun rises, eventually. You are still on the road.

And not long after that, as the valley opens out like an Eden, you encounter a drinking fountain. A small metal box, a gushing spout, a glass tumbler neatly rinsed and upside down in a corner. So perfect, it feels like a trap, a fairy tale temptation you will pay for, once you drink of it. But you drink anyway. Quench your thirst.

Not long afterwards, you pass two more water fountains, and two sets of early morning hikers, wearing proper shoes and with proper hiking sticks. Then a third set of hikers. It transpires this is a famous and well-serviced walking trail, inspired by a famous writer's famous travels with a donkey, apparently pioneering the art of travel writing. The only thing you take from this is: in this night of thirst and terror, were you constantly passing water fountains?

The sky is blue when you reach Florac; your story trails off in little endings – the bus out of town, train station goodbyes, the long wait in departures.

Loose as you are with your stories, this one you will tell again and again for a time, over beers in college bars, in the kitchens of house parties.

In the telling, it changes. Elaborations, exaggerations. You do not lie, in the sense that you do not introduce untruths. Certain absolutes: you do not assign to yourself the vague bad things that you heard happened to Beth, you heard happened to Ellen. The blackberry incident never features, though tangibly, it was the only thing that happened to you. It is, you decide, too tame, or maybe too dismissible. And you have come to learn that if one element of the argument can be dismissed, it weakens the foundation.

The story is told by you, and as you tell it, so it becomes about you in a way. Everyone you know has a travel story about a creepy encounter, a near-miss, and so to differentiate your own, you play up certain elements. Both rational terror and irrational bravery are not very interesting, instead your story becomes about 'us and them' mentalities, the danger of groupthink, turf wars between men, and aren't you just so intelligent, so articulate?

Over time, you acquire new stories. You live through a period of history that you experience as a series of job interviews, coffee breaks, TV box sets, Sunday brunches, haircuts, familial obligations, morning commutes, boyfriends and not-quite boyfriends, unfulfilled aspirations, and things you buy that disappoint you.

Anyway, this particular story becomes one that goes untold. Not forgotten, but more you have no reason to tell it. There are other things to say.

Now

In your flannel pyjamas, in your hotel room, remembering, reliving.

The *look* on his face.

You didn't *know*, you had reiterated, not for sure, not the details.

How the conversation had flipped, him righteous, you defensive, trying to make him look at you.

"I don't think it matters," Patrick pronounced, "whether he explicitly threatened her or whether she was just scared."

Detailing body parts used, he told you, about that one time in the woods, and how afterwards, she had all these abrasions, her knees, her hands. The way things catch on skin.

Now, rubbing creams into your own hands, greasing the creases of your fingers, a memory, unbidden, the smell of antiseptic, Patrick reassuring, Ellen wincing, and you, looking on.

You were just a kid, you tell yourself, turning off the light. Even as you swim in memories, you feel the gulf between the child that you were and the adult that you are. You remember the fear, but it feels alien to you. You are perfectly safe and warm and comfortable, in your hotel room bed, ensconced in luxury behind an auto-locked door.

That's not quite true; you feel disturbed. You realise, as too warm, you kick back the bed covers, that it has been preferable to believe that you were just stupid kids, overreacting.

Preferable to thinking that in reality, you brushed up against a predator.

And you have been telling the story wrong, all this time, and this too troubles you – not that you didn't know the things that you didn't know – no, what bothers you is that you didn't understand the nature of the story you have been telling.

Not used to being wrong, an uncomfortable feeling, and is it this that makes it impossible to settle, the complimentary hotel water already drunk, too hot in your pyjamas, the sudden lamplight too bright for your eyes, the window that won't open, because that's how they design hotel windows (fall-proof, suicide-proof), the city lights blurry in the rain, thoughts and images and half-remembrances, spooling and unspooling with meaning, real, projected –

That one time in the woods.

The smell of pine. A sky so blue above the treetops it hurts your eyes when you crane your neck to look. A riding crop lying across the long grass. Horses running down a mountain.

And like a lens refracting your vision, in and out of focus, or an old camera reel, choppy, blinking, Antoine and Ellen, there, Antoine and Ellen, gone, you remember now, it comes to you, they were meant to be there, but when you looked back, only trees, woods, forest.

And you think questions beginning with *if* and *when* and *while* –

You remember now. A scream in the forest.

You remember now. On your way back, you were eating blackberries. Under dappled light.

Angharad Williams

Angharad is a Welsh-Irish journalist based in Dublin. Her work, published in both English and Welsh, has appeared in titles including The Sunday Times and The Irish Independent. A keen hiker who grew up in the Welsh countryside, she often draws inspiration from nature with wild terrain and stunning vistas.

She returns to our collection with two poems that follow our tour of autumn into stormier weather. 'One Autumn Day' *captures a moment of seasonal beauty in the natural world, while* 'Souls in Stormy Waters' *embraces the wildness of the Irish Sea, drawn from the memories of her many ferry journeys between Ireland and Wales.*

One Autumn Day

One day in October I take in the view,
slowly breathing in the cold autumn air.
The changing colours of trees, fields and bracken
create a tapestry of beauty I cannot describe.

The leaves have turned brown and quiver in the wind,
circling and dancing until they rest on the ground.
Yet there is still life beneath these fallen leaves,
life busy preparing for harsher months.

The breeze picks up and I pull my coat tight,
despite the feel of the October sun.
The dried, crisp leaves tumble down paths,
resting again as the world becomes still.

There's the song of birds that I do not understand,
preparing to take flight for their migration.
I envy their journey and what they will see,
before they reach their lush promised lands.

Angharad Williams

I sniff as the cold kisses the tip of my nose,
the sweet scents of summer now gone.
Smells of soil and wood become overpowering,
as nature reclaims all that is dead.

I lie back and look up to the sky,
some blue just visible behind the clouds.
Days are shorter but full of value,
as nature puts on its colourful display.

As the sun descends the land is bathed in light,
ablaze with reds and golds of sunset.
Such a sweet way to end the day,
crows roosting as I make my way home.

Souls in Stormy Waters

Thunderous winds sway a ship heading to port.

White sea foam creates a trail behind the stern.
Deafening waves break on the bridge and hull.
They hear creaks of metal with each slight turn.
Then some silence for a moment during each lull.

Fearful faces seek comfort in the relentless sea.
Clearly sick from motion and longing for land.
This ship battles on through whatever will be.
Not the journey any of the passengers planned.

Blanket clouds flung wide hide the moon.
The salty wind rumbles on with a low roar.
Those on board will the storm to end soon,
as it continues to shake each one to the core.

Feet face towards home waiting to step on land.
There is silence from the souls on board.
Some pray and stare at each wrung hand,
asking for salvation from their lord.

Then talk begins as lights are seen ahead.
People stumble as they try to see.
Relief and joy replace the fear and dread.
Delighted someone heard their anguished pleas.

This journey is one they won't forget.
Now life seems to continue just as before.
Until they reach land there is still some fret.
But for now the storm will rage no more.

Now in dock there are tears of relief and joy.
Time for family as their journey finally ends.
About their ordeal some of them are coy.
But, they share tales of their new ship friends.

William B Wood

Paul Carreo seems to think he's a publisher first and a writer second. His alter ego William Wood, however, strongly disagrees. William is a rambling satirist caught between two nations, his work leans American with splashes of Irish and world wandering.

Apple Cider Pumpkin Pie is an autumn-in-New-York tale of the slow formation of self and the pitfalls of nostalgia. In these troubled times of pining for a better tomorrow or stewing over misremembered yesteryears, this allegory is a reconciliation of our life stages, nudging us off the barstool to confront the day.

Apple Cider Pumpkin Pie

Between two spaces of what was and what will be is a churning liminal space. A season of inbetweens that tugs your gaze from scaffolds to sidewalks, from leafy canopies to the squish of the fallen. There are many occupants living in this frozen forever. Fresh mums blooming through dying wildflowers. Dry-aged aspen leaves clinging defiantly against the wind. An early frost melting in the last lashes of the siren sun. And you live there too. Darting between city crosswalks and neighborhood borders, spending a Sunday morning at the edge of Monday and a weekend wasted.

The sidewalk stench of New York's summer rot fades, giving way to the redolence of crunching leaves. There is no sound, other than the soft wanderings of brunch crowds strolling slowly. You're weaving through them like a commuter with somewhere to be. At twenty-five you're always feigning somewhere to be. Zigzagging aimlessly down Murray Hill through Washington Square, you're on a fast approach to nowhere. Every step edging you closer to tomorrow's cluttered inbox.

This crisp fall day is lost on you. The only seasons you see turning are the changing neighborhoods and the slippage from morning to afternoon. You find yourself muttering aloud, "Is it too early for a drink?" Is it ever?

The Indian summer is piercing your eyes with smoky sunglare. You want to spoil this splendid day. Like a sick day watching Star Trek in bed, or a dorm room binge on Call of Duty. Or perched on a bar stool in a small college bar, elbow to elbow with the old locals, playing the part of a day-drinking barfly. Among fellow bar dwellers, retreating into something without dread or regret. A space of no troubles, like you used to feel.

This craving consumes you, the longing for a hideaway dive with a classic jukebox. And before you know it, your feet make a new plan. Striding a straight line through the cross-streets of

Greenwich, deep into the pit of the Lower East Side. Past the boutique shopping bags. The glitzy nails, holding loud speakerphone calls. Past the dreadlocked vapers sitting on their skateboards, scowling at consumers. Past the fathers crouched on one knee, caramel apples dribbling in their hair as they tie their crying kid's shoelaces. These aren't your people. Searching for the crossroads between anarchy and conformity, you find your tribe inside Iggy's Lounge.

You glide past this mosaic of swirling people, escaping through the swinging red door where the breeze follows you inside the musky tavern. Ornate stained glass cast dancing prisms across the walls scribbled with glowing graffiti. You pull up a barstool at the corner and unsling your waxed messenger bag as your fingers fumble past old gum for a coat hook. A blunt inscription is etched into the wood by your elbow: *Sato was here*. You're sitting here now, waiting for the barkeep to spot you past the row of grumbling locals.

She's busy flirting with a quiet, vintage-clothed man in his fifties. She's stretching herself long over the bar and playfully lifting his chin out of a tattered dime novel. She's at least fifteen years his junior, wearing her lost dreams of fashion school with retro thrift clothes, freshly seamed and stitched. Horn-rimmed glasses and pink silk button-down, torn off at the shoulders around her full sleeve tattoos, and tied in a knot above her pierced belly. She's unaware of her fading youth, salty but still capable of catching the side-eye of her regulars. She seems to prefer the quieter man and the way he takes off his reading glasses to look deep into her eyes.

You never expected to envy an old man, but you can't help staring subtly through the smudged barback mirror. He sits apart from the rest, letting her whisper in his ear, and nodding to whatever she seems to be apologizing for. She pecks his cheek gleefully and turns sharply on her heels to swagger your way. She's in front of you now, shifting to her tilted hip and biting her bottom lip expectedly.

You panic and glance down the row of locals and count up an assortment of empty pint glasses, shot glasses, cigarette packs and over a dozen hard cider bottles. They're all drinking their own brands of beer, but the bald freckled man at the end keeps insisting on buying rounds of Magners. Perhaps it's the man's reminder of his youth in the motherland. Perhaps it's the only taste of autumn he could think to share.

Apple cider is hardly the image of hard boozing you'd expect from this lot. You want to order cheap beer like Pabst Blue Ribbon, but no – this would mark you as a hipster. And you don't want to disappoint the barkeep tapping her foot. So you order a cider loud enough for the others to hear. You pause briefly and add a shot of Fernet to the order. The 'bartender's handshake,' so you've heard. Something an older, classier coworker once told you at a company party. She looks you up and down and decides to allow it.

You get a long pour from her, as you spot the cracks of her makeup around her otherwise dazzling moonpool eyes. You're hypnotised by an alternative future, dating a woman so bohemian punk, so abrasively beautiful. Someone worlds away from your corporate bubble. Someone settled in the subculture who could ground you. Someone who would really see you and the fake laugh you affect with your coworkers. You could never bring her home to mom of course, or dinner with your boss. A perfectly settled bartender, full of pepper, littered with body piercings and signature tattoos. It would never work.

Then she winks at you and you melt. She pours herself a Fernet too and clinks your glass before turning on her heel back to her suspected boyfriend. You flash a wink back but don't feel quite as cool. You're a toddler wearing his cool uncle's sunglasses. Your smile is a little too oversized, too eager. She's leaning over him, tucking a streak of grey behind his ear and whispering in it. The envy rushed back over this image of a refined man, so settled in his own skin. A western denim shirt and clean fitting chinos, tucked into motorcycle boots. A stickered MacBook and an empty coffee cup traded for a pint of Guinness. Or was it a Zero?

He catches your eye in the mirror and you flinch, grabbing your shot glass as cover. You wince a little as the rush of hot licorice syrup washes down your throat. Get it together for god's sake, this isn't spring break, the old men are watching. "Ahhh," you should exclaim. Pretend you needed this. You're not an alcoholic, just one in training. Drinking the way you were taught to drink from independent movies and detective noirs. Assuming the slouched position at the bar you were meant to, swirling the glass and gazing into it like the abyss of all your sorrows. It's rehearsed despair, not the real thing. That would come decades later.

These patron refugees know real pain. They're clutching their pints to stave off the withdrawal tremors. You're clutching your pint to stave off last week's performance review. You rise up to pump some quarters into the jukebox. They're putting on classic rock songs from the 70s, from before they had property taxes and child support. You're putting on grunge rock songs from the 90s, from when your biggest problems were finding a soulmate and finishing exams. One of them yells at you for selecting Nirvana, and the other winces when Smashing Pumpkins queues up. You take your seat again, a little closer to the crew. At least you can all agree on Bowie.

The trim older man seems to be packing up now and your envy fades again. He's not part of this tribe, perhaps he used to be. But now he's leaving a half touched pint and shuffling on. Where's he going, so content? Does he think he's better than you? What secret is he hiding behind that coy smirk? Part of you wishes you had somewhere to be that could be more important than flirting with this barkeep. The other part of you would rather settle in here forever. You turn your attention to the locals instead and you barnacle yourself beside them. Forgetting for a time what's ahead of you. Ruminating on glory days gone by for the rest of the afternoon. And every Sunday since.

The mirror doesn't just reflect you, it reminds you. And before long, without noticing, you're looking back down the bar from the other side. You look over your tattered paperback at the old familiar faces. Mikey, Tommy, Bobby, Mick. You could recite their names in a jingle as they file in like clockwork, always in the same order, to their assigned stools. You could recite their drinks and cigarettes just the same. Scattered glasses of cheap draught beer, packs of cigarettes and vape pens, empty shots of Jack, extra glasses of ice for the cider. Mick must've won a scratch-off, he's backing them all up with extra bottles of Magners faster than they can choke them back.

The young man with the familiar face in the mirror seems eager to break the ice and is having one too. That people-pleasing eagerness of youth. So recognizable – and so thankfully left behind. At least he had good taste in music. He got yelled at for putting on Nirvana and Smashing Pumpkins. Songs that you would've put on yourself if you wanted to lose yourself on that barstool all afternoon. Everyone here plays what transports them backwards. Mikey plays The Stones, Tommy plays The Clash, Bobby plays Kiss, Mick plays The Pogues. Thank god we all agreed on Bowie.

Mick is buying another round and includes the kid this time as a peace offering. You aren't offered one but he nods and acknowledges you all the same. In a local haunt like Iggy's, everyone strikes an ecological balance over time – who wants to talk and who wants to be left alone. Iterations and iterations of clunky small talk. Those seasons of becoming a regular, getting sloshed together, giving each other life advice, wife advice, job seekers advice. Those shit-faced late nights, figuring out who's an honest friend and who's just a reliably unreliable drunk. Hot breath confessions, turned to angry politics, turned to months of silence.

Seasons of staying away from Iggy's at certain times, on certain days. Seasons of going off the drink for months on end. Seasons of settling back into these compromised routines. Rituals of nursing your Guinness 0 in disguise, reading and writing on a Sunday and flirting with your on-and-off again girlfriend behind the bar.

You know why they're here. For the same reason you can't stay much longer. Of all the other seasons, none stunk with sulking quite like autumn. Nostalgia is that dark illness that seduces you to seek safety in stewing. Seasons of music and better music before it. Seasons of market bubbles and bursts, 401ks and welfare checks. Seasons of elections for your guy, then their guy, blueberry pie, then pumpkin pie. They can keep their pie, you can't sit here and grow fat on ruminations of the past any longer.

The day is ticking away and you're at risk of breaking your oath. You've made your amends for last night, you've read the paper, you've finished the chapter you said you'd write today. You've had your tight and tidy Sunday morning.

Your old sanctuary of Iggy's Lounge will soon be waning to younger crowds. Piling in for the ironically cool and cheap Pabst Blue Ribbon. Soon the jukebox will reek of corrupted old classics, fouled by fist pumps and woo girls. It's not their fault. You were young and obnoxious once too. In fact, you yearn for the freedom to be imposing and indulgent.

Like that young man you catch spying on you through the back mirror. He sticks out like hard gum, striking a pose, pretending not to notice Linda's thong line. This dive smells of those days, so unsettled in your skin, so panicked with life. You come here to take one breath of yourself, in those days when you celebrated being a beautiful disaster. The young man's face resembles your own, creaseless and smoothing over someone terrified. That old familiar Monday dread. Something you couldn't say you missed. You want to tell this yesteryear man to quit that job he obviously hates, to stop living between the divide of Peter Pan and Wall Street. College alumni tee shirt and cargo pants on the weekend, white collars and chinos during the week. You want to tell him the secret of being at ease with yourself. But you don't want to spoil the surprise. He'll find his way to where you are eventually. After he's wasted enough time finding no answers from that barstool where you used to sit. Someday.

You've shaken those bad habits a long, long time ago. So remind yourself now not to linger, to pack up before you're tempted to join Mikey, Tommy, Bobby, Mick. It's one thing pining for lost days. Another to be lost in pining. And you have no patience left for the misrememberings of all those seemingly better yesteryears. All those false promises in how to stall, how to forget, how to delay the turning world. None of them balms the pain better than what you've found. The peace in persistent forward motion.

You slide a twenty to your girlfriend as you fold your laptop to signal your morning work's done. She leans in for a kiss on the cheek, and you pull her lips closer for a full one. She lets you. All is forgiven, you'll see her tonight.

The young man is still stealing a glance, disguising his envy. When you were him, years ago, you'd rather have a splitting hangover until Tuesday then take a chance asking her out. When you were him, you'd probably love knowing the secret to getting through the week. When he finally becomes you, you'll have had enough of barstools and stewing. Only then, will he find what you've found. Closing the circle with a clean habit-chain, motion without friction.

You sling on a cashmere scarf and give the familiar young man a knowing nod in passing. You both have the same brown leather sneakers on, yours just a little more scuffed. On your way through the red door, you bid him good luck. Leaving them all behind as you unchain your bike from a streetpost. Leaning in the sun-washed streets of a closing farmers market, it's practically wagging its tail as you hop on and pedal onwards.

Somewhere between the fading deciduous and the rotten detritus there is a liminal space. An inbetween of aromas from candied apples and funnel cakes where you dare not linger. The overhanging tree boughs are swaying in the churning winds. They offer no dread for hard winters ahead, no seductions of a glorious summer lost. Each fallen leaf is a tempoed beat to the left then the right, keeping signature time for everlasting change.

Children are zipping around the market tents, while their parents watch from a sidewalk cafe. Exhausted shoppers, canvas bags bursting with gourds and corn and crusty pumpernickel, trade their spiced lattes for chardonnays and Heinekens. Some of the kids are sitting on a curb sharing an overstuffed bag of kettle corn. The rest are running wildly apart from the adults, playing hide and seek in the closing street tents. The leader speeds up his countdown, peeking through his hands, shouting a warning to the whole street in hiding, what's coming for them.

"Apples, peaches, pumpkin pie, who's not ready, holler aye!"

Stephen Brock

Stephen is a new writer, poet and playwright who blends weighty stream-of-consciousness with rich cultural context. His work spans from historical-gothic realism to sharp modern satire. As evidenced by his first published poem for The Martello Journal's *sixth edition, 'My pint is spilled and I shall never be whole again.'*

Ushering in the gothic side of our work, his story 'Green' reads like a travelogue through the apocalypse. It follows an unnamed teenager during the Great Irish Famine as he journeys across the country, pursued by death – both figuratively and literally. A meditation on grief and cultural scars, it traverses the enduring presence of the Famine in the Irish consciousness.

Green

See the green hills shivering in the wind, blemished with the bodies of the dead and dying alike in silent liaisons between this world and that one yet beyond. Pockmarks on the face of creation. See the Lad descending, bent, exhausted. His mother some three hills back lay where she would forever, flesh and bone to nurture the very earth that starved her. He passes corpses with mouths agape and eyes fixed skyward, their lips and dead tongues the finest shades of emerald, tufts of rainwet grass clasped in cold hands. Wandering afoot through days shawled in clouds bibleblack and pregnant with rain. He trudges on absently. Here but not here. Homesick and in his heart homebound. But he will not see his place of birth again. The last of his kin now perished under such a weary sky as this. He falls into walking among families half complete and they rove as if sequenced by some drunk puppeteer. Passengers all, hostages to an optimism that will like as not sustain their travels.

Memories recur in the widening gyre of his hungeraddled mind. Moments out of time swimming to the forefront of thought, crying for recollection. Such was this distant morning. He stirred from sleep to the sound of damp footsteps trailing outside. Quiet throughout the house. Not even the birds sang. The day paling incrementally into view. He dressed in the half darkness and stepped outside. Smell of rot in the cool morning air. Down from the fields yonder his father passed through shadow and shade. In his hands the rotted crop gone black and bruised green. Deepset features that could once only frown now showed naught save horror. Panicglazed eyes, slackjawed mouth.

"It's gone bad. All of it. Every morsel, every crumb. We'll starve."

His father said it again and looked to the soil beneath his feet and shook his head.

He can recall the sound of his mother and father talking in muffled panic in the back room. The hapless play of his siblings. He stoked the fire with turf cut the previous morning. A queer light coloured the memory. This mosaic of moments divorced from one and other, something that could not be put back the way it had been. All of time in a state of fading, of gentle disintegration. It started raining that day and did not seem to stop. His mother drying teary eyes with a ragged kerchief fashioned from some old green fabric her own mother had left her. How many tears had it dried through all their lifetimes?

Come nightfall having drifted from the path he found himself alone within the heart of a forest dark. Trees imbrowned the leafstrewn earth, slivers of sickly moonlight coloured branches pale. Not a soul in that lonely place. The dull crunch of leaves underfoot as he wandered that heliographic feverdream. Directionless. The Lad wept without noticing, meek cries carried by the breeze that oozed through treenbranch and bush like the whisper of a candle snuffed out. He prayed the wind be his messenger, to carry forth these pleas to a God who might hear him through the din of a million souls begging for the same. Let me be a leaf and assume the wind, let my spirit fly back to you. Father, I hunger. Father, I am lost.

Somewhere in that shadowed, shifting mirage of limbs he beheld fire. A divot of flames licking at the sky betwixt two great leafless oaks. Like sentries to some sleeping evil in the earth. The Lad moved slowly toward the fire, hands reaching to guide him through the dark. By the flames he found a ragged priest squatting.

"I see ye lad. Come. Warm your bones."

He gestured with longnailed fingers, bid the Lad sit. The Lad perched by the fire's edge. The Priest watched him for a spell, his unshorn visage motionless against the trembling light of the flames, a single eye catching the orange glow.

"Where came ye from?" he asked.

"West. We were plotters. Crop failed and soon enough landlord had us thrown out."

"Aye. And your family lad?"

"Gone. All gone now. My ma the last to go. It's not right, Father."

The Priest looked deep into the flames.

"Methinks there is no rightness nor wrongness in this land no more son."

The Lad ran a finger over his torso, felt the outline of ribs protruding.

"Do you think God is still out there, Father?" he said.

The Priest scratched at his beard.

"I was giving last rites to a soldier, lad no older than yourself. Typhoid it were. He remained lucid for much of his passing. We spoke of the Lord, of the country, of his village. He told me the blight came on the wind. This rot that has poisoned every crumb we could eat, travelled the same way as the birds and the clouds. It confounds me to no end. What be the message of such a thing? Have we strayed from the Lord? Has He strayed from us? What make ye of it lad?"

The Lad spat into the flames, saw it fold inward for a moment. Great canyons of light and heat arcing in infinite spirals. A vista of some hell he was surely bound.

"If He is here, I have not found Him."

The Priest nodded.

"The Lord doth work in guises a mystery to mine own mind. And mayhap He intended it so. For He gave me this mind to reckon his ways. And mayhap it is not for me to comprehend. That's faith lad. How can I reckon with the Lord had he not endowed me the mind to parse his will? I have been bequeathed enough to serve God but not to understand his holy plot."

The priest reclined from the firelight. A cadaverous outline of skull endarkened by night save only a pair of eyes blazing like dying coals. That starved countenance writhing in shadow. Looking to the flames, to a moment not heretofore known.

"These last weeks I have wondered perhaps if this be an evil beyond our Christian reckoning. Something older. Deeper. Older than the Celts or the Normans or indeed these Britons. From a time when the blasphemers prayed to the trees and the soil, the setting sun. And I feel it, son. I feel meanness in the soil when I grasp a handful of it. I taste it when I drink from a stream. Behind the eyes of so many of God's creatures I behold a darkness like the coming of a storm. The depths we men can plummet to in times of strife. Hunger turns us into little more than beasts. We turn from the light of the Lord, find our souls out in the cold and what may beset them here where God's light cannot reach? It worries me sick."

The Priest turned his head to survey the woods and returned his gaze to the lad.

"Hear this lad. Hear this. I have seen in my dreams a black rider. Down the old Brehon roads. The rider cannot be lit by no manmade spark. He carries some rope fashioned from bone and viscera. He'll take your eye if you look at him. In these dreams he circles my father's house. And I am but a boy there. I do my damnedest to gather enough kindling, enough kerosene and turf to build a fire. Something bright enough to throw a light on him, even but for a moment. Alas, 'tis naught enough to view him. I don't believe our God can relieve us from this starvation for He is not the arbiter of it. Our forefathers drove out the blasphemers, the pagans and their affronts to God. But what of their Gods? Is this blight not some vestige of their revenge? On a people who have turned away from them?"

"Do you ever see the rider when you're awake?"

The Priest met the Lad's gaze and his lips curled to answer but he fought himself and spoke not, turning away to face the dark. In silence they sat listening to a curlew sing out. After a spell the Lad curled up by the fire and fell into a restless sleep. That night he dreamt he swam to a lakeshore and on that shore was an ashwood dining table attended to by diners clad in lush garments of blue and yellow. Candles near down to their wicks flickered about. Among the diners sat his mother in a chair cut from limestone with her back to the table and she faced the lake with a grassy rag stuffed in her mouth that flapped dimly in the breeze like a dog's tail. On platters of fine silver a feast fit for a hundred men though none ate. They paid the Lad no mind, no matter how hard he tried to wake these sleepless dreamers. That none shall disturb their halfdead gaze. The Lad took it to be some foretoken but of what he could not say.

When he woke in the bleak midmorning the Priest was nowhere to be found. A smoking pile of ash was all that remained of the fire. The Lad started walking and emerged from the woods onto an old Brehon road. Passing unturned fields with rotten harvest. A dolmen by the base of a hill. Some emaciated souls by a riverstream nets in hand to divine where their next meal may swim. By the roadside a makeshift cemetery of shallow graves, bulbous swellings on the land like the bellies of the dead who lay beneath it. Little shrines of wilting sunflowers about. A single tree against the hills, hulking crucifix in mud and there from a naked branch hung a man. What wrongdoing the inevitably starved won't commit. What sleeping evil slumbers in the prism of some men's hearts, waiting for the beck of hunger to rouse it from sleep. Some townsfolk had scrawled *bradach* on the thief's bedclothes. Swinging gently in that soft breeze. Candlewax eyes unblinking and unclosing forever to witness this terrible beauty. The land bares a thousand scars. The Lad watched an evicted family drink from a puddle. A thousand earthly agonies he watched that day. Episodes not even Dante could verily describe. Watching and weeping and walking on. Having forgone all wants, praying only now to be fed. On a ridgeline distant he watched a horse and rider trail along the horizon itself, trapesing where earth and sky articulate viridescent. And though too far to say he was sure the rider looked to him and he back. Death shall have dominion here in this land. The air. You could feel winter approach. That same wind that harboured the blight and disseminated it on every crop in every corner of the country. How quaint a force without form that can tousle a boy's hair, could carry the engine of ruin that would render everyone he had ever loved weak and sickly until such a time that they could walk no more and only perish, consigned to the nonmemory of the eternal dead. Apocalypse loosed, the likes of which will silence song for a generation.

As the anthracite sky dimmed to darker hues yet he came upon some settlement. Kinder eyes might have called it a village. Rain slowly came to fall in faint drizzles. The village was a single main street flanked on either side by thatchroof cottages of mossbearded stone. Further up an old public house and mill. In the valley beyond this antique land the hills climbed upward in jagged zigzags of bare limestone and much further on clouds congregated by the base of a mountain. Streams fit to burst divvied up the hillside into a series of diagonal islands in the rain. A pang of hunger shot through his gut. The Lad moved with a dizzying gait into the village, scrounging for some meagre sustenance but finding none. Torrents of rain came down.

The final cottage stank of rot. Through an open door he entered giving neither courtesy nor consideration for any who dwelled therein. Come upon a room of stone barren of utensils and furnish bar a rusted poker and a halfhacked chair used for firewood. He stopped a moment. Heard a rustling from yon bedroom. He edged slowly toward. From an open door a foul air drifted. On a bed lay a corpse and on the corpse a sheet and from the sheet an arm hung across the floor and here a mess of rats gorged on the jadecoloured flesh. The Lad stopped in the doorway, watched for a few moments and returned with the poker. One rat was gnawing a thumbnail with mute crunching when he brought down the poker with what failing strength he could summon. It whistled through the air, through the pitter patter of rain. The fuzzy mound of chirping mouths separated and fled. He managed to kill three.

With flecks of turf mounded in the hearth he commenced to stoking a fire. A dulled flint dashing against rock until sparks spat onto the paper and thatch before him. Until weak flames appeared and he carried them hands twitching in pain and lowered them upon the turfmound like a newborn. He knelt over the hearth. Blowing his sick breath. Soon a meagre fire burned. The Lad sharpened the flint on a rock, cut the heads and tails from the rats. He then dressed them, shearing away what little meat he could yield. He went outside in the rain and broke some sticks from a nearby tree and returned. A rumble quaked through the sky. He lanced the bloody ratmeat, held it firewise. Hands trembling with hunger. In the crackling flames the meat hissed and blackened. The Lad ate frantically. By the time he finished his stomach ached. He fed the fire some turf and lay down foetal before it and slept. Somewhere long into the night he woke to hoofs crossing the soft earth but saw nothing on those hills. He sat up listening. Through the thrumming of rain came the falsetto squeal of a horse frightened by the lightning, then silenced by thunder. Come morning there was a neat set of hoofprints through the village that had not been there when he arrived.

By noontime the storm broke. In that lull where the forces of wind and sky abated he stole off into the hills. Rising up and beholding the country. There was a nakedness to the land that invoked a world before the first men had come treading upon it. The lad journeyed until the village was little more than a speck on the horizon at his back. Hours passed before he saw a soul. A cavalcade of starved proceeded down a dirt trail. He fell into walking among a group of two dozen or so. The road ahead bepopulate with the hordes of famished damned shivering and weeping mute prayers, clothed in threadbare rags, tragedy guised in myriad form, a father carrying his lifeless child bloated and palefaced, man of cloth gone halfmad who had divested himself of goodbook and collar, widow with eyes bloodred from tears who sang some nursery rhyme, snotnosed boys barefoot and confused, bodies in motion with scant sentience, shrunk with hunger, hunched over in genuflection to any listening deity, lumbering along such grim byways and the dead were left where they fell for attending to by priests and nuns speaking last rites for the thousandth time that day, all horrors abound on that road and green was the colour of the country and green the colour of their rotted crops and green with greed the masters of the land.

The Lad watched it all. An unfolding bedlam. He trudged along. The road seemed without end. Fields fit for grazing now barren. All livestock slaughtered or stolen. Bandit country this. Some unkindness of ravens had perched along the arms of a dead tree to watch them pass and when a girl cried out for her daddy they startled and took to the starspecked sky above, darkness unsheathed. Between corridors of black clouds the Lad could see a pusscoloured moon hanging between horizons and against that celestial body the jagged outlines of rocky hills like the underbite of some great shadowed beast. Rearways far down the path already crossed, a horseman sidled along to survey the last dwindling moments of a boy and his dad. The breath in cold air rising from the pair as they spoke final words to one and other. Or prayed. The Lad could not tell. Nonesuch vapour left the mouth of the rider nor his steed. Too far and too dark to discern any particulars. The rider turned to look at the Lad as if he had known the Lad had been watching all along. The Lad felt his blood run cold. Breath left his lungs and he faltered on the path and fell.

He lay waiting to die for some time before a trio of nuns hauled him onto a wagon with other sickfolk. On his back facing the sky, tracing silver rivulets arcing across the nightblack tapestry. The wagon trundled on. So many stars. Incandescent flecks of day sown on a coalcoloured canvas. His mother had called them sparks from the hammer and anvil of God. Toiling away at some interstellar forge to birth as many stars as there are eyes to gaze upon them. With blinding sight he looked at the unfurling cosmos and wept. The last gasp of beauty in this roughshod world. He would will the image a permanent fixture in his mind. A candle he would carry into the dark. The wagonman stopped here and there to collect more sick and dying, ferrying them along. The Lad sat up to watch the road behind trail off into austere dark punctuated by moonlit breaks in the sky and with dim canter the horseman followed.

The Lad came to wake in a darkness that slowly revealed a room of cold stone. In the company of some sleeping sick and unsleeping dead. Pockets of moonlight from a window on haggard faces, limbs astrewn on the floor. He rose from a corner and stood to look through the window. A town of sorts. Cobblestone roads vacant save a pair of soldiers on guard. Yonder a stream and further yet a web of trees. He was not sure how far the wagon had taken him. Amid the howl of wind and gnashing trees he listened and listened for it: hoofsteps. He leaned closer and scanned at the horizon. There. On the edge of the treeline something moved. Where overhang branches had been broken or bent thin shafts of greenish moonlight spilled and in a halfmoment passing between these shafts he spied the horseman. Riding madly in the dark. Riding beyond view of the window the Lad watched from. He listened.

The horseman returned again. He rode round the town in awful revolutions. Circling like some deathbird, getting closer to where the Lad stood looking down. The horse was armoured with the bones of a dozen creatures, children's jawbones crisscrossed the saddle like hovering smiles in the pureblack dark. In one hand the horseman hauled a long whip which trailed along the damp ground, a serpentine instrument of human spines bound with what appeared to be hair. Yellowed with rot in pale moonlight. The horseman glanced up and though there were no eyes in his head the Lad felt the sickly touch of his gaze. The Lad shuddered backward into a mass of bodies in the room, some cold with death already. All became a blur. All became crescendo. Running through rooms and bursting through doorways, down stairs and streets. And all the while the staccato rush of hooves drew closer. The sky had gone the colour of a bruise. He ran past a pair of soldiers on patrol and though they bid him stop he went on. His ears rang with the chorus of a million cries. The horseman trailed along far behind him and his horse seemed it would never tire. Galloping in that awful dark. Ragged robes dyed in night's colours fluttering in the gale, whip of spines clickclacking on the cobblestone, cadaverous horseman with tallowcoloured skin and eyeless face watching and following, always following. The wind screamed. As the Lad looked back a final time he saw in that moonlit street the horseman clutched a green rag in his hand and he knew it was his mother's. He did not know how but he knew he knew.

As morning fell upon the land he summited a hill and looked about. The country in a state of becoming. Soon to be shorn by winter. Birdsong, the gentle whisper of breeze like his mother shushing him to sleep. He closed his eyes and listened deeply to the busywork of all God's creatures. The humming earth. A corncrake singing out to herald the new day. Deer plodding somewhere on the far side of the hill. Hooves now approaching. He knew a time would come not long from this moment when he'd lose the strength to walk on. He would lay himself to die in a green field on a bed of leaves autumnal orange and copper and earthy brown. Under such a weary Irish sky he would lay and as body and soul separated like parting lovers he would think a final time of his mother and her green kerchief and hope only in another time she could dry his tears once more and sing him to sleep, to ferry him to a new dream, all moments made disintegrate like ash on the wind, memories of that green kerchief dissolving into a greener world yet, fading, fading, fading. The Lad looked back and then forward and started walking. *Cast a cold eye on life, on death. Horseman pass by.*

Ruairí McDonnell

Ruairí is an emerging fiction writer in our community with a sharp eye for satire and a tilted reality. When asked for a short biography, he claimed to be the patriarch of an alpaca farm, contributor to Lithuanian Tractor Review, and a fan of acrostics. We can't confirm any of that - but it does say something about the spirit of his work.

He rejoins our collection with 'Sidhe,' a story that deepens our delve into the gothic and the historical while introducing some supernatural intrigue. Here, paranormal punishment is meted out to a squad of Black and Tans for their crimes, a haunting reckoning in a reimagined past.

Sidhe

The occupants of the lorry felt every jolt in their bollocks as the chassis bounced along the rocky road that cut through bleak bog. A couple retched, but did not vomit. Robinson seemed to be in a worse state than usual. O'Connor had noticed he usually had some kind of strange attack of nerves mornings after drinking and hoors. He would become possessed by weird thoughts and preoccupations; needing assurances that they weren't things to be thinking. But this seemed worse than usual. O'Connor had overheard Robinson ask Davies if predestination was real and if they were all destined for Hell no matter how they lived.

Davies couldn't read so probably wasn't best equipped to deal with theological questions, thought O'Connor. But Davies had a patience with the nervous soul and they were friends after a fashion. He just said, 'Fucked if I know.'

Hill was driving, seemingly not as affected by last night's imbibing. He had disappeared for a long portion of the evening. O'Connor had seen him at one stage through his own drink bleary sensoria emerging from a bedroom. He had been followed by a pathetic waif, whom he promptly smacked in the mouth and pushed back into her cot. Hill had slammed the door behind, and O'Connor had thought no more of it.

The next morning they had emerged from the boarding house into a blue-grey world. An urchin stood looking at them as she idly chewed the tip of an index finger. Hill had walked calmly over to the girl, leant down, and said something that made her suddenly cry and run into the boarding house.

They had 'requisitioned' the hostelry on behalf of King George V with authority to do so as constables of the Royal Irish Constabulary. Dúchrónaigh. Black and Tans. It was all the same to the locals and all the same to them.

The lorry continued to seemingly hit every contour of the road. A small boy walked on the verge.

'Watch this', said Hill as he veered towards the boy and slowed. He reached out his large, uncouth paw and in one deft movement caught the boy by the nape of the neck. The boy did not immediately seem to understand what was happening but then clawed helplessly and pitiably at Hill's thick fingers.

He screamed a babyish scream and cried as he tried to run alongside the lorry. The bridges of his feet helplessly dragged between the few steps he managed. Chalky residue that stained his legs and the hems of his short trousers soon spouted red rivulets. Pathetic little squeals.

The soldiers laughed, jeered, goaded perhaps out of duty or fear or genuine amusement. Hill absorbed their glee and then pulled the boy in to toss him from his pincer into the bog; tossing him clear of the lorry's wheels an altruistic act to such a man.

O'Connor looked back at the pale figure lying on the bank between road and bog. It did not move to look up in fear, anger, confusion. It just lay.

A dizzy nausea overtook O'Connor that was distinct from the alcohol-induced one. The soldiers continued to cheer and slap Hill's shoulders in praise. O'Connor thought he heard a low shriek but put it down to a sudden lightness of head and bad blood coursing through him from the hangover.

'I... I think you killed him', said O'Connor in a wobbly voice that didn't pierce the sounds of the soldiers' animal glee.

He said it again. The soldiers stopped their revelry.

'The boy, Hill, I think you killed him.'

'So fucking what?'

'I... just think...' O'Connor began to offer.

'Think what?' said Hill, staring forwards.

'I just think we shouldn't kill the children...' O'Connor caught himself veering into something that would only provoke so he changed tack. 'Roughing up Mick bastards is one thing, but I don't think...'

'I don't care what you fucking think', sprang from Hill in a leonine roar that stunned O'Connor into frozen timidity.

'Only the son of some fucking whore grows up to be a drunk; they aren't like us. They only exist for our entertainment. Fuck the mothers, kill the others. Get that through your thick skull and you'll have an easier and better time of it.'

O'Connor said no more.

They continued on through a featureless land. O'Connor had heard there were places like this at home. Moors he thought they were called. He had never seen them. Only the red brick slums of Leeds. 'Dark satanic mills' of that rubbish hymn.

Mist was descending as they left off several of the soldiers to pay a crofter a visit. They had spotted a pillar of smoke presumably attached to a cottage and decided they'd go to see what they could see. To see what they could defile.

After the soldiers alighted, the lorry continued along the road in its unrhythmic bounce. A mass in their path hove into view and the vehicle mercifully stopped.

'Dead 'orse', said Wright in his heavy Yorkshire accent.

'Ah for fuckssake', said Hill as he glared at the animal. 'How the fuck did that get there? Gerra out and see if you can move it.'

The remaining soldiers looked at him and each other.

'I don't think we are moving a horse, guv', said Lord, a shrill malnourished cockney. O'Connor thought he saw him flinch as he said it. Like a child about to be slapped despite being at the far end of the truck from Hill.

'Just get out and have a look ar' it', said Hill in a flat tone that left no one in the lorry five seconds later.

The soldiers plopped down onto the ground and approached the horse. A flash and then pop-pop broke over the top of the horse's mass and O'Connor suddenly felt the side of his face wet. Lord fell to the ground.

'Fuckssake lads, someone's shooting.' They turned and scrambled back towards the lorry.

Hill brought the Lewis gun from the passenger seat up atop the lorry's bonnet and opened up on the carcass, blood jumping from the impacts. The constables' rifles shot madly at the horse.

O'Connor always thought his colleagues ill-disciplined and skittish. They were soldiers who had seen the Great War, but now in Ireland they appeared to have lost respect and discipline under those fit for Bedlam. Under those like Hill. The officer class was replaced by boors who reveled in terror and idiocy. Or perhaps the officer class was ever thus, just better at hiding baser behaviours.

The Lewis stopped. The rifles stopped at this as if in an obedient hierarchy of weaponry; as if at the insistence of the bigger gun. The carcass sizzled.

Hill shouted for Robinson and Wright to approach the dead horse. Davies ran to Lord as he lay on his front. He had been spun around by the velocity of the shot. The matter of the abattoir fanned out on the road from the crown of his head. Davies said coolly, 'He's dead'. A redundant statement that didn't seem meant for anybody.

They approached the horse, gingerly with rifles raised. O'Connor sensed there was no one behind the animal. And there wasn't. Robinson and Wright seemed to sense it too as they upped their pace in the last few feet. They went around the horse almost bored.

'Where did he go?' roared Hill after Wright shouted back there was 'Nowt a sinner.'

'Fucking Mick, fucking disappearing leprechauns', said Hill with a touch of amusement O'Connor couldn't square away with having been ambushed and one of their party killed.

Robinson vomited and, after wiping his mouth, started babbling again about strange things. Wright told him to shut it. Hill beckoned O'Connor and he approached the lorry.

'... what if you are trapped in a perfectly carved out room of rock, not big enough to stand or sit... and you are millions of years underground and you... You feel like you are choking for eternity...'

'Hell better not be real for men like us... now just shut up. You're drunk...' O'Connor couldn't listen to these exchanges. They now scared in a way like when he considered eternity as a child. Like in a way he presumed everyone just tries to keep tamped down.

'I want you to find these arseholes, these Mick fuckers who were shooting at us. Use your Irish fairy powers. You have that Paddy name', Hill said, still sat in the Crossley Tender. He looked comfortable slouched back and did not look a man fearful of being killed by whomever was in the mist.

O'Connor walked back towards the horse. The horse was odd to him. The face too long, too distended. Eyes too bulbous and wild. It was white but too pale. Not a horse of this world, he thought, before banishing such nonsense.

'What the fuck are you on about Hill? What do you want me to do?' O'Connor shouted from behind the horse's carcass. It provided a defense between him and a man he didn't want to admit he feared.

They advanced along the road, no idea what they were really looking for. Hill had sent them to find the other soldiers, but they were only vaguely aware of where they had gone and through the mist couldn't see the column of smoke from the farmstead anymore.

Robinson was distracted. Looking out into the mist in a stare as he walked. He now seemed to O'Connor on the verge of some sort of full-blown nervous attack like the kind his mother used to have when she was alive.

Davies seemed to sense it too and waited while Robinson trudged up to him.

'Alright mate?' said Davies as he took a swig from a canteen O'Connor knew for a fact didn't contain water.

'Yes... Just...' Davies could tell he was about to say more on mortal ends, or religion, or some such rubbish he didn't understand so he thrust the canteen at him.

Wright was on ahead. Always a bit keen, a bit grasping. O'Connor didn't like him. Even though Wright seemed to possess more of the discipline that he so deplored the lack of in the other recruits, O'Connor knew that he was only a less boisterous sort of dangerous than Hill. Hill would make you watch while Wright would go back later to sate himself with the violence or...

O'Connor looked at the ground in front of him while he walked and thought on what he had seen in this forsaken country. He knew this was hardly a sensible place to be looking if Micks were out in the bog watching through the mist.

He couldn't explain why, but he knew no one and nothing was out there. But in the no one and nothing there was an all-enveloping *something*. He just knew being alert though had no bearing on anything that had transpired or was to come.

A commotion behind him took him away from his awareness of a force that seemed to have already decided... *something*.

'Robinson, shut it-I don't want to hear it', Davies said as he emptied his 'water' and threw the canteen to the ground. 'It's this mick rot making you mad.'

'No please', said Robinson 'Just hear me out. If we are only animated on this Earth for a short time and then stop and rot and what are we? Do we exist at all? What is preferrable? Hell or nothing? What if in Hell they make your nervous system the size of a planet and you can feel nations coming and going and warring within you and you can feel all this pain...'

Robinson's words made no sense to Davies and his arms flicked out wildly this way and that as he spoke. As if to prove they were his and he were him and he were alive.

'And, and, we go around as if there is no death and what we are and see and hear is constant and unceasing and unchanging... but it's not... it's not...'

Robinson was now pulling at his clothes and twisting the fabric of his ill-fitting uniform into bunches. Davies went towards him, striding up as if to hit him, determined to stop this thing he didn't understand. But when he reached Robinson, he saw in his eyes a fear that made him stop.

'Shut up Robinson.'

'I can't.'

'Well, I'll make you.'

O'Connor had no further interest in Robinson's ramblings or Davies's threatened intervention, so he walked on and left them to sort it out between them.

He looked up expecting to see Wright, but he couldn't see him through the mist.

Wright looked back expecting to see the three others, but they weren't there. The road was straight, and they weren't that far behind last he looked. There was a boulder to his right-the only thing someone could be behind besides the mist curtain.

He went around it to satisfy himself there was no one behind it.

O'Connor looked at the boulder to his left-could Wright be behind it? Perhaps he had sat himself against it to wait for them to catch up, he thought. He went the full way around it, but Wright was nowhere to be found.

Wright thought it strange and decided to continue on as that is what Hill wanted.

O'Connor looked back, Robinson and Davies were nowhere to be found now. 'This is ridiculous', he said aloud to mask what he was actually feeling. He was impelled from somewhere to continue on.

'They aren't behind this rock', said Davies as he appeared to Robinson from the other side of the boulder. As Davies rounded the granite, he caught in his periphery a flicker of limbs and a waif's face looking out from straight raven hair atop the boulder. He looked back and there was now only featureless sky.

'You saw her', said Robinson pointing at him.

Davies had, but not wanting to encourage Robinson, he said he hadn't.

Wright saw the strange earthen work rising up on the field like ringworm on the landscape. He strode up it and down the other side just for a bit of diversion. Micks are afeared of these, he thought, stupid fuckers. He stomped through it in defiance of the superstitious ramifications of his act.

He could make out in the middle of the circle what looked like a table. He went closer to it. His ears pricked as if invisible twine pulled at them. He suddenly realised he was feeling like a nervous dog as he went towards it. On the table was a pie. What the fuck is this? he thought.

He smashed it with a fist. He didn't know why. He didn't know why he did most things. It felt good.

The innards of the pie were a vivid purple which dripped from the side of his hand. Unidentifiable berries rolled from his hand into the grass. He brought his hand up and looked at the filling and then greedily put the edge of his hand into his mouth.

It tasted incredible. Like some shite rich people probably eat, he thought. He started to scrape up the pie and put it into his mouth with too much alacrity. A greed overcame him, but the more he ate, the hungrier he felt. When it was finished, he smashed the dish on the edge of the table.

He wiped his mouth with his sleeve. He felt hungrier now than he ever had before.

He realised there was a wetness in the front of his trousers. He thought it was pie filling that had spilled down there when he was stuffing it into his face. But it wasn't; it felt like it was inside his trousers.

He put a hand down inside his string belt to investigate. He rummaged around and brought his hand back out. It was alive with vivid dark red blood.

'What the fuck?' he said aloud.

He quickly put his hand down his trousers again and felt his bollocks. His frantic fingers slipped into an open wound on his scrotum. A rush of sickening panic into his jowls and ears; he became dizzy; he thought a swoon was sure to overtake him... horror as he felt two small eggs slip down the inside of his right leg.

He turned and in his turn crushed a testicle under his boot that had reached the end of its journey. He held the wet front of his trousers attempting to keep something together. Insanity inducing pain radiated up into his torso as he stumbled towards the edge of the fort while trying to stay conscious. He scrabbled up the side of the fairy fort with one hand and then felt himself falling. The gentle undulation of field now sheer, cliff-faced drop.

'What if Hell is real? What if it's inescapable?'

Robinson was hueless; a blanched face drained of life.

'Stop talking', said Davies.

'Why do we go around like it matters? Denying the fact we are the same as the cattle? Trapped in a corpse that we can't control the death of.' Robinson was frantic again now; his breathing was shallow.

'Robinson, you have to stop. Hill will kill you, give you the death you're so afraid of.'

'Meat. It's just meat.' Robinson was suddenly aware of all his organs. His eyes in a skull. He felt unmoored from the denial that keeps humans from the madness of their end.

Robinson saw in his mind's eye a man on a seemingly endless marble plane. The whole alabaster world tipped and the man started sliding down it; trying as he slid to get purchase on the perfectly smooth surface. He was sliding into fire with a mad desperate look on his face. His slide became a sickening tumble as the angle became steeper. His limbs slapping the marble in pitiable ways as he thumped down the slanted world. This is the maw of Hell Robinson decided. It *was* inescapable. Nothing could be done.

Nothing, but one thing.

Robinson stumbled out into the bog, his feet rolling onto their sides in the pock marked ground. He picked up a rock. Davies looked on from the road. Davies didn't know what to do so he just watched.

Robinson heard a voice. The voice was female and benign, and it said, dulcetly, 'Bash your fucking brains out.'

The one thing he could do. He brought the rock up beside his head. His instinct made his animal body shiver in a weak hesitation before he brought it crashing into his temple. The one thing he could do was control the hour of his death.

'Robinson, you stupid fucker.' Davies ran from the road towards him. Robinson struck himself again, and again, and again, and again.

Davies reached him and could see the right side of his face was caved in. Robinson looked at Davies with an eye of too much white; nearly the full orb of his eyeball was exposed in exploded socket. Robinson looked a pathetic thing.

Robinson collapsed into the mire. Davies got sick.

There was no field hospital. There was no nothing. Davies looked at the bloody rock and didn't think there was much point. He wasn't to be saved. Nothing to be done. Davies sat in the mud. A mood stole over him which became an intense grief for the whole of humanity.

He thought he heard someone say sweetly but with a scratchy vulnerability, 'Kill yourself you worthless fucking nothing.' A bullet in the brain would be his control over death.

Cold steel pressed into soft willing palate.

O'Connor heard a shot. From where it came, there was no telling. It felt like it was right beside him and elsewhere at the same time.

O'Connor knew for some reason the cottage must be close. He felt impelled to go there. For what? Reinforcements? Against what? He heard unnatural screaming again. It was in all his senses. He had to sit on a bank to compose himself. He found it hard to catch his breath. The screams hit him again. Physical thumps in his chest but at the same time somehow feeling like they emanated from within him and went outward, out across the landscape of mist.

Just a few feet more; he could see the farmstead now. He picked himself and his rifle up and went on towards it. As he approached, he noticed a strange talisman affixed to the planks of the gate into the yard. It was some kind of crude face made of chicken feathers and some kind of bone. There was a small mouth under large black eyes. Eyes that seemed to be dark onyx.

He did not like it. It was on a backing of twigs in some kind of star pattern. He did not like it.

He pushed the gate open. The whole yard's churned up muddy ground darkened with... no, it couldn't be, he thought. It would be a lot of blood if it were... He noticed there were bright streaks and smears of it on the squat cottage walls and it was undeniable as to what it was.

The other soldiers... He didn't feel sick or sad. He knew he had to keep going. He heard a baby mewling from inside a building. He went in. He could see the back of a young woman bent over a hayrack that appeared to be the crib.

'Are you here to violate me too?'

'No... did they...'

'They did not.'

'...why?' O'Connor felt the presumptions in the question.

'They wouldn't let it happen. They wouldn't allow it. There's a protection in the land and they wouldn't allow it to continue...'

'...why?'

O'Connor admonished himself silently for asking the question, giving this nonsense credence. The Micks had done this to scare them. Bleed a few chickens; spread the blood around...

'The invader. The coloniser. The ancient ones won't allow it. They don't intervene often. But they did today.'

O'Connor found himself slipping into believing this and caught himself. It was poppycock.

'There are Fenians somewhere, they did this-where are they?' O'Connor began to raise his rifle but didn't. It wasn't who he was.

'Nowhere.'

'Where?' If he wasn't going to raise his rifle he was going to be as forthright as if he had done so.

'Everywhere.'

O'Connor was about to call her a cunt but stopped himself.

'Is the child harmed?'

'It's not a child.'

'But I heard it cry.'

'You may look at it.'

O'Connor stepped forward and looked into the hayrack. The face of the child was grey and long, contorted and evil, with serrated teeth that cut its own lips. Its eyes were red with tight pupils and seemingly no irises.

'What is wrong with the child?'

'It is not a child. They provide protection but extract their price.'

O'Connor realised he was walking backwards and had already decided he was to leave as there was nothing he could do here. He couldn't explain...

'They will allow *you* out.'

'What?' O'Connor said feebly before he remembered he was the soldier and added 'I don't need permission... Out of what?'

'You *know*', said the woman as she rose suddenly, pulling the demonic child up by an ankle and smashing its mass against a wall. The child cried and she smashed it against the rough stone wall; again, and again and again until it made no sound at all.

It had all happened before O'Connor could have done anything at all.

But something had lifted. The air had a new quality to it he couldn't explain. He did not say another word to the woman and left her to her howling grief.

Hill looked up to where the horse had been. There was no horse, but a smaller mass now. Blaming the drink, he climbed down from the Crossley Tender bringing the Lewis with him.

Going toward the mass he realised it was the boy he had 'roughed up' earlier. Well, he thought, we didn't know for certain if the little chap was dead. Looking around, he could see nothing and no one only mist and mizzle.

The boy's legs were now clean, and he was lying on his side. Hill put a hand to the boy's shoulder and leapt back. A shock had gone through Hill. He imagined this was what happened when you touched one of those galvanic batteries wrong.

He had heard about them making the severed heads of prisoners move their mouths and eyes with their shocks from a drunk who claims he had seen it done in Italy.

He looked at his hand and looked back to the boy. The boy still lay there on his side.

This is a trap, thought Hill. He shot off into the mizzle. He shot this way and that, wheeling around when he thought he felt someone behind him. 'C'mon let's be having ya. Cunt.'

Fingers like wicker strands slid from behind him and spread over his left cheek. A voice that seemed a thick freezing cold stream into his ear canal.

'Tá an sigil de ifreann ort.'

He spun left and shot at nothing. On his right cheek the same and now hot into his right ear,

'Ní ghearrfar pionós ort; beidh tú pian ionchollaithe. Cinnteoidh mo lucht aitheantais é.'

He strode back to the lorry and got another drum for the Lewis. Something caught his eye in the bog. Hill wasn't having this anymore. He struck out into the mire and mist.

Something this way and that. He fired this way and that. He was out of ammo. He took the new ammo drum from where he had hastily tied it to his belt by its handle. As he did so, he absentmindedly drifted backwards; unconsciously going away from the threat he couldn't see or even be sure was there at all.

He stumbled back and fell onto his back, awkwardly catching his leg between two rocks.

‘Fuck these Irish rocks’, Hill roared.

Three lithe, extended figures slank through the mist almost uninterested and somehow, they felt to Hill, unimpressed. They were female but had the aspect of trees.

He saw cavemen he had seen in a book once. They were around a fire. In the picture in his memory, they were now loomed over by these figures. He had feelings of intense insecurity and hunger and looking out over lonely dark plains and feeling helpless.

Faces and limbs too long. Long hair dark and lank. Refulgent red eyes with the rawness of tears and weird reflections and he saw in them every unwilling girl and it made something well up. All at once all of their grief and pain and everything was his. Survival, but not his. A feeling of falling but he was on the ground.

He pissed his pants and thought of his mother. Desperately trying to reload. Our father who art in bullshit.

He had broken his leg, but it hardly mattered now.

‘Irish cunts what the fuck is this?’

He managed to affix the drum onto the Lewis but then stopped. He just knew now there was no point. A wooziness came over him and surrender beckoned. It wasn’t a bad feeling now; it was acceptance. His vision closed in with dark reeds growing from every side. He felt a cold like he couldn’t know.

O’Connor had been walking for… he had no idea; the light hadn’t seemed to have changed.

‘Bollocks’, said Taylor as he took another slug of Guinness from a can in the hotel room overlooking Smithfield Square.

‘No, it’s true’, said Wilson.

‘Your great-grandfather didn’t find a death cult in Eye-land in 1902 or whatever.’

‘In 1921.’

'It didn't 'appen. Black and Tan, maybe. But this stuff with the farm and the monster baby didn't 'appen', snorted Taylor. 'I can imagine one of these savages killing a baby though.'

Wilson didn't like Taylor. Or the rest of the squaddies. He was in Ireland for his brother's stag party. 'Wilson' was now included in the surname naming convention due to the seeming inability of the party to use people's first names despite it causing confusion with his soldier brother.

He had somehow gotten stuck with Taylor, and they had nothing in common. He had told the story he only half knew about his great grandfather coming across some sort of atrocity in Ireland nearly a hundred years ago in the hope of building rapport. It seemed to have made Taylor dislike him even more.

The soldiers told stories that ended in dead ends when they realised that Wilson was there. Stories that would start sinister enough so he couldn't imagine where they went. The most intriguing one to him was whatever had happened in Basra.

Taylor had said something to him on the Ryanair flight over that morning about 'Mexican Valium'. Wilson had no idea what he meant and had to look it up later. When he learned what it was slang for, Wilson couldn't tell if Taylor had been serious and if he had meant him to be shocked, or impressed, or even maybe somehow emasculated by its mention.

'I'm just going out for a minute', said Wilson.

'Eye don't give a fuck, just be back before we 'av to go. And don't forget your Hawaiian shirt.'

How could Wilson forget that ugly piece of tat?

He closed the door softly behind him and walked down the corridor. Suddenly he felt a tightness in his skull. He gripped his head. He fell to his knees. The corridor felt endless. Screaming shattered the whole world.

Sylvia Konstantinova

Sylvia, our returning Canadian poet based in Dublin, writes to express her understanding of others and to connect deeply with the world. Her minimal style offers space for the reader to lean in with open ease. This year, she has challenged herself with new and diverse artforms, including her first open mic performance.

We pause here on the supernatural to share her four poems, which help to trace the weight of fear, survival, and reclaimed self-worth. From the rare magic of belonging (Open Doors), to the quiet severance of a longing (the cut), to the guarded grief of love (Armour), and the harsh maths of injustice (Fifteen Hundred to One), these poems reconcile vulnerability with the cost of moving forward.

Open Doors

Let me tell you about open doors.

They are El Dorado, and
I have bled my feet, exploded my lungs,
broken my back on absence and ghosts
to find
just one.

Unbelievingly,
open
wide,
I have walked through.

To a place where I am not wanted
for labour or profit, my body
at others' disposal, disposable

but to a place where I am seen
and taken, beyond my depletion,
with all my limits and all my strengths.

A place where I can settle
for a season, or forever
to refill my lungs, straighten my back
and walk my rested feet anew,

to live wondrously, expansively
for myself and all the others.

All the others.

Open doors, I tell you, are magic
needlessly so.

the cut

you have quit, you have cut my yearning
a second skin which I had painfully peeled,
balled, and swallowed to forget
but which I could not digest, sat
and got sad from time to time

my hunting, hungry heart is stilled
the nearness of you, still nearing
and constant, catches me unawares, looped
though I am watching, pupils black
beholding all that light gouging scarcity

you have quit, you have cut my yearning
in a part of me, I am something new
an opening bud, and you are you

Sylvia Konstantinova

Armour

My saddened heart had armoured itself,
fortress high, ready for retreat and
retraction, activising the muscle of loneness.

I mistook the walls for something other,
muddling over minute notes that matter
almost not, but which will be sounded in time.

In clouded humour, I didn't see,
and forgot the stars of your fabric
that illuminatingly I loved and continue still.

Fifteen Hundred to One

Broken and breaking ground
where all stirring is titled,
so the sun shines askew,
leaving hours uncertain
and bellies naked inside.

We take until the corners fill,
and back against the wall,
the only move left is forward –
an exchange of danger where
any hurt inflicted is survival.

A punishment, misdirected,
is calculated: fifteen hundred
lifeful bodies felled for one human.
To roam the burgled greens,
by permit; aren't we deserving?

Aayan Atiq

Aayan joins us as a crafter of fiction steeped in understanding and longing. He describes himself as a 'writer of sad stories, maker of chaotic beats, part-time overthinker, full-time romantic.' His atmospheric style has a way of challenging the reader to absorb density and long for more. His influences include Kazuo Ishiguro, Virginia Woolf, and Wong Kar-wai – anyone who knows how to ache beautifully.

He brings us 'Reflection' here as we continue the gothic with blurred recollections and the literal ghosts of our past. At a quiet wake, a soul lingers – adrift in remembrance, music, and silence – confronting the boy he was, the man he became, and the love he never dared to claim. This is a quiet confrontation with identity and the lives we leave unlived.

Reflection

Old. Sunken. Still.

He lies in the casket with a strange kind of peace, the kind reserved for people who no longer need to perform comfort. His hands are folded neatly, as if someone else arranged them – someone with a sense of decorum, or duty, or shame. The suit is a size too large, or maybe the body has shrunk into it. The skin is pale, sagging at the temples, the lips thinned into a line that doesn't look like any expression I remember making.

I don't recognise him.

Around the room, people move like whispers – muted, gentle, reluctant. A woman sits on the edge of a sofa, rubbing at her eyes with a crumpled tissue – one of a few here who seem genuinely moved. A man loiters in the hall, drink untouched. Their voices are hushed, their footsteps quiet.

The air is thick with lilies, beeswax, and something medicinal – antiseptic, maybe, or aged drawers. Sunlight slants through half-drawn curtains, warm in hue but cold in meaning. A bird trills beyond the open window, cutting the silence. There's warmth out there – and it pulls at me.

My steps make no sound as I move forward; the floor registers nothing. Light brushes past my shoulder, but it carries no heat. I'm not certain what I am, or what this is, but I know that the world beyond the frame is in motion, and I am no longer part of it. Dust floats in the sun as I near the window, and something unnameable loosens inside me.

At the edge of the hallway, I catch a glimpse of a mirror, tall and narrow – uncovered, leaning slightly – as if it had been forgotten. The custom would be to shroud it, as someone had done so with the rest – fabric pulled tightly across the glass, ghosts smothered before they could take shape. But this one has been left bare, and for a moment, I wonder: an oversight or an offering.

I turn toward it, and the face it reveals steals whatever momentum I had.

The reflection stares back at me, but it isn't the man in the casket. This face is still mine, much younger – sharper in the lines, cleaner in the shape, more certain in its posture. The hair is thick, dark, and curled in the way I used to love. There are no creases pulling down the edges of the eyes, no slackness in the skin around the jaw. The mouth is familiar. I know this version of myself. It's the one I used to carry in photographs, in passing glances at shop windows, in the way strangers used to look at me with interest rather than pity.

I stay there, suspended, between the ghost in the mirror and the body in the box, unable to decide which version of me is more real. Slowly, I walk back toward the casket, and this time, I let myself really look at the man inside. The features are the same, but softened, sagged, altered by time and burden and whatever griefs accumulated unspoken. I search for myself in the face, and for a long moment, I find nothing.

And then, quietly, like the last note in a song that no one heard begin, the thought comes.

How did I become him?

The question hangs in the air, unanswered, unanswerable, and for a moment longer, I remain by the casket. But the house around me begins to whisper in quiet recognition, and my curiosity pulls me away.

I drift slowly through rooms that must have been mine. The faded wallpaper, roses pale on cream, peels gently at the edges. I pass an old cabinet standing proud in a corner, rust tracing intricate patterns down the brass handles, the lacquer peeling back like dried petals. A clock sits on the mantle, stopped at half-past three, its pendulum frozen mid-swing as if caught between breaths. The house feels both familiar and strange, like an old friend who changed just enough over the years to make recognition difficult.

As I move farther, the faint scent of something sweet and stale – tea, perhaps, forgotten in the bottom of a cup – draws me into a smaller room at the back. A reading chair, well-used, sits beside a lamp. Books line a shelf, spines softened by years of gentle handling, pages filled with the scent of paper long undisturbed – dry, faintly sweet, almost brittle in the air. I reach out to touch one, but my fingers pass through nothing.

I reach again for a book I almost recognise when a sudden chime cuts through the stillness, sharp and insistent. The doorbell rings sharply once, twice, thrice, and footsteps rush to answer. Bright greetings jar the somber hush. I hear a laugh – too loud, too forced, as a man strides into the room. He is older than most here, settled comfortably into middle age with greying hair carefully combed, yet he wears his casualness awkwardly – faded jeans beneath a suit jacket, an unlit cigarette tucked absent-mindedly behind his ear. He pumps each hand in turn. "Terrible business, isn't it?" he murmurs, nodding solemnly as though rehearsing empathy.

He drops onto the sofa, crosses one leg over the other. "Quiet in here, should we liven it up? Did the old man like music?"

His words land awkwardly, like the discordant notes of a piano out of tune. Something shifts inside me – tightens, hollows. Did they really know so little of me?

Before anyone else can reply, a girl I hadn't noticed before steps forward. She's young – mid twenties perhaps – hair dyed a vibrant shade of violet. A small silver earring glints in one ear, catching the muted sunlight as she walks. There's something quietly assured in her movements, something that feels familiar though I can't place her yet.

"He loved music," she says gently. "More than most things, really. Have you seen his record collection?"

She moves across the room with purpose, kneeling beside a large wooden cabinet I'd somehow overlooked. Her fingers trail affectionately over the spines of dozens of vinyl sleeves before she selects the right one, carefully sliding it free. She holds it delicately for a moment, as though honouring its weight, before placing it reverently onto the turntable.

The needle touches down with a faint crackle, like rain murmuring against a window. The first warm note slips into the room like an exhale, wrapping around me with a softness I had forgotten. I recognise the song, and something within me responds – deep and magnetic. I turn slowly back towards the hallway mirror left uncovered.

And as the singer's voice drifts into the air – *Moon River* – the glass before me ripples gently, the familiar shapes of another time sharpening: lights and laughter, swaying silhouettes, petals forgotten on a dance floor.

The years begin peeling away quickly, like pages turned backwards through an old book, until the reflection staring back at me is younger, softer, more hesitant – fifteen, maybe sixteen. My features are smooth with youth, my hair carefully combed, my body thin and awkward beneath a sharp navy suit, new, crisp, stiff at the collar. I touch my reflection gently, tracing fingers across the glass that gives no warmth. The mirror melts away quietly, and I step fully into memory.

I am standing in the corner of a dance hall – grand, polished floors reflecting the soft golden glow of hanging chandeliers. Paper streamers twist gently from the ceiling, balloons drift lazily in corners, forgotten. The scent of cologne and hair pomade mingles with the faint undertone of floor wax. Boys stand clustered together, shifting nervously, while girls in pastel dresses with cinched waists, their hair set neatly into careful waves, laugh behind delicate hands. At the front, a small band sways beneath the lights, *Moon River* flowing softly from a silver saxophone.

My heart flutters like something caught in a web, anticipation tangled with dread. I stay near the wall, careful, safe. The music flows around me like water, carrying laughter and whispered conversations. I keep my eyes fixed on the floor, watching shoes scuff and shuffle, afraid to look up too openly, afraid of giving something away.

A burst of laughter cuts through the music, clear and bright. I glance up involuntarily. It's him, my best friend, smiling easily as he guides a girl back to her friends. He walks towards me, adjusting the sleeves of his jacket, slightly breathless. Even his hair – usually wild and tangled – is neatly parted tonight, smoothed back carefully with Brylcreem.

"Don't tell me you're going to stand here all night?" he says, nudging my shoulder gently. His voice carries a teasing warmth.

I force a laugh, shake my head slightly. "I haven't decided who to ask yet," I reply, careful to keep my voice neutral, calm.

He raises an eyebrow playfully. "You'd better hurry up, or all the good ones will be taken."

My throat tightens, words catching halfway. Instead of answering, I simply smile again, pretending ease. But my eyes betray me – I can't help it. They linger on him: the gentle line of his jaw, the grey suit perfectly tailored to shoulders broader than mine, the flushed colour in his cheeks from dancing, the way his breath comes quickly, softly, his chest rising and falling beneath the fabric of his shirt, the nervous rhythm matching my own. I notice how his tie is slightly loosened already, his collar unbuttoned, as though daring the rules to challenge him. I notice too much, too intensely, too openly – and quickly look away.

He laughs, oblivious to my panic, eyes returning to the dance floor. "Pick quickly," he says lightly. "Tonight's going faster than you think."

He's right, of course, but it's not the girls I see, it's him – sharp and shining, standing close enough to touch yet impossibly distant. I watch the way the shadows fall softly across his face, the faint curl of his hair at the temples, his hand resting casually in his pocket. My heart races as the music swells, and even though the song fills the hall like an embrace, it can't drown out the quiet voice in my head – a voice warning me not to step too close, not to linger too long, not to reach for something I can't afford to want.

So I remain silent, anchored by hesitation, the music washing over me, its promises just beyond reach, while the night slips away, never daring to ask for even one dance.

The final notes of the song fade slowly from my mind, dissolving gently like mist caught in sunlight. My vision blurs momentarily, and the vibrant lights of the dance hall drift away, leaving behind only the quiet stillness of the house and the empty reflection staring back at me – older again, a little more familiar, but tinged with something softer, sadder. A feeling catches in my chest – a phantom heartbeat racing even though I have no heart left to beat.

Music. How had I forgotten the way it shaped my days, defined my nights? The records were more than a collection – they were a quiet refuge, where I could safely feel everything forbidden elsewhere. I glance back toward the cabinet where my albums rest, untouched now, save for the careful hands of the girl with violet hair. Her fingers had brushed them with a tenderness no one else had shown, and it fills me with both comfort and sadness.

Across the room, the older relative who had questioned my love for music chuckles softly, leaning back, his eyes only half-attuned to the conversation. Beside him, another – a cousin, perhaps – shakes his head faintly, gaze drifting to the stopped clock on the mantle. I watch them both, searching for some trace of recognition, some quiet acknowledgment of the man whose life they've gathered to mourn. But their expressions remain casual, unburdened by memory. Had I left so faint a mark that they could sit comfortably at my wake, speaking lightly of anything but me?

Troubled, I drift again through the house, retracing my steps with a clarity I hadn't known before. The wallpaper's pale roses now carry echoes of tenderness left unsaid. The cabinet, rust-traced and tired, feels more intimate, emblematic of small comforts I denied myself. Even the frozen pendulum of the clock seems to mock the moments I let slip by, irretrievable.

I return to the small room with the reading chair. The scent of forgotten tea lingers – sharp, sweet, laced with quiet regret. Books line the shelf, some cracked with use, others nearly pristine. Their titles whisper softly now: *Great Expectations* beside a worn *Persuasion*. A volume of *Leaves of Grass* lies bookmarked halfway, as though I never allowed myself to finish. In these simple objects I see something deeper – afternoons spent carefully alone, quiet companionship pushed aside for solitude, caution, silence.

A soft rustling of paper draws my attention back toward the living room, where relatives sit murmuring around an old photograph album. Curiosity pulls me closer, each turn of the page invoking forgotten moments briefly illuminated again.

"Look at this one," someone says softly, tapping gently against a worn photo. It's small, slightly creased from being handled often. Two young men smile broadly at the camera, bicycles propped beside them, the sea stretching endlessly behind. The face next to mine in the photo is half-turned towards me, caught mid-laughter, eyes full of warmth and quiet intensity.

"It just says 'Antibes' on the back – does anyone know who the other person is?"

Julien – the name rises before I can stop it. As if it had been waiting just beneath the surface all this time, patient, unforgotten.

In that instant, the photograph's edges start to blur, brightening as though lit from behind. The sound of waves, the warmth of sunlit afternoons, the gentle murmur of conversations held beneath endless skies – all of it begins to spill forward. I am pulled, gently but inevitably into another memory, of the summer I turned twenty-eight – old enough to know better, still young enough to believe there was time.

The first thing I remember is the warmth, a sun softer and kinder than any I've felt since, settling comfortably across my shoulders, soaking gently into the thin fabric of my linen shirt. I breathe deeply, tasting salt and sunlight, the bright edge of summer still lingering on my tongue. Beside me, Julien pedals effortlessly, the sleeves of his shirt rolled up, his light hair tousled by the warm breeze blowing off the Mediterranean.

We glide along the coast, through towns with names like poems – Villefranche-sur-Mer, Saint-Jean-Cap-Ferrat, Èze. Each blurs into the next, stitched together by the sapphire sea. Lavender, salt spray, and freshly baked bread drift on the air. We stop sometimes for no reason other than to stand at the water's edge, toes digging into sand still warm from the afternoon sun, and watch the waves break gently, endlessly, against the shore.

Just outside Nice, he finds an oyster stand set against a rugged outcrop of rocks, its bright-painted wooden boards faded slightly by sun. He laughs as he hands one to me, its shell rough and glistening. I pretend not to hesitate, tasting brine and the cool rush of the ocean, and he watches my face with quiet amusement, his eyes bright and knowing, green like sunlit olive leaves.

"You don't like them," he says softly, smiling, reaching gently to brush the salt from my lip with his thumb.

"I do," I insist, unable to hide the way my face twists involuntarily. "I just – I haven't learned how yet."

"Maybe someday," he replies easily, as though the future were endless, a promise stretching forward rather than something slipping quietly away. From a beach café, Chet Baker's *I Fall in Love Too Easily* drifts over the road, trumpet as lazy as melted ice, winding itself around Julien's laughter and the salt on my lips. Then he's moving again, calling over his shoulder, challenging me to keep pace as we pedal faster, laughing breathlessly beneath the late-summer sun.

At sunset we swim, slipping quietly into water that mirrors the indigo sky, our clothes folded neatly on the sand behind us. The sea is cool against our skin, welcoming rather than cold, and the last rays of sunlight paint his chest gold and amber as we float side by side. His laughter is soft against the rhythm of the waves, blending gently into the fading daylight. He speaks quietly, words dissolving into whispers and smiles, promises too fragile to say aloud. Yet in the gentle rise and fall of the tide, I hear everything clearly.

At night we lie beneath a sky so full of stars it feels impossible – too vast, too bright, too endless. He points upwards, naming constellations, tracing lines between points of silver that I can't quite follow, and I don't mind; it is his voice I care about, quiet and warm in the dark, anchored by the soft rhythm of his breathing. The air holds wild rosemary, distant campfires, and faint sweetness of ripe figs. Beside him, the world feels gentle, generous, infinite.

The days unfold slowly, beautifully – morning blending into afternoon, evening slipping into night – each hour a quiet affirmation of the life I have always wanted, but never dared claim. It feels easy here, beneath the open sky, to believe that life might be like this forever, a gentle cycle of sun and sea and laughter.

On our last evening, we sit quietly on the stone wall at Cap d'Antibes, our feet dangling gently over the water as the horizon fades into violet and rose. His shoulder brushes mine, warm and comforting, a gentle pressure I wish would never leave. Neither of us speaks. There is no need for words now, beneath a sky like this, the stars softly claiming their place once more.

This, I think softly, is happiness.

The memory of Antibes recedes like a reluctant tide, leaving only dust and silence. The turquoise sea, the taste of salt, Julien's laughter – fade into a hush heavier now. The warmth lingers briefly, a phantom sun, before slipping away. I wait, hoping some trace remains. But the house is mute. Only absent, unmoving air.

The mirror waits, dulled as if tired of remembering. I drift toward it, facing the reflection, seeing only a man forgetting what wanting truly felt like.

He didn't go back.

The thought arrives like a chill – sudden, impersonal. In the third person. And I can't change it.

"*He*", not "*I*".

He didn't return to the sea. Not to Julien. Not to the boy who once laughed without looking over his shoulder, sun-warmed and certain the world might still bend toward joy.

Instead, he returned to something colder. Smaller. A world of cautious conversations and silent edits. His vibrant joy felt illicit under muted skies, too bright for shadowed rooms. Quiet guilt took root – happiness felt transgressive, freedom mocked the ordered life awaiting him, and the mirror stood ready to reflect the faces of those who taught him to hide.

The flickers in the glass – too quick for memory, too sharp for invention – settled, and my face emerged, more worn now, the first shadows of the man in the casket beginning to take shape. A table. Relatives. Someone smiling a little too brightly, head tilted with a theatrical concern: "No special young lady to tell us about yet, dear?" – the 'dear' – a velvet hook. An uncle's voice, all stage-whisper and elbowed suggestion: "Still burning the midnight oil at work? Or just haven't found the right sort of companionship?" The laughter that followed, threaded with speculation, slid like ice splinters against bruised skin.

Each seemingly casual query felt like another stone sealing the entrance to the sunlit world I had known. In the mirror, his shoulders slump, eyes dimming with the quiet acceptance that joy like that was never part of the script. And with it, the light in mine faded too.

It wasn't only those pointed questions, those gently raised eyebrows that felt like accusations. The deeper shame was already there, an insidious seed planted long before *he* even understood it. I watch my reflection again, a little older now, more slumped, as I recalled myself, perhaps six, excitedly recounting a dream where I flew with a flock of shimmering, multi-coloured birds, only to have a gentle hand smooth *his* hair, a soft voice murmur, "What a funny little imagination. Boys usually dream of airplanes, don't they?" – and the birds abruptly vanished. That was how the lessons came, in the air itself. To speak too clearly of inward, unconventional landscapes made one strange, suspect, an outlier in a world that prized conformity.

So, I – *he* – folded himself smaller. The quick, eager way he once moved stilled into something more contained; the laughter I remembered now rarely reached his eyes. The face in the reflection now was clearly *his*, the hope I held onto as "I" receding with each compromise.

The mirror released me, its depths having claimed the last of my offered youth. I drifted back to the casket through the now-familiar heavy air. I looked down at *his* still, powdered face. We were identical now: the same lines, the same thinning temples, the same mouth muted by a lifetime of silence that led to this epilogue, steeped in the room's weary scent of antiseptic and old grief.

All that meticulous care, the thought coiled, sharp as the cold light from the window, *all those years tiptoeing around joy, sanding every bright edge from your soul... for this? This hushed reverence, the faint rustle of a forgotten mourner's tissue?*

Silence pressed in, suffocating. So, *you achieved it*, I conceded bitterly, *the perfectly unremarkable life.* Not a ripple stirred the funeral lilies; barely a breath disturbed dust motes dancing indifferently. That vast, chosen stillness – his curated nothingness – felt cold, threatening to draw me into its –

A flicker of movement at the edge of my awareness. Not the hesitant rustling of other mourners, but something purposeful. Before I could fully turn my attention, a shadow fell gently beside the casket. It was the girl with the violet hair. She stood there for a beat, a small, vibrant punctuation mark in the room's muted greys. Through the air's quiet hum, a faint, ethereal music drifted, a song I couldn't quite place, its melody shimmering just beyond recognition.

Then, she reached out. Both hands. One, small and pale, came to rest on the polished wood of the casket's edge. The other, just as gently, she laid directly over *his* folded, lifeless ones.

The contact, even seen from my detached state, was like a spark in the oppressive stillness. My spiraling thoughts of ash and nothingness fractured, scattered. My focus was snared by the image before me: her living hand, warm and definite, covering *his* cold, still one. The contrast was absolute. Her defiant violet-painted fingernails, against the waxy pallor of *his* skin. A gesture of such simple, unalloyed tenderness it seemed to radiate a warmth that even I could perceive.

Her hand on *his*.

The air around me shimmered, the room with its lilies and hushed mourners beginning to blur. The image of those joined hands – one so alive, the other so irrevocably still – drew me down a sun-dappled path, into another time, another touch... My own hand, reaching out, closing around another, much smaller, trembling one.

She was there, no more than seven, face streaked with tears, clutching a brightly beaded bracelet – a splash of colour against her drab school uniform. Another child's taunt about it, sharp and cruel, still hung in the air. I-*He* didn't speak at first, simply offered his hand. When her small, trembling one crept into *his*, *he* held it, a quiet, steady anchor. Then, *he* spotted a single, perfect daisy nearby, picked it, and with gentle fingers, tucked it amongst the bright beads of her bracelet.

That image of shared, fragile beauty dissolved, and as my gaze returned to her vigil by the casket, the familiar silk of *his* old scarf knotted at her throat blurred my spectral sight, pulling me sharply back into another room, another year.

She was older, perhaps fourteen. *He* found her in the spare room, standing before a chipped mirror, old silk scarves of *his* draped around her like a makeshift gown. A look of fierce, fragile longing in her eyes as she saw herself transformed. She hadn't heard *him* approach. When her startled gaze met *his* in the reflection, *he* leaned against the doorframe, a softness in *his* expression, and said gently, "The green one, I think. It brings out the colour in your eyes."

That moment shimmered for a heartbeat before fading into another: an evening just past dusk, she had sat beside *him* on the porch steps, hair freshly dyed violet again, luminous in the twilight. She hesitated, then softly admitted, "Sometimes I feel like I'm just pretending – like someone's going to find me out."

He had paused, feeling the weight of years and silence pressing behind his own words.

"Yet we keep going anyway."

She nodded, eyes bright with something like belief, and in that stillness, something passed between them – unspoken, understood.

Her small smile on that porch dissolved before me. I felt the air shift, grow heavy – the silence no longer gentle but taut with the palpable ache of an unspoken question, pulling my focus sharp to another moment.

She stood before *him*, small, her gaze clouded with a thought she seemed almost afraid to voice – one of those thoughts too easily punished if spoken aloud. *He* met that gaze, held it, *his* own eyes filled with a gentleness that was a balm. Then, *his* voice, quiet, steady:

"Boys can dream of whatever they want to."

Her head lifted sharply, a flicker of desperate hope igniting in her eyes.

"And what about girls?" she whispered, the words so soft they were almost carried away by the silence. "Can *they* also dream?"

For a bare instant, I saw the shadow of *his* own unvoiced longings pass across *his* face, a fleeting echo of the boy who hadn't dared. Then, it was gone, replaced by an immense, unwavering tenderness. *He* didn't offer words. *He* simply opened his arms. She immediately stepped into them. *He* held her then – a long, encompassing embrace that seemed to gather up all her nascent doubts and fears, offering in their place a silent, absolute affirmation.

And I, watching, felt a profound shift, as if a tightly locked door within me had finally, irrevocably, creaked open.

Cherry-coloured Funk. Of course. The soft, ethereal melody I'd half-noticed earlier seemed to crystallize in this new openness, its swirling notes suddenly familiar. A gift from her bright, burgeoning world to *his*-my quiet, shadowed one. Something *she* had given back.

"*His... my...*"

The words resonated, a new chord struck within the silence of my being. The weight of *his* choices, my regrets, suddenly felt... different. Not lighter, but rearranged, as if seen through a prism gifted by her song, her memory.

A fragile warmth spread through me. The air in the room still held the scent of mourning, but the sharp edge of judgment within me had dulled, softened by the melody of her unexpected gift.

I began to drift, one last time, through the rooms that had been *his-ours.*

The faded wallpaper, its roses worn pale – the conversations *he* never had still whispered there, a faint, lingering sorrow. But beneath it, I sensed the quiet continuity of *his* days, the silent witness to countless mornings, the simple turning of pages. A life, in its unremarked unfolding. *My life.*

I passed the old cabinet, rust on its handles, lacquer like dried petals. The comforts *he* denied himself were still a palpable ache, yet it was a keeper of *his* small, private world, the things I chose to hold onto.

The clock on the mantle, forever stopped at half-past three. The sting of lost chances, those moments *he* let pass, hadn't vanished entirely. But the frantic mockery was gone. It was simply *my* clock, from *my* time, a quiet fixture in the landscape I inhabited.

In the small room, the reading chair still sat, well-used. The scent of forgotten tea was no longer just a sharp tang of regret for *my* unfulfilled solitude. It mingled now, softened, with the clear memory of listening patiently there, as a young girl with searching eyes spoke of futures I helped build.

On the shelf, tucked beside a stack of those unread volumes, almost hidden, I saw it now: a small, brightly beaded bracelet, its colours still defiant, like a pressed flower kept between pages. The daisy was long gone, but the memory of *my* hand placing it there, her small one in *mine*, still bloomed.

Each object, each scent, each slant of light no longer testified only to unfulfilled desires. They were fragments of *his* existence – our shared passage. A life, yes, profoundly tinged with sadness, but a life lived, in all its quiet complexity. And woven through its muted fabric, that thread of unexpected, luminous kindness which had, indeed, changed another's world. Perhaps, in those fleeting, incandescent fragments, my life had bent toward joy more than I'd realized.

The ethereal notes of *Cherry-coloured Funk* softened, mingling with the scent of lilies and dust, weaving a sense of fragile, completed peace. The violet-haired girl had stepped back from the casket, her small act of tenderness concluded. Her eyes, scanning the room, paused as they fell upon the uncovered mirror by the hallway wall.

A small frown touched her lips. "Oh...," she murmured, her voice a soft echo in the quiet space, "...missed this one."

She looked around and then, spotting a length of dark velvet, she moved with that same gentle purpose as at the record cabinet. Carefully, she lifted the velvet, draping the glass. The images of my younger self, echoes of joy and regret, began to dim. Each fold felt like softly closing a book.

The music played on, a gentle, swirling farewell, but I was no longer there to hear its final notes. I was simply gone.

Gabriel Graves

Gabriel is an established theatre-maker – born in Spain, raised in Argentina – who has now built an active career in Ireland. He has premiered over twenty-five plays and attributes his writing to 'opposable thumbs and a highly developed prefrontal cortex.'

Following our laments of fading time, he leads us deeper into Irish horror with a subverted vampire tale. 'Persistence' is a gothic elegy for monstrosity and endless decay, where memory and flesh erode, but desire endures.

Persistence

Si cette partie m'a causé du mal à la fin, elle m'a aussi procuré bien du plaisir au commencement. Ce serait ingrat de ne pas le lui reconnaître.

– Michel de Montaigne

He masturbates without purpose, driven solely by friction. No thought in his mind, the harsh back-and-forth of his hand, his gaze lost on the peeling rocks. His skin, dry as a palimpsest, worn by layer upon layer, raises dust with every stroke. He squints, fixated on the rocks. Perhaps he tries to recall if this had been one of the lavish rooms with heavy drapes and intricate tapestries, or if, instead, it was another chamber of stone. Stone upon stone, now crumbling too. Being there is, in its way, a form of prayer.

He has long nails. Longer than ever before. There must have been a before. Though 'before' means nothing now. Back then, it meant something. A beast as terrible as a woman, or perhaps a woman, sank her teeth into his neck, birthing in him a taste for blood. Her bite was sweet and long. It was, perhaps, a woman. But what is a 'woman' to him now? His rigid member, the relentless motion rising and falling, waiting for a sudden burst. By the sheer persistence of being there, he confirms his own existence.

He toys with a thread of memory sometimes, unraveling it strand by strand. But in the end, what for? How long can a memory last? A lifetime? And what is a life, an individual 'life,' even his own, in this circumstance? He continues his task, born from the depths of existence, surviving amid stone and oblivion. He runs his tongue over his gums. There is still a tongue, yes. It doesn't click anymore, but it's there. There are still some gums, he confirms. It must have been, yes, a woman. Generous breasts. Time wore away his teeth. Except, of course, the fangs. He can still rub fang against fang, and something like a smile emerges. His arms reveal blue patches, clots in what was once blood. Back then, he had to restrain himself from lunging at his own arms. Sometimes he failed. The old taste was gone. His 'blood,' now foul, thinned further each time it returned to his veins. Less blood each time. Yet, the urge to feed lingered long. Until, one day, he forgot it.

He has seen everything. He no longer salivated. Never again would he, as in the days of games, receive a guest. Times when he could still invite someone to the castle, perform his little ceremony, his courteous 'Enter freely. Go safely' ritual, all that paraphernalia, only to then, yes, let himself go.

He has been loved. Perhaps he had loved her back. Loved her for her bite, for her curse. Even now, in this current state, whatever this 'state' is, he was, in a way, thankful. If 'thankful' still means something. Because what was he without his curse?

He has been hated. The hatred lasted long. Sometimes, even now, he snarls when, far off in the desert, something flickers. A spark, half-imagined, half-seen, a memory of when men gathered with torches, hoping to lynch him. The memory of hatred warmed him for a long time. There was still hope back then. When they came with stakes and crosses. An era of stakes and crosses that weren't enough for all. The fortunate ones departed that way. He remained.

He came to crave the swift oblivion of the stake. For a long time, he yearned for those days when villages lit a thousand fires in his name. When there was fear, and there was blood. And through others' fear, and others' blood, he could feel his existence. He never thought he'd miss that. He learned to hate those men far more than the crackling fire. He hated them for being worse than other men, for failing to drive the sharpened wood into his chest. Eventually, the memory of hatred became a memory of a memory. Then nothing.

He still sits in his chair. His tall chair, once commanding respect. It can hardly be called a chair now, but long ago, it signaled a, let's say, hierarchy. When did his chair cease to be a chair? It wasn't a single moment, nor the span of a life. It was longer. Yes. It had to be. It doesn't matter. Measures are blurry now. He has no tears left. No words left. Not because there is no one to hear them, as was true at first, but because they are gone. They had abandoned him along with the cities, the names. There are sounds, yes - grunts, occasional gasps, the wind, the sounds a body makes. He clenches his fist, and a new cloud of dust forms. He continues. Back and forth.

He saw his enemies pass by, his executioners. His friends. His biographers. He saw the ideas of one era become the mockery of the next, and he saw it all repeat. His reflection always eluded him. It was dark, yes, but what is 'dark' in this circumstance? Sometimes there seemed to be another sound, a knock from outside. Once, lifetimes ago, he rose to investigate. He transformed into another, flew aimlessly. Nothing. One time, he thought he saw a girl, but a 'girl' meant no longer anything. He wavered between killing her and letting her die. It was the last time he tasted another's blood. He did it without hatred, without haste. In time, he wondered if it was only a dream and longed to hear that knock again. Then it passed.

The moon turned reddish.

He tried to write his memoirs. He started them. Then abandoned the project. He found it much later, forgetting he had begun it. It didn't seem like his life. It entertained him, yes. He tried to write his memoirs again, new memoirs of his new old memories. He wrote an S, a large, menacing S like a butcher's hook. He looked at his hand, surprised he could still do that. He looked at his veins, like if they belonged to someone else. He stared at the quill as the red ink dried. He clicked his tongue. There was still a tongue. It still clicked. Dizzy, he set the task aside for later. He never returned to it. He forgot writing and the old dreams he used to dwell on.

Laughter stayed with him a long time, long after he forgot what he was laughing at. He dragged his body to the chair and began. His hand on his flaccid member. Once. And again. And again. And so on. Until, in the end, there was only dust after each effort. Sometimes a grimace or a long exhalation.

He had lived centuries. He had, I insist, loved. A woman. There has been a woman. He had been bitten. He had devoured. Now he does this. The world had emptied of blood, but his body endured. Perhaps he suspects that even an absurd curse like his will end. Because gravitational forces dictate that the planets must crash into one another, and that at some point, destruction must claim every living thing. Such is the universal promise. Meanwhile, he waits. His hand moves. He presses with force, the memory of his body compressed in his hand. He resists his ghostly condition, the unyielding judgment of mirrors and shadows. For the mirrors, I insist, refused to reflect him, but the mirrors had passed, and he was still here. His absent shadow mocked him and his vanity. His shadow never followed. He persists, without a shadow. He touches himself. If he doesn't, time passes anyway. In the flaking of his hand, there is still something to keep destroying. The filthy moon, stained by centuries, is still there. The sand is still there. The sea is still there. And he is still there. And the friction. Little else.

He is unique in his kind, as every monster is. Even when there are no monsters anymore. Only remnants of a forgotten, let's say, hierarchy. The last vestige of a body that moves from time to time. After his prayer, his hand seems to move, covering himself with an imaginary cloak. Then he leans back, and his vertebrae, that old machine where his vertebrae once were, creak. Almost beatific, he reclines, his fangs collide and something like a smile appears. And the bloody moon grows, and the wind still sings its song, as the faint grim claims his lips further, and his eyes open wide, and he stares. There he still is, if you wish to see him.

Lorraine Hester

Lorraine shares once more, showcasing her range from historical fiction to speculative worlds anchored in vivid realism. Based in Phibsboro, *she's infatuated with the nearby* Botanic Gardens *– her favourite place to dream up new story ideas or mentally work through plot tangles.*

Here we layer in speculative futuristism onto our examination of uncertainty, aging and the echoes of past relationships. 'Six of Cups' follows a woman who escapes to her seaside hometown and turns to a popular Tarot *app for guidance. Its uncanny readings stir old longings, blurring the boundaries of nostalgia and desire.*

Six of Cups

She scurries along Main Street. The sounds and smells have not changed; jangling arcade music and malt vinegar. Crystals of sea salt settle into her crow's feet and grit her eyelashes and lips.

She blinks and the ghost of her younger self eyeballs her from the clumps of teenagers loitering outside the supermarket. Strange how much she looks at home there. Fashion has cycled back to the trends of her youth – layered camisoles, wide leg jeans, slip dresses, and butterfly clips. She's read that, for women, the forties are the decade when self-assurance beds in. She's sure that she's been leaking confidence since she was nineteen, like a slowly deflating party balloon.

Now she's hurrying again. She's early but the pub will have WiFi and she's excited to check her *Readings* on the app before Paul arrives. There's no internet or cell reception in the mobile home she rented at short notice two days ago. Being completely offline sounded like a selling point before she arrived. In practice, impotently unlocking her phone multiple times an hour has sparked the kind of prickly restlessness no amount of cheap white wine can smooth away.

She arrives. The pub is darker inside than she expected and she pauses a few steps inside the door, disoriented. Stale air resettles heavily behind her. As her vision adjusts, she sees the place is empty save for a couple of older men invested in making steady solitary progress on their respective pints. It's a faded establishment, but the bartender is disconcertingly young and trendy. Bleached hair blossoms in curly chunks around his face. He takes her order and delivers a poorly executed Aperol Spritz, the soda water floating unmixed at the top of the glass.

"Happy hour at four, if you're sticking around." He taps on the plastic straw dispenser with dove-grey press-on nails.

She nods, hurries to a table, logs into the app, and scrolls back through her activity history. She wants to be sure she's revisited every *Reading* before Paul arrives.

May 10th 2025

On behalf of all the students, masters, and mavericks of The Tarot before you, welcome back to **R*CANA**. Here are a few tips for using the app:

1.Start a daily practice. Turn ON notifications to get alerts for your daily tarot reading.

2.Your package includes one daily reading and one daily personalised clarification via **Delphi**, the AI-powered tarot reader in your pocket.

3.Remember, depending on your life situation and mood, it may be healthier to explore The Tarot with a friend or trusted partner. If you feel upset or triggered by certain cards, consider exploring your feelings with a licensed therapist. Click here for a discount code you can use with our on-demand, online therapy partners.

What would you like to do?

1. Learn more about the Tarot
2. Explore your Daily Reading
3. Draw a Spirit card
4. Draw a Love card
5. Draw a Career card

>>><<<

Draw a Love Card

>>><<<

> Six of Cups: The card of nostalgia and childhood memories, a reminder of happy times gone by. In a love reading, this may represent warm memories of a past relationship, or the early stages of your current relationship. The Six of Cups could also denote the possibility of an old flame reappearing in your life.

Re-reading the card description sets off the same sequence of bodily reactions as it did one week ago. Heart speeds up. Stomach clenches. Skin behind her ears burns, hot and prickly.

She takes a long sip from her drink, relishing the cold clink of the ice against her teeth. Daylight spills in from the street, illuminating the sodden beer mats and grubby smudges on the table top. Her head lifts in anticipation but Paul is not in the doorway. The door is open but the doorway is empty. Her glass feels heavy in her hand. She squeezes her eyes shut. When she opens them the bartender is smiling. She follows his gaze down, and down again. She releases her breath.

A small child is pressed against the base of the door, bracing himself with all his strength to keep it open. There is sand on his forehead. He is dragging a beach towel on the ground and vibrating with urgency.

"Can I hide in here?"

The bartender hesitates, "I don't think you should be in here, sweetie."

"Quick! They're coming, can I hide in here?"

"Who's coming?"

The boy shakes his head in exasperation. He releases the door and barrels across the floor, tucking himself beneath the table adjoining hers, alongside a tall wooden partition. She squints at his little head in the low light and waves to the barman to show that she's not bothered by the intrusion. Maybe it will be a charming anecdote to recount when Paul arrives. Wiggling her fingers at the boy conspiratorially, she reopens the app, scrolling back through her activity.

What would you like to do next?

1. Get a New Reading
2. Speak to **Delphi** for a personalised AI Clarification on your last Reading

>>><<<

Speak to **Delphi** for a personalised AI Clarification

>>><<<

What would you like to ask **Delphi**?

>>><<<

Question: Is this a reading about my ex?

>>><<<

Delphi says "Ah the mysteries of the heart. It is with those we love that we weave the most complex tapestries. I applaud you for your insight and dedication to exploring the meaning of the Tarot as it relates to your one, beautiful life. You pulled the Six of Cups - a card steeped in nostalgia. The Six of Cups represents comfort, memory and familiarity. In the context of love, it can represent an opportunity to reconnect with former partners and even to rekindle former relationships. Perhaps emotions that once burned strong still have relevance in the present day? Perhaps there are valuable lessons to internalise from past romantic entanglements?"

Would you like to go deeper? **R*CANA Premium** offers almost unlimited personalised readings and progress reports. Learn more and review pricing plans here.

A tug on her pant leg jerks her back into the present. The little boy is gesturing to her drink.

"Can I have a sip of that?"

"Oh! No. That's only for grown-ups to drink. That's not for kids."

"Do you have any kids?"

"I do. I have a little girl about your age."

"Where is she?"

She looks around her for help, but none is forthcoming.

"She lives with her father at the moment. Where are your parents?"

"It's ok, they let me go into town with my friends. Are you hiding from your friends too?"

"No! I'm....I'm meeting a friend here soon."

"A boy or a girl?"

She smiles, "A boy."

"Boys and girls can't be friends."

There is a snort from a nearby table.

"He's right, you know." A man – she guesses in his late fifties – two tables over is swirling the end of his pint slowly. "It never ends well."

She laughs politely, then hates herself for laughing politely. "We'll just have to agree to disagree", she says.

She reopens the app.

May 11th 2025

On behalf of all the students, masters, and mavericks of The Tarot before you, welcome back to **R*CANA.**

What would you like to do next?

1. Explore a New Reading
2. Subscribe to **R*CANA Premium**
3. Speak to **Delphi** for a personalised AI Clarification on your last Reading

>>><<<

Speak to **Delphi** for a personalised AI Clarification

>>><<<

What would you like to ask **Delphi**?

>>><<<

Question: Is it a good idea to contact my ex?

>>><<<

Delphi says: "I honour what matters most to you in this moment. You can and should trust in your own emotional intelligence and instincts. Hold space for yourself and your true desires. There is no one else like you. We should all be so lucky to have you in our lives."

She looks up. Paul is late now. By more than a couple of minutes. A sharp hook of anxiety catches and twists. Could she have given him the name of the wrong bar? She checks her recent sent messages and confirms that all the information is correct. Including all of the map hyperlinks.

The little boy is now crawling commando-style across the floor of the bar. He looks back at her, points towards the man at the nearby table, taps one ear twice, then gestures two fingers forward urgently. Unintelligible SWAT sign-language. The man catches her eye again.

"Meeting someone local?"

"He used to be."

He examines the dregs of his pint, letting her curt response hang there in the silence. "Didn't mean to offend you, love. Just speaking on my own experience of men and women. Learned some lessons the hard way."

He finishes his drink and taps his fingernails one by one against the pint glass, first slowly, then quickening. The sound sends off little bursts of static at the base of her skull. Her hands tighten reflexively around her phone.

"It's absolutely guaranteed that someone is looking to get the ride. Forget friendship – they're not in it for tea and chats and sympathy. Someone's being led up the garden path in that case."

"That's a very depressing view of the world."

"Realistic, more like. So a local fella? Would I know him?"

She hesitates. "Paul... Paul Healy."

"Oh aye. Moved back just last year." He squints at her slyly, "Lovely wife."

"As I said, just an old friend."

Her phone pings with a notification. Her fingers tremble as she unlocks the screen.

> If you've enjoyed using **R*CANA**, please rate us on the App Store. It helps us reach more people, just like you!

She turns the phone facedown on the table and slumps back in her seat.

Her neighbour catches her attention again. "Can I buy you a drink?" he asks, raising an eyebrow at her and one finger to hail the bartender, "As a friend?"

Jamie Samson

Jamie, another long standing group contributor, brings his trademark blend of deep resonance and understated satire. His fiction has appeared in The Irish Times, RTE Culture, The Four Faced Liar, Channel, Metro Eireann, and Hektoen International, earning him a reputation for sharply-crafted storytelling about humanity.

Extending our focus on self-perception, we shift to a new examination of technology for human intimacy. In 'Good Egg,' he takes us into a near-future gig economy where bodies and minds are rentable commodities. A young woman spends her weeks inhabiting another person's desires while suppressing her own – an arrangement that pays the bills but frays her sense of self.

Good Egg

ILLUSIONS

It is Sunday. A young woman is sitting alone on the roof of a white institutional building. She keeps turning her hands over, both hands, over and over. She is entranced. She keeps pinching her skin. She breathes in the bright rich windless air. She keeps fluttering her fingers, watching the bones move under her skin. She thinks they are like worms wriggling in sand. She cries. It is the middle of the day, the very middle. The sky, untouched by cloud or contrail, is a strong cold azure. Far away in the distance she sees the gleam of two trams moving towards the same point. They seem like they might collide. But they don't. They sail past each other, shining, on separate tracks. It's just an illusion. The young woman thinks: today has been a good day. She wishes she could have more, just a little more, but she knows that wanting more is not good for the soul. Later, at dusk, great clouds amass on the horizon. They are complex, glittering things, full of creases and chasms, knots, pleats, veins. They rise up before her like a firing squad. She would like more but she will not ask for more. Today has been a good day. She will not ask for more.

_HOST_NATASHA_

"Come and have a drink with us, Natasha! You shouldn't be hiding away in your room like a little mouse. Let's have the chats."

Natasha's three flatmates are spread out across the common room's musty couches and armchairs, holding cups of wine and vodka spritz. Alina, Gabriela, and June consider Natasha, with her weird job and foul moods and bedroom drinking, a bit of a curiosity, a source of amusement. She has overheard some of the things they say.

"I can't tonight," Natasha says. She smiles shyly. "I'm at the centre tomorrow."

The mention of the centre introduces a silence into the room. The girls all assume tight, blank faces. Natasha can't tell if they're concerned for her or holding back laughter.

Gabriela sits up in her seat, feeling emboldened enough to ask for details.

"They don't let you drink?"

"Not the night before a session. It's in my contract. I have to be fresh."

Gabriela makes a face. "Fresh?" she says. The others giggle.

"I have to have... they call it a HBE? A hospitable bodily environment. If I'm sick or hungover or anything they cancel the session. And then I don't get paid."

Natasha is a BodyShare host. Every Sunday she takes the tram out to a large research facility located deep in the northern suburbs. It's a pretty Victorian-era building, with glassy modern extensions, that's surrounded by birch trees and alders and a very tall fence. It was once owned by the Sisters of the Blessed Sacrament and is now owned and operated by BodyShare Technologies Ltd, trading under the ticker symbol BSTX. There are three other such centres across the country, with more planned to follow.

At the centre, Natasha undergoes a non-invasive operation that puts her consciousness on ice for roughly eight hours, allowing someone else to take over her body and mind in the meantime. In return for this service, Natasha receives just over €2,000 a month, roughly 8% of the full client fee. The rest of the time she works at an office building in the Docklands, as a cleaner.

"So when you go to the place tomorrow, some old dude will just, like, take over your body for the day? And what happens to you? Are you just asleep for it?"

Usually Natasha does everything she can to exit conversations like this. Tonight, though, she decides to go along with it. The girls are being a bit less bitchy than usual. She sits on the closest armrest and explains.

"I mean, it's not sleep, technically. Technically, I stop actually existing for those eight hours."

The girls take a moment to absorb the strangeness of this remark.

"So, it's like being dead?"

Natasha thinks about this.

"It's not really like anything. It's new, you know? The whole thing is so new. They don't have names yet, for what happens at the centre."

June says, "That must fuck you up though. It must. Renting yourself out like that..."

Gabriela comes to Natasha's aid. "Renting yourself out? You're making her sound like a *prostitute*."

"I'm just saying!" June laughs. She gestures to Natasha with an open palm. "I mean, *clearly* it fucks you up..."

The last comment hurts. Natasha knows what June's getting at. The girls have seen her in some rough states, have seen the sour, haunted, hateful creature that staggers through the flat from time to time. And even on weekday nights they are all too familiar with the spectacle of their weird flatmate drifting across the common room, acknowledging nobody, on her way to the cupboard for a cup or glass. They know she keeps bottles of wine hidden in her room. She hides herself in there, in that nasty-smelling depression box, all night, every night. Sometimes they spot her emerging with a discreet Aldi bag full of clinking empties.

"And do you know anything about your... what's the word, *tenant*? The old man who enters you."

The girls smirk at Alina's phrasing. Natasha can feel herself becoming more dour and defensive.

"They're called guests," she says. "And no, I don't know anything about him. They call him Guest Eamon, in the forms."

"Guest Eamon," Alina repeats. "He sounds hot!"

Soon she grows tired of the questions and says her goodnights. She sits in her bedroom, on the windowsill. The window swings all the way open. She hears the girls giggling again through the wall and guesses that the laughter is at her expense. She hopes they'll decide to go out tonight so she can have some solitude and move about the house as she pleases.

She always finds herself thinking about Guest Eamon the night before a session. Tomorrow, at dawn, as she makes her way to the centre, an old man on the other side of the city will be doing the same thing. She wonders who he is and what he gets out of occupying her body every week. She wonders what he does for a living to be able to afford such an expensive hobby. He's been renting out Natasha's body for two years now. She struggles to imagine what he gets up to in her skin while her own mind floats in nothingness. She doesn't really want to know. She assumes he's some kind of creep. She pictures him as a short, bald, well-dressed man with eggy eyes and a bad back. But that is how she pictures all old men, really.

Guest Eamon. Sometimes she thinks she feels traces of him, little visions of the life that blends each week with hers. At night she shuts her eyes and sees through a haze of snow-grey dust and brownish light the shadow, the outline, of an unfamiliar woman, in a country kitchen, making bread. She sees horses galloping over wet grass. She sees a chest of drawers covered in pinkish lamps, the bottom drawer portentously ajar. The woman in the kitchen, these lamps and drawers and horses – they are not hers. They are like dreams that don't make sense, calm, sorrowful, unfocused, washed in the light of someone else's memory. She has been meaning to ask a BodyShare support agent about this. It must be some kind of glitch.

It's bedtime. She desperately wants a drink. Outside, the city makes its bleak music – shouts, sirens, and rain. Down on the street a man is splayed on the steps of a derelict building, out of his mind on something. A breeze is developing. Scraps of rubbish bounce along the curb like hares.

*_THE_CENTRE_*

People ask what happens at the centre. What actually happens, step by step? People want details. Natasha can only speak about the part where she's conscious.

She arrives at eight o'clock and leaves just after four. On winter mornings the Victorian redbrick facade glows hot and pink and dripping, like a rare steak.

To protect the privacy of guests and hosts alike, the BodyShare building has two entrances. The guest reception, with its pillars and ferns and brightly uniformed staff, resembles the lobby of an upscale health club. The host reception, where Natasha surrenders herself, is dark, low-ceilinged, purely functional.

She signs a check-in form. She follows a technician into a small bedroom full of alien machinery that smells of surgical scrub and air freshener. She changes her normal clothes for a plain clean pocketless frock. For the HBE test she huffs into a breathalyser and has her temperature checked. She signs a consent form. She lies down on the bed.

Then comes the worst part, the bit she has nightmares about. The tranquilisation. The gas. A busy, tired-looking nurse places a mask over Natasha's mouth, secures it with straps, pulls a lever to tighten it. The gas makes her brain feel tinglingly dull, like a limb that's been sat on. It smells like permanent marker. The nurse tells her to recite the alphabet. By the time she gets to F the letters come out sluggish and slurred. She never gets as far as M.

People want to know what happens next. Does she feel anything, however faint, when Guest Eamon's consciousness replaces hers? Does she sense this transition at all, or anything that follows, if not in her brain, then in her blood and skin, her nerve endings?

But she feels nothing. Nothing. There is no pared-down, immaterial version of Natasha watching what Guest Eamon gets up to in her body. For those eight hours, *there is no Natasha*, plain and simple. Her mind, her identity, her personhood (a word used often in the BodyShare debate), whatever you want to call the part of her that isn't nailed down in flesh and bone, simply gets put on pause, suspended in a void outside of time, while an old man she has never met takes control of her physical body, bringing his own subjective experience along for the ride, like a suitcase thrown onto the backseat of a rental car.

Until she is resurrected, that is. Then she's back. And it's time to endure a long, slow headache and start assessing the damage.

A slight strain in her neck or inner thigh, or throbbing in the soles of her feet, or the taste of food she has no recollection of eating (guests are supposed to brush before handover), is about her only evidence that she hasn't been sleeping the entire time. The muscles in her face often hurt. Then there's the tiredness. Sometimes she wakes up feeling like she has just run an uphill race. And she's always dizzy and fog-brained as she nods her way through the check-out inspection, as she retrieves her belongings and says goodbye to the girl behind the desk, whose name she never learned.

Then she goes home, showers for at least forty five minutes, and drinks most of a bottle of inexpensive white wine.

This lets her know that yes, to answer the next question, she does feel violated by the whole thing. And yes, she would like to stop doing it. The idea of some rich old man possessing her body and mind for eight hours every week gives her the horrors, plain and simple.

Being a host does not, on balance, make her feel good about herself.

Maybe it was mildly interesting, or at least novel, the first couple of times. But that was two years ago. These days it's just an upsetting chore.

The problem is, she needs the money.

_WHAT_DO_YOU_MEAN_DOWN?_

She calls the BodyShare Guest Helpline. She needs to talk to someone. She can't talk to her flatmates about it. They are too scandalised by the details to be of any help. She can't talk to her sister about it, who has made it very clear that she doesn't approve of this freak-show job of hers. And she can't talk to her mother, because her mother doesn't know, and can never know.

"Hello, welcome to the BodyShare support centre. If you are a host wishing to register a complaint against a guest, please press one. If you are a host requesting access to our emotional support service, please press two."

Natasha presses two. Absently she watches a fly crawl up the windowpane, drawn to the lights of the traffic jam outside. Its tiny buzz reminds her of distant lawnmowers in summertime.

"Hello, this is Debbie from BodyShare Support. Please state your name, BodyShare ID number, and your reason for calling today."

Natasha answers the first two questions without hassle but pauses on the third one.

"I suppose I'm just feeling a bit..."

"Mm-hm?"

"Just, you know, a bit... not myself?"

She is surprised to find she has difficulty holding back tears.

"Mm-hm, mm-hm. Go on. Go on, darling."

Natasha imagines the woman on the other end of the line looking gravely at a sign saying, "If in doubt, refer to the caller as *darling*."

"I guess I'm just feeling a bit down."

"And tell me, Natasha, what do you mean *down*? Down how?"

"Just a bit..."

"A bit depressed? Would you describe your state at the moment as depressed?"

"Yes I guess I might say I would."

"And tell me, Natasha, have you had any suicidal thoughts in the past forty eight hours?"

"Just I think in a vague way. But no. Not really."

"I understand. Well Natasha, as one of the co-ordinators at your site might have explained to you, you are entitled to a weekly prescription to Eudamodil. It's a mood stabiliser. Very mild side effects. It wouldn't affect your ability to perform your role at BodyShare. Will I sign you up for that?"

"What are the side effects?"

"Diarrhoea would be the main one. But mild diarrhoea."

"Oh."

"Will I sign you up for that?"

"For diarrhoea pills?"

A silence follows. Natasha seems to have offended Debbie. She rolls her eyes, and decides it's better to have them than not have them. She can worry about whether she wants to take them later.

"Yeah go on," she says. "Sign me up."

_THE_WALLS_ARE_MADE_OF_GLASS_

It's Monday. Natasha in her blue apron and yellow rubber gloves smiles tightly at a pair of young workers as they pass her on their way to the elevator. They are the last to leave tonight.

"You're doing the Lord's work, Natalia," one of them says, loudly. "Fair play to you."

Natalia.

She pushes her trolley from Conference Room A to Conference Room B. She empties the rubbish bins. She hoovers the floor. With a microfibre cloth she wipes down the tables and shelves. She clears a pie chart off the whiteboard.

She's on the top floor. The walls are made of glass. Through the glass, and the streaming rain, she can see people in suits, framed by office windows, harshly illuminated, typing. She sees traffic jams of double-decker buses, their windows fogged. She sees the river and the bridges going over it. Lights from see-through buildings wobble across the water's black surface.

In the men's room she gets a call from BodyShare. She has to put down the mop and peel off her gloves to answer it.

The woman on the phone tells her that she has some unfortunate news. Guest Eamon passed away this morning.

Natasha lowers herself onto the plastic bin.

"Oh? Well, that's..."

"I'm very sorry, Natasha."

"That's sad," Natasha says. "I just had a session with him yesterday."

"Unfortunately I must inform you that Guest Eamon's death means that the income stream associated with his account has been terminated. This in turn means you will not be receiving any further payment from BodyShare, not until you've been matched with another guest. However, Natasha, I have some further news for you. Guest Eamon left you a sign-off tip, which he specified was to be given to you in the case of his death or inability to continue using the service."

"A tip?"

"We recommend that guests who are happy with their hosts leave a sign-off tip of 100 euro per session. However, your guest insisted on leaving more. Are you sitting down, Natasha?"

"I am."

"Guest Eamon has left you a tip of twenty five thousand euro. This will be deposited into your account within five business days."

Natasha doesn't say anything. She looks absently at the cubicles and urinals around her. She catches her reflection in the polished mirror and notices her eyes are red with tears.

"Natasha, are you still there?"

"I'm still here," she says.

_B41_

Later that night when Natasha steps out of the shower she notices something behind her ear. At first she thinks it's a mole or a freckle. She looks closer. In fact it's a dense ball of writing – a letter followed by two numbers. It says B41. The B is especially thick. She recognises the handwriting as her own, more or less.

A code, she thinks. A message.

B41. She writes it down on a piece of paper. She spends a long time thinking what it might mean. She types it into Google. She reads about the B41 bomb, the most powerful thermonuclear device ever developed by the United States. She reads about B41 FG alloy wheels. She reads about the Bundesstraße 41, a federal highway in Germany. None of these seem right.

Finally she discovers the website for a pub called Bar Forty-One. It's located in Sandymount. She scrolls through the pictures. Hanging over the door is a golden sign saying B41. The B is especially thick.

She gets her jacket.

On the train down to Sandymount she keeps thinking of Guest Eamon. It disturbs her that only a day ago he was occupying her body and now he's cold and dead. She also can't stop thinking what a big number twenty five thousand is.

Bar Forty-One is a warm, elegant, thickly carpeted neighbourhood pub. Natasha steps in from the rain. Four or five drinkers, all men, lift their heads with curiosity at the soaking young woman who approaches the bar. They have the flushed and restful appearance of old regulars. A rugby match plays on mute from a widescreen TV attached to the wall.

"I told you me fuckin prayers would be answered," one of the old men declares upon seeing her. The others wheeze with laughter.

Natasha approaches the bartender, a tall, big-eyed man who seems slightly afraid of her.

"Hi," she says.

"Hello, young lady. How can I be of service this evening?"

A man perched on the stool next to Natasha grins.

"Tommy, how come I don't ever receive that level of professionalism in how I'm greeted?"

"Because you're not a feckin *lady*, Jim. You're a feckin eejit is what you are."

This Jim man now slams his pint on the counter in mock outrage.

"This is a bit unusual," Natasha says. "But do you happen to know someone by the name of Eamon?"

A degree of melancholy enters the barman's face and the room becomes detectably quieter.

"I do. I did, I mean. He passed only this morning."

"I heard."

"Was he a relative of yours?"

"No, he wasn't. He was... a guest of mine."

"A guest?"

"I don't know if this will mean anything to you, but... I'm Natasha."

She registers the soft thump of many pints being set down as all attention focuses on her.

"It is very good to meet you, Natasha," the barman says, deadly sincere. "He left something for you."

He retreats into a back room. While she waits, Natasha looks around the room and recoils at the intensity of the gazes directed her way.

The barman returns with a shoebox. Natasha opens it there and then. Inside is a black notebook and a small thick envelope. She is too intrigued to take it elsewhere. She orders a glass of white wine. The barman pours her a generous serving from an expensive-looking bottle. "No charge," he says, and grins sadly.

She takes the box and the glass to a booth at the back, on the far side of a billiards table. The pub's eyes are still fixed on her, but gradually, as she settles in and opens the notebook, the men return to their conversations and she fades into the background.

She begins to read.

Today I had my first BodyShare session with Host Natasha. She is twenty three. Soft blemish-free skin. Long, blonde, slightly wavy hair that practically glows. Firm flat stomach. I couldn't believe I was "in". I walked around the centre, trying out activities. I swam a few lengths of the pool. I played tennis with another BodySharer, a Belfast fellow occupying the body of a young Indonesian. Tennis! I visited the trampoline room. The best day I've had in years! It was such a deprivation to return this evening to my own frail, broken, dying body. I felt like a homeless man who'd been permitted to spend the day in a glorious firelit palace, only to be sent back at the eleventh hour to his park bench. Natasha is my palace! And everything else, it feels, is my park bench. The park bench is my tumour, my wheelchair, my hospital bed, my aches and pains, my bowel movements, my sleepiness, my loss of memory, my Lisinopril, my ThyroLux, my Omeprazole, and the empty spaces where my people should be. I will count down the hours until next Sunday morning. The hours, and the minutes, and the seconds too.

Natasha looks up from the diary. The barman looks at the rain through the window while polishing a glass. The customers are mildly absorbed in the rugby match. The fire crackles behind the stove guard. She turns the page.

I cannot understand why I didn't spend every moment of my youth in a state of transcendent joy. Natasha has reminded me of how magnificent it is to be young and beautiful and flexible and clear of mind. It seems like magic to me. Today I woke up in my usual state, a confused and groaning corpse. But then I got to inhabit Natasha again. It was even better than last time. I sprinted, I swam, I danced, I stretched. I spent fifteen minutes doing jumping jacks, the joints moving so seamlessly, the lungs working so painlessly, the golden hair flying everywhere. I even did the splits! I feel such a strong connection to Natasha. I hope that she is happy. I hope she has a good life and will continue to have a good life without old pests like me stealing hours from her day. She is a good egg alright. I hope she realises how divinely beautiful she really is. I was a bit naughty today, in fact: I snuck in a disposable camera and took some pictures. I like to look at them sometimes and just take in the loveliness of the face.

It goes on like this, two years' worth of entries. Over and over Eamon praises every facet of Natasha's youth and flesh, wishes her nothing but love, laments his own sorry state. Natasha feels strange reading the diary, as if somehow she is a voyeur on her own life. She sits in the booth for hours, reading. She gets to the final entry.

This is the end. I know it is. I am just so grateful I had a chance to inhabit Natasha one last time. This last time was different. I didn't do many activities. I did however eat an implausibly delicious meal – a double portion of roast beef with plenty of potatoes and for dessert an enormous bowl of mint chocolate ice cream. I hope Natasha won't mind the unhealthy food choice. It's just, you see, this particular flavour of ice cream brings me back to childhood summers in the farmhouse in Kerry. It's funny, I never really liked mint chocolate as a boy but today it tasted like everything. It tasted like life itself. After lunch, I wanted to be alone. I found a way onto the roof of the centre. I spent most of my time just sitting there, breathing in the rich cold November air and enjoying the colours of daytime and sunset. I just wish I could have stayed for the stars. But I know it's wrong to wish for more days than you've been given. Someone else who's young will enjoy tomorrow's stars, I hope – not for what they mean or might mean but for what they are. Perhaps Natasha will enjoy them.

I did something naughty once again. I left a little message for her, in biro, just behind her ear. I'll leave her some money, and this diary. Perhaps she'll figure out how to get it. I like to believe she will. Sometimes I think I can sense her inside me. I've felt this for years. Not the body I borrow, but the life attached, the life that must pause itself to let me in. I think I can sense a kind of sadness at the heart of that life. Even the sadness is hard to say goodbye to.

Natasha, it distresses me that we should part ways like this, with the handing over of cash. Makes it seem like that's all it ever was – a transaction, a fee paid for services rendered.. For me, though, it was closer to a gift. It has always been a gift. Squeeze from it everything you can, every gold and silver drop.

Natasha has been doing more crying in the last few days than she's used to. She puts the diary away and opens the brown envelope. These are the pictures Eamon took with his disposable camera. They show Natasha on the tennis court, at the cafeteria table, on a yoga mat, on the dance floor. Seeing them, she understands at once why her cheeks always hurt after sessions. In every one of them she is smiling enormously, with an ease and a radiance she has never seen on herself before. Here the nose she's always hated is cheerfully crinkled; there the eyes she's never liked – the eyes she thought morose, bitchy, dull – are absolutely glittering with joy. She wants to know: *Are these pictures of me or pictures of someone else?* She tries to mimic the expressions, the smiles, and finds it difficult. Does that answer the question? She doesn't really know, nor does she know how to feel about Eamon's words, however sweet, or his money, however generous. All she knows is that these pictures, these pictures... She is glad to have them. She clutches them tight against her heart.

It's late. She says goodbye to the barman and walks towards the station. There are many things she has to do.

The train, when it arrives, is jammed with people. She's never seen it so tightly packed. Something has ended, an event, a football match. Through the glass doors she sees a muddle of green scarves, gift bags, funny hats. She takes her place among the warm bodies. Some of the adults are singing. Some of the children are drinking hot chocolate from paper cups. The train goes slow at first, then fast. It surges northward, through the radiant city, under the night-blue sky with all its stars.

Thomas Waelkens

Thomas continues to lend diverse genre work to our group with science fiction capers and the odd subversion of gothic tales. He describes himself as having the soul of an artist and the mind of an engineer. Although he writes for fun, his work shows his spirit of willingness to workshop a word prompt and experiment with unique character-driven plots.

In 'The Clockmaker's Curse,' he pairs our gothic work with a mechanical mystery and a literal exploration of time's uncertainty. When a stranger arrives in the isolated village of Silverglen, Luke learns the place he's lived his entire life is cursed. Together they must find the clockmaker to unravel the age-old spell.

The Clockmaker's Curse

When I arrived back at my house I found a stranger leaning against my front door. A tall and slender man, wearing a long brown coat and a feathered hat. The presence of any stranger in Silverglen would put me on edge but his man in particular looked like trouble. He had his eyes cast towards the ground but looked up once he heard me approach.

"You Luke Harrison?" The man asked, overly articulating the R's as he did. If there had been any doubt before, it was obvious now he was not a local.

"I am." I said, wondering how he knew where I lived, "Why are you looking for me, stranger?"

"I apologize for the ambush, my name is Solomon Clarke, I arrived this morning. I am in need of assistance and the people I've spoken to so far have pointed me to you as being my best bet."

"If you need any repairs done, please visit my workshop tomorrow." With only an hour of sunlight left I wanted to get my cooking done before dark.

The man shook his head, "I am in no need of repairs. I came here looking for a missing person. A woman who visited this village about two months ago."

I could not recall any strangers coming to the village in recent times. Silverglen was an isolated place, a day and a half away from the nearest paved road, concealed in between the mountains and mostly forgotten about by the rest of the kingdom. We still received mail once a week so our faraway rulers were aware of our existence, and we of theirs.

"I haven't seen any strangers in months," I said.

"I did not think you would have," Solomon said, though I still detected a hint of disappointment in his voice. "The truth is I need your help to investigate something."

"Investigate?"

"Silverglen is cursed."

"Cursed?" Did he take me for a fool? Not all people in rural villages were superstitious.

Solomon looked at me and smiled, "You said you did not recall seeing anyone visiting your village the past two months, correct?"

I nodded.

"Well, do you remember anyone visiting at all, during your entire lifetime, can you recall ever seeing any visitor coming here other than myself today?"

I thought about it. Really thought about it. In my thirty years living here I ought to have seen and interacted with at least a couple of them. Hell, Silverglen even had a little hotel, so there should be visitors. Yet, I could not recall any of them. Someone's relatives or travellers must have visited before? I recalled seeing stacks of newspapers and letters delivered to the hotel but had I never paid attention to the people delivering them? How was that possible? I tried to find a reason to object to his statement but it seemed that what Solomon hinted at was correct.

"The village is cursed." He repeated, as if reading my thoughts. "Will you help me?"

"I'm the village's repairman, I fix tools, clothing, furniture, whatever needs doing. I know nothing about curses or magic."

"I'm a witch-hunter, I will deal with the curse. But I need your eyes and ears to see and hear things which I might miss. I do not know Silverglen the way you do."

Part of me still thought this was ridiculous. I had heard of curses in fairy tales and campfire stories but had always considered them just that, fiction or exaggeration. Now this stranger was telling me that not only did they exist, one of them was active here in Silverglen. My rational mind objected, but could not deny that it was impossible for me to have never seen any visitors before. I couldn't quite trust the man in front of me, but I also wanted to know what the hell was going on.

"Alright, fine. Tell me what you need from me and I'll see what I can do."

"We're going to need to find and release the clockmaker."

Before I had a chance to tell him there was no such person living here, he said, "Meet me at the cemetery entrance at midnight."

Stunned by the strange request, I simply agreed without thinking.

Solomon left without waiting for a reply, perhaps not wanting to give me the time to change my mind.

I spent my dinner and the rest of my evening thinking about the conversation and my decision. If he had wanted to cause me harm he could have easily done so, he did not need to lure me to the cemetery. The witch-hunter had seemed genuine in his request and I couldn't shake the feeling he was telling the truth. I would trust my intuition and go with him. Besides, I figured I could use a change of pace. While peaceful, Silverglen was rarely an exciting place to live.

At midnight I headed to the cemetery and Solomon stood there waiting for me, leaning against the fence and looking up at the sky. A lantern and two shovels lay at his feet.

"It's a beautiful night." He said.

"So, what are we doing here?" I asked.

Solomon smiled, "Finding the clockmaker. Let's get on with it."

He then turned around and effortlessly scaled the fence. His fingers gripping the narrow steel beams as if they were handles. Once on the other side, he gestured for me to follow. I made an attempt, slipping and struggling as I made my way over. My teenage, trespassing, fence climbing days were years behind me.

It seemed he had done some scouting and we walked up straight to a gravestone in the far corner of the cemetery. It stood isolated on its own plot of land away from the other graves. I leaned over and read the name on the tombstone, 'Edward Archer.' He'd been dead for almost two hundred years, yet he was the one responsible for the curse somehow? Why had he been buried here alone, should he not at least have some family members around him?

We started digging. At first our shovels struggled to pierce the cold dirt but as our rhythm synchronized our progress accelerated. The hole in front of us deepened with every passing minute. I wasn't religious but this still felt wrong to me. Even if Edward Archer had been forgotten by the village, isolated in the graveyard, that didn't mean we should disturb his peace. But that was too late now. I had committed to assist this witch-hunter and if desecrating graves was part of the job, then so be it.

Eventually my shovel hit something different, something that did not feel like dirt. Solomon noticed as well. We wiped the sweat from our foreheads and worked on revealing a wooden lid.

Once we had cleared enough surface Solomon plunged his shovel into the wood to crack open the coffin. He kept cracking away at the wood until half of it was gone. We looked at our work and saw the coffin was empty.

That was the first time I'd seen him hesitate. He bit his lower lip and stared at the empty box.

"That is... unexpected," he said.

He dropped his shovel, knelt down and reached inside of the coffin with his right hand. He probed for something, anything and eventually retrieved something from the inside. No bones or other remains but a round silver object with a small chain attached to it.

He held it up in the moonlight. The locket opened and revealed a little clock. What we had found inside the coffin was a pocket watch.

"Disturbing. Hold on to this for me please," he said and handed it to me.

I took the watch and inspected it. For all I could tell it was completely ordinary. It was still ticking, the time set to one thirty. Since we started at midnight, I reckoned it might even be accurate. How long has it been in there? Even the best clocks coming from the city wouldn't retain their accuracy for very long. It could of course be by chance, but seeing how things were going I doubted that was the case.

"What now?"

"Let's leave it at this for tonight. Our investigation continues tomorrow." Solomon said, "Meet me at nine tomorrow morning underneath that Sycamore tree in the village square."

"Sure, I'll see you there."

Solomon did not look back and climbed over the fence. Only once he was out of sight did I realise I was still holding the watch. I put it in my coat pocket, where I supposed it belonged and headed home.

The next morning, I waited for Solomon. I glanced at the pocket watch, ten past nine, he was late. People walked by, some saying hello and good morning, others ignoring me. Ten more minutes passed by without a sign of the witch-hunter. Had he overslept? The hotel was the only place he could be so I decided to go and find him.

Roger, the hotel owner, was sitting at the reception, reading a newspaper.

"Morning Roger, have you seen Solomon, tall guy with the feathered hat?"

Roger looked up from behind his paper and scratched his head. "Can't say I have."

"He should have checked in yesterday."

He sighed, "Nobody checked in yesterday. Let me check the book."

He wasn't that old, and even if he was, characters like Solomon weren't easy to forget. Roger retrieved his giant ledger from a shelf, put it on the desk and flipped it open. He scanned the pages for a moment and then looked up at me again.

"Solomon, you said? I have him noted down here, he's due to check in tomorrow on the fifteenth."

Tomorrow? Wait, the fifteenth? "Yesterday was the fifteenth," I said.

He shook his head and pointed towards a calendar on the wall. "Are you alright there Luke? Today is the fourteenth. The fifteenth is tomorrow."

Roger marked off each day with a big cross and the calendar showed that today was indeed the fourteenth and not the sixteenth. I swore I had seen it marked differently yesterday and I certainly had not imagined meeting Solomon.

I went through different scenarios in my head. One: Roger was really confused, suffered from memory issues and had marked his calendar wrong. Two: I had lost my mind and had hallucinated yesterday. Three. I hesitated. Three, Solomon was right and this was the effect of some kind of curse. I supposed that if a clockmaker had left a curse on our village, it would involve time. Other people had calendars, other people would have seen Solomon yesterday, maybe they remembered him. Though the biggest clue lay perhaps in the graveyard. I assured Roger I was not crazy and headed to the cemetery.

The gravestone was easy to locate. It stood there, just as we had found it yesterday. The soil looked untouched, like no one had dug here in years.

I wandered around the outskirts of the village trying to collect my thoughts. I visited Frank the blacksmith and asked if he remembered selling anyone two shovels yesterday and he didn't. Everyone in the village except for me seemed to have lost yesterday. As if it didn't happen to them. Solomon was nowhere to be found. If time went back, did that mean he was still on his way?

I could also go back tonight and dig up Edward's grave again but could not figure out how that would help me. I thought about heading out and trying to find Solomon on the road. Then I remembered why he had come to the village to begin with. He said he'd been looking for a missing person. What if that was what happened to all visitors arriving in Silverglen? That would explain why I could not remember a single visitor coming to our village. They'd come here, time would roll back and they'd disappear. But I remembered now. Something had changed. Was it the pocket watch?

I went back home and stared through the front window for a while. More thoughts came and went but nothing helpful passed by. The sun crawled across the sky until it disappeared behind the mountains in the west. The grumbling of my stomach kicked me into action. I realised what the problem was. I got up, ignored my body's need for food and headed over to the hotel.

Roger was still sitting behind the reception desk. He looked surprised when I walked in.

"Did you find that man you were looking for?" he asked.

"No," I said, "But I thought of something I'd like to ask you about."

Roger gave me a faint smile, "Go on."

"I can't seem to recall anyone ever visiting our village. As it, not a single person, ever. So, I was wondering, if no one visits, then, why do we have a hotel?"

Roger stared at me with a blank expression. Then he blinked a couple of times. Having spent too much time thinking about watches I pictured the gears in his head spinning as he tried to come up with an answer.

"You must be mistaken," he said, "We do have visitors. Not many, but people do come. Besides, I don't need much to survive here."

The dismissive tone of his reply sounded dishonest to me. "Then why can't I seem to remember ever seeing any strangers in the village?"

He shrugged, "Must be something with your memory, I can assure you, people do visit from time to time. Mostly folks from the cities who want a retreat from their busy lives over there."

"Is there anyone staying at the hotel right now?"

"No, just have the one man you asked about coming in tomorrow."

"When's the last time someone stayed?"

The question seemed to upset Roger, "I don't remember precisely, I would have to look it up in the ledger." He took a deep breath and stood up. "Listen, if you're that interested in meeting city folk, I can let you know the next time someone arrives. But it's late, the sun has set, why don't you go home, get some sleep and come back tomorrow to meet this Solomon guy?"

His tone and posture showed he had no interest in talking to me. I thanked him for his time and left. Part of me hoped that coming back tomorrow would cause me to meet Solomon again, but my gut feeling told me the witch hunter would never arrive.

Hours later I found myself outside again. Up in the sky, the moon was hiding behind dark clouds. Up until yesterday I couldn't recall ever being out this late, and here I was, out by lantern light for the second night in a row. The hotel was just a big house with a sign stuck to the front door but now I felt there was something ominous about it. It was the only three-story structure in the village and that was enough to make it tower over everything else.

I was about to break into Roger's house on a suspicion that he was hiding something. If I was wrong, and if I got found this would be the end of me. I'd be outcasted, exiled, I'd never be able to return to this place. And what if I discovered something, there was no guarantee anyone would believe me. I shook my head, no, I was committed to this now. I had been committed ever since I crossed that fence into the graveyard last night.

The front door was locked. People may be trusting of each other here, but it still felt natural to lock the door at night. I did the same. I circled around the building looking for a more concealed entrance. I checked every window and found one left open on the side of the building. I paused and looked around me, making sure nobody was around to see me. Then I pulled it open, the frame swinging outside. I put the lantern on the windowsill and climbed into the hotel.

With only the faint light of the lantern to help me, I observed my surroundings. I found myself in the kitchen. A couple of pots and pans stood scattered around on a large wooden table and I could still smell the remnants of burning wood coming from the fireplace. Nothing of use in here so I continued on into the hallway. What I was even looking for? Signs of guests, or the lack thereof? I made my way to the front of the building, to Roger's reception desk and located the ledger he'd consulted to find Solomon's name.

I put it, and the lantern down on the desk and started leafing through the book. Most pages were empty, save for a date written at the top. I found the page for the fifteenth and did indeed see Solomon's name on there. No indication as to which room he'd be in or how long Roger had been expecting him to stay. No indication of when he received the request for lodging either. He must have gotten a letter at some point. Solomon said the missing person had been here a month or two ago. I flipped pages until I found another name. Naomi Watts was registered on the twentieth of August. Identical to Solomon's record, her name was the only piece of information in the book.

At very least this proved I wasn't completely mad and Solomon had been right about a person having visited here. I put the book back on the shelf and snuck through the hotel, taking care not to make any sounds.

I climbed the stairs to the second floor, where the guest rooms were supposed to be. I opened the first door on my left and walked into an empty room. No carpet, no wallpaper, no furniture, just bare wood. I tried another room and found it in the same condition. Then a third room and a fourth and final room. I ascended to the third floor but took a step back downstairs as I saw a faint speckle of light coming from underneath the door in front of me. This must be where Roger was staying. I couldn't risk exploring around there. But why was he still awake? What was he doing in the dead of the night? No time to ponder about it. I went back down to the ground floor and started entering the rooms there only to find them empty as well. All except for one. Behind one of the doors there was no room at all, instead I found a winding stone staircase circling down underground. I peeked around the corner and could not see the end of it. It looked like it went on forever. Whatever was down there was certainly no ordinary basement.

I descended. My heart was pounding in my chest and my finger's grip on the lantern strengthened with every step I took. The stairs kept going far longer than they should have. This was what I had been looking for. Something that shouldn't be here. The grey stone walls surrounding me grew darker the deeper I went. After what must have been minutes I reached the bottom and found myself in front of an unassuming wooden door. I paused for a moment, taking in the strangeness of the situation. Part of me relieved to have found something, part of me trembling at what may lay beyond. I took a deep breath and pushed open the door.

I entered a long and wide hallway. I couldn't see the end of it. Torches hung on both sides, illuminating space. I covered my eyes for a moment to readjust to all the light. A cold breeze blew through the place and the only sounds I heard were the flickering of the flames. This did not look like Silverglen at all, it's like I had walked into a different world. I started walking straight ahead, the only direction I could go.

My sense of time ceased to exist in this place. I had no idea how long I had been walking until I heard a soft grunting sound in the distance. I stopped dead in my tracks and listened. It sounded like someone was in pain. I approached, keeping my pace slow. I peeked into an alcove to the right and saw Solomon. I let out a sigh of relief. He was still wearing the same brown coat, though his hat was gone. He was chained to a massive dark wooden grandfather clock which reached all the way to the ceiling. Metal chains around his ankles and wrists held him in the air against the clock's body.

I moved into view, he saw me, but did not react. Sweat rolled from his and though he had no visible injuries he was clearly suffering.

"Solomon, what the hell is going on here?" I whispered, still weary of alerting anyone to my presence.

The witch hunter looked me straight in the eyes and gave me a questioning look. He did not recognize me.

"You don't know who I am?"

"I do not," Solomon said, his voice sounded exhausted.

I gave him a brief rundown of what had happened.

He nodded. "I see. Could you hand me that pocket watch? Just place it in my right hand."

I followed his instructions and placed the watch in his hand. Solomon closed his eyes and chanted a couple of phrases in an unfamiliar language. He made sounds I didn't even know humans were capable of producing. The chains around him loosened up and fell to the ground. The impact of the metal hitting the stone floors reverberated throughout the underground. If anyone was around and hadn't noticed me yet they would now. I helped him stand up. The witch-hunter leaned against the clock, panting.

"Thank you." Solomon said, "It seems my future-self prepared for a scenario like this."

"What now?" I asked, wondering about the exact purpose of the pocket watch.

"We pick back up where we left. We must find the clockmaker." He looked back at the construct he had been chained to, "I believe we have come to the right place."

Solomon started moving, stumbling around like a drunk man determined to get home. As we marched on, Solomon's strength gradually returned to him. We passed by more alcoves and clocks with different people chained to them. Men and women in travel gear, none of them looked familiar. Were these the people who went missing in Silverglen over the years, the people we couldn't remember? Unlike Solomon all of them were unconscious.

"Some of them must have been here for years..." Solomon muttered.

"Can we save them?" I asked.

"Perhaps, but this is not the time. Unless we deal with the source, nothing we do will matter." He looked away from the people and stared straight ahead into the distance. "Let's move along, I do not know how much time we have left."

In the distance and end to the hallway came into view. A giant blood red clock face had been painted on the wall. In front of it stood a gallows and from the gallows hung a man dressed in a blue uniform with silver linings. He looked old, his face full of wrinkles but there was energy in his wide-open eyes. Despite his predicament the man was awake and he did not seem to be in any pain. He ignored me, but his gaze tracked Solomon as we approached. This had to be the clockmaker.

"So, at long last I've been found," the hanging man said. Neither his mouth nor jaw moved as he spoke but his voice sounded loud and clear.

"Is this how you met your demise?" Solomon asked.

"It is. Accused of witchcraft, hung without a trial." I detected a faint hint of sorrow or regret in his tone.

"Seems like they were right accusing you. Hard to deny the witchcraft now, isn't it?"

A grin formed on the man's face, "I would still have liked a trial."

"And this... installation?" Solomon looked around, exaggerating his movements and pointing in all different directions. "You're draining energy from them?"

"Correct, witch-hunter. Just a couple more years and I should be able to walk again."

"And what happens after that?"

"Celebration and revenge, I haven't decided the order yet." The man sounded happy now. Like he was enjoying this conversation.

Who knows how long it had been since he talked to anyone. Had he been down here in silence since his death over a hundred years ago? If he hadn't been insane before, he sure would be now.

"And I suppose you are expecting me to let you do as you please? Imprison and kill innocent people so you can live?" Solomon took a step towards me and as he spoke he pushed the pocket watch into my hand. I did not understand why he wanted me to have it again. If this was his protection, then why would he not hold on to it?

"Your little tricks won't work here, witch-hunter." The man raised his right arm and pointed at Solomon. Space around him seemed to distort, go blurry as if my eyesight temporarily went bad. Then the witch-hunter's body exploded into tiny fragments which evaporated in the surrounding air. My instincts screamed at me to run, but I found myself frozen in place.

Edward Archer now finally looked at me. "I don't know who you are, or why you were unaffected but you can take the hunter's place on the clock. I am in need of more bodies. My servant will be with you shortly."

Servant? My thoughts went to Roger. Someone must be maintaining this space, hanging the people, it could only be him.

I fiddled with the pocket watch in my hand, hoping it would do something. The clockmaker noticed, "The witch-hunter's trinket won't do you any good. I might not be able to make you disappear but you are powerless to stop me."

I did not know what to do. For what must have been minutes I stood there, looking at nothing in particular. Too afraid to look at the clockmaker, too afraid to run or do anything. I assumed Roger would come for me at any moment. When finally footsteps started sounding in the distance I jolted into action. I might not know anything about curses but I could try things. I was the repairman, the handyman. I didn't know how to fix chairs until someone brought me one for the first time. I hadn't studied or practiced how to sew back together a coat; I kept trying until I could. I looked at Edward Archer again and felt he did not look as scary. He was just a greying bald man in a fancy suit, hanging from the gallows that should have killed him. His hand waving might have removed Solomon but it did not seem to affect me. I walked up to him. Hesitating at first, but step by step I approached. This distressed him. The look on his face changed from bored to worried, to panicked as I got closer.

"Go back," he said, unable to hide the fear in his voice. But what was he afraid of?

I remembered Solomon's words now. Find and release the clockmaker he had said. Why had he specifically said release? Release from what? I circled around him and started to untie the knot keeping Edward Archer in place. I pulled on the rope, twisted it but it was thick and the pressure of the hanging man impeded my progress. If only I had brought a knife.

The approaching footsteps sped up; the walking transitioned into running. I pushed my fear away and with more strength than I had ever felt before I continued pulling at the rope until it came loose.

With a thud the body fell on the platform. The moment it did, my head started to hurt. A sharp pain surged from my skull all the way down to my feet. I grasped my forehead in pain and collapsed on the floor. The last thing I saw before I blacked out was the image of Roger standing over the skeletal remains of a man.

"I guess this is over," I heard him say.

When I woke up again I was back in my workshop. I patted down my body, pinched my cheek, I was alive. I checked my pockets and noted the watch was gone. Through the open window I saw the sun was setting. I scrambled up from my chair and ran to the front of the room where I kept a calendar on the wall. It was the fifteenth of October. The day this had all started.

I ran out of the workshop and headed home.

And there he was, leaning against my door, a tall and slender man, wearing a long brown coat and a feathered hat.

"You Luke Harrison?" the man asked, overly articulating the R's as he did.

"Yes Solomon, you've come to the right place. Though I suspect the curse you've come to solve has already been dealt with."

The witch-hunter stared at me for a moment, then took out a silver pocket watch from his coat. He studied it, then looked back at me and gave me a nod of approval.

Cormac P Walsh

Cormac says there are two versions of himself: one writes and directs stage plays for neurodiverse adults; the other crafts experimental fiction from word prompts, portraits, and music – from pop to punk to opera. He rejoins our collection with his gift for theatre bravado and darkly humorous narration.

Continuing our meditations on the figurative and literal ghosts of the past, 'Chapelizod' follows Rexine as she prepares for a crucial audition while a volatile figure's shadow from forgotten days closes in. The result is a dreamlike blend of naturalism and absurdism, where dialogue dances between razor wit and performance theatre.

Chapelizod

Frank wasn't good or indifferent. Frank was bad.

Two years out of college. Progress?

Shielding her eyes with her script *Carlos the Arsonist* Rexine yawned to the softly falling evening on the river deck and went inside.

Johnny and Sarah were Johnny and Sarah. Stoners on a sofa.

"Give me the Vera's".

Sarah gently licked and ripped the side off of a cigarette. She looked at Johnny.

Johnny tossed her a pack of rolling paper skins, which she nimbly caught and flicked to her assembling of the joint.

"I need a roach."

"Again?"

"Yeah. Rolling two Spliffs."

"Hmmmm!"

Rexine flopped on the sofa and offered her current second favourite script.

"Maybe the *Carlos the Arsonist* binder is good for something?"

"Perfect."

Johnny slowly ripped a narrow strip of cardboard from the script and passed it to Sarah.

"Have you got the lighter?"

"Yeah."

Sarah regarded Rexine for a moment.

"So how goes it?"

"More Alice than Lucy."

The house was a smoky mess, late September evening sun defined the closed blinds.

"I should read some more."

Rexine went out onto the deck. Birds had eaten the mouldy tomatoes and dried-up grapes she had left out for them. Their ungrateful shit littered the table and leaf strewn ground. One prodigious splat dappled the edges of her play script. *Alice is Light* By Rex Tarrant.

Her favourite of the two scripts looked forlorn amid the detritus of the bird's dinner. She was auditioning *Alice* at the Gate Upstairs to a group of twenty Influencers and Agents in a week's time. The only thing that had touched her script this week was that bird shit.

Frank.

Marc had joked, "Let's capitalize on his good points."

Neither of them were here but they wouldn't go away.

She sat on the bench determined to clear her mind.

One moment passed into another on the old wooden bench. Her breathing was stressed. Violent sobs racked her body. She cried. She bit on the back of her hand. Two years out of Drama School. Living with Johnny and fucking Sarah. What a mess.

Drifting Autumn leaves coloured the gently flowing Liffey waters.

One year in Chapelizod. It was beautiful. Such a fine river house. So old. With a cool balcony and a deck below, even a quite loud working antique cuckoo clock by the dartboard on the landing.

Such a cozy room inside.

Her thoughts drifted with the water, gently swirling through eddies on the river's curve.

Inside Sarah yelled, "Rexine do you want a toke?"

"No thanks!" Rexine put her head in her hands.

"You still reading that 'Wonderland'?"

"Our Alice!" Johnny yelled.

Rexine bit her lip and reached for the script. Rex Tarrant's *Alice is Light* by fucking birdshit.

"Focus."

She opened the script and read.

> **Hatter:** Personally, I stopped listening when you lot entered with that rowdy gaggle of servants and hangers-on. Accidentally conceived wastrels all.
> **Alice:** You cuddly Crumpet. You can't pee in your middle pants after Christmas.
> **White Rabbit:** How dare you say such a thing? You chronographically opinionated bauble!
> **Alice:** Your timepiece is festered.
> *Pause*
> **Ghost:** This is an uncomfortable silence.
> *Pause*
> **Twit Faced Fetchers:** I attended an uncomfortable séance once.
> **Alice:** Séance's are most disagreeable. They are like reading braille with one's teeth.

Inside on the sofa Sarah and Johnny were snog swapping the joint.

> **Hatter:** The Bishop's wife did recommend that I kept my legs apart while delivering a reading.
> **Alice:** I almost never know whether to sink or sing.
> **Twit Face Fetchers:** When I look at you everything is pointless.
> **Alice:** Love and scandal are the best sweeteners of tea. But not with you sweetie.
> **March Hare:** Then you should say what you really deep-down mean and plant me in a basket.
> **All:** Bonkers moocow thoughts.
> **Alice:** You are all quite thick. I deserve better.
> **All:** Why, thank you very much, Alice. You are so sweet. Keep us warm in your love. Do, please do.
> **Alice:** Condescending sewer of mithering gobshites.

Johnny jumped up clutching his calf.

"Fucking cramp! Jesus fucking Christ!"

Rexine dropped the script and rushed inside.

"What's up! What's up?"

"Johnny's a crypanzy."

"Fuck you!"

"Oh me. Oh me-oh me-oh me-oh me-"

"I have a fucking cramp!"

Rexine returned to the deck. It had rained heavily overnight, the Liffey flowed languid and strong. Two Swans and their adolescent cygnets preened on the islet by the far bank.

Shadows lengthened. Pealing bells from the Church up beyond the hill rang a pointless perch for her thoughts.

Somewhere over there under the river. That was where her phone possibly lay. She shuddered, remembering her fury as she had flung it away.

Saturday night, Sunday morning......The part was drug fuelled.

You're just too good to be shrewd. Everyone who wasn't dancing was. A firework broke the sky.

A huge projector rotated paint splatter Rainbows and Pop Art on the cloudy sky.

The house and the deck were well populated by boisterous revellers.

This is where Rexine hated her phone. Marc had fucked up for the last time.

In the living room a bunch of people celebrated a pagan mass. "Don't call me Ismael," intoned the priest.

She held the Chalice high, displayed it to all sides and lowered it to her lips. "This is a very unpretentious Wine."

Everybody was wearing counter masks. Klimt Scream, Munch Kiss and so on and on. Unimaid and Mercorn chattered on by.

Rexine drifted through the party. The masks reminded her of characters and people she had played and desired to play.

Neither Extravert or Introvert, DJ Chime Charm Chime was a Moodievert pausing for what she called "Exactly scattered Pigeons. No cats cast." She always found a sound to fumble the mind. Her rapt audience slowly danced on the landing.

In the attic the ghost of Leonora Piper was holding a Seance. A firm believer of the afterlust, this was no Lady of the Lake.

"You can shove your lines up your arse." Madame Fortune was intimidating, scared of the boredom of truth. East Fife 4 Forfar 5. She remembered his face, his hideous breath. They first met as employees at Frank's lawyers Ocont, Ilwillbe & Wownt. It was also the last place she met him, for they had got married and she disappeared up her husband. In time divorce perceptually solved and somewhat quietly unsolved that. Leonora Piper played gentle wistful music. Madame Fortune was calm.

Vivid and livid, Frank didn't do calm.

"All stories are bullshit. Reality is bullshit. Tell me how many words were in the last sentence I said. What was the last sentence you said? You want to be a fucking actress? Remember lines? All people want to do is fucking forget!"

Frank's rant echoed in Rexine's mind. Two years.

Frank wasn't here. Madame Fortune was in a dream where all cats knew a come hither look.

Girl you've been a naughty Boy. Banjo Emzerr passed her a pipe of blazing Red Leb. Rexine went back downstairs past a gaggle of dancers to see great Hercules whipping a gig. How big would a Budda be? She was breathing with the Mindful Group on the Balcony. Sally Wigwam asked her whether she wanted a ponder of calm. She thought of Jonathan. That fucking charlatan always trying to impress someone. Off in Transylvania. For Mina. Dear Mina, such a good friend. Or was it France?

Drawing from her boisterous quiver, Lucy stretched her bow and went firing a symphony of the greatest flowers ever grown and known that went quaffing flailing air at the Dartboard by the Cuckoo Clock.

A disheveled tapestry of petals beautifully shambled and coloured the Landing.

Underfoot and aurally all around the party pumped. Rexine didn't know who she was.

"We can never settle the brilliance of the mind. That unstinting machine nagged by the ever beating heart. "

Until it stops.

Marc kept ringing and messaging. Fucking Twat!

"How does it feel!?" Sarah was piggybacking her on the deck. "Can you make a fucking deal!"

"What is Marc doing?!"

"I don't fucking know Sarah!"

They were flat on their backs, laughing wildly.

Emzer was ranting at her. Idiots of time. His unruly beautiful face was becoming unpalatable. She started talking to the Australian guy with the pliers.

"Not a child wasted. Don't ask when this party is going to end."

"Reality is a colossal mess."

"Are you listening to me?"

"I hear both laterally and horizontally."

"The present is a language you can't speak."

"Do you remember when your first Pope died?"

"I'm not into funny stuff."

Splashy DJ lights fought sporadic fireworks for supremacy of the Autumnal Liffey sky.

"You need to know how to get required both by and with the soon forgotten."

"I could have danced all night."

"That's a lot of fucking dancing."

A disturbing person with a Graham Norton mask danced and screeched "Andromada is doing a celestial double feature with the Milky way. DJ! Dj! DJ! Danger of Moon Suds! Turn off those lights!"

All the lights failed. And flashed. And failed again. And flashed. And failed again. And flicked flickering. And failed, again.

Rexine noticed an absent God slowly moving through a love triangle with Tweedledum and Tweedledee in the dark. She quietly rejoined the conversation.

"Never trust a Man or a Woman."

"Is that comment directed at me?"

"Not exactly."

"Love has a Letterbox in the vicinity of the Arsehole of Sincerity."

"Neither snow nor rain nor heat nor gloom of night stays these couriers from the swift completion of their appointed rounds."

Dawn was shadowing a bright-ish Liffey morning. A fading season and a straggling party entwined with done things.

Sarah was snoring loudly, her face squished on the detritus strewn deck. Her slow slumbering breath rhythmically troubling a stubborn beech left snot stuck to her face.

Yawing freely Rexine slowly got to her feet.

Bodies were slumped, entwined and wasted. Some were still awake. A vinyl record player was playing a warped and scratched LP.

Good old boys drinking.

Earnest, almost visionary conversations drifted past as Rexine walked through the house. Wondering what breakfast might look like, she went back to rouse Sarah – who was the better cook – on the Deck. Her phone was humming somewhere around her slumbering friend.

"Marc?"

"I've been ringing you all night!"

"Marc..."

"This is not about us Rexine!"

"Marc, come on, I-"

"Frank knows."

"What!?"

"Frank knows."

"What? Marc!"

"He is flying into Dublin."

"He tracks us!"

"He tracks fucking everything."

Rexine flung her phone high into the dawn.

Three days.

Was Marc still alive?

The deck was almost dark. On the gently flowing Liffey fallen Sycamore leaves swirled in the slow fading light.

She thought she heard her phone ring.

Marc?

It wasn't his phone. It was a Blackbird impatient for grapes or tomatoes or whatever.

They exchanged dirty looks and the Blackbird flew off. Rexiene moved inside.

Sarah and Johnny were stoner arguing. They knew about Marc, they knew about Frank, and they had killed their phones in Town, but they could still do this banter. Rexine felt reassured by their voices as she entered the room.

"I orbit opinion, Johnny!"

"Are you racing butterflies?"

"Bees. Bees. Bees."

"Why is the word 'sin' the opening act in the word 'sincerity'?"

The doorbell rang.

Sarah, Johnny and Rexine were each silently terrified.

The bell rang again.

The three of them slowly moved together.

The doorbell rang repeatedly.

They cautiously scrambled up to the Landing.

An unnerving twist of metal sounded the front door lock being tried.

Sarah pulled Johnny and Rexine into a scrunched huddle on the petal strewn floor under the Cuckoo Clock.

"Rexine?"

Sarah's whisper was loud.

"Sarah?"

"I just want to tell you-"

Above them the Cuckoo Clock doors whacked open.

Joe Mc Kiernan

Joe is a loyal contributor and man of all seasons, writing short stories across sci-fi and fantasy, contemporary drama and historical fiction. His broad perspective has no doubt benefited from living abroad and his extensive travels across six continents. His most modest ambition in life is to one day afford to become a full-time writer. Many of us believe he's well on his way.

Rounding out our segments on identity and self-deception, 'Royal Blood' layers in an ambiguous narrative that dismantles the borders around class, legitimacy, and self-grandeur. In this second-world chamber drama, Prince Edgar has staged a coup against his father, the king, and makes a final visit before the execution – but the encounter doesn't unfold as he had imagined.

Royal Blood

King Harald, Ruler of the Four Kingdoms, liked to say he ruled with a firm hand. The truth was that he ruled with an iron fist. As he told his son, Edgar, benevolent leaders are more likely to lose their heads. He schooled the prince, from the earliest age, in the art of treating both enemies and subjects in the same uncompromising manner. The prince took this instruction so deeply to heart that, on the day of his seventeenth birthday, he staged a coup against his father.

At three in the morning, his personal guard of four loyal knights ghosted to the royal quarters. At the door, they met two of the king's guard who extended their hands in greeting. Edgar's men met the greeting with their right hands and slit their throats with daggers held in their left.

Outside the royal chamber, the resistance they met was even weaker. The two guards on duty were asleep in chairs. Each awoke in time only to feel his life ebb away as blood pumped from his throat.

The king and queen roused to the silhouettes of four tall men surrounding their bed. When Falcon, the leader said, "Your Majesties, you will come with us forthwith," the queen began screaming, only to be met with a savage punch in the face from the nearest man. Her screams were replaced by the sounds of her sobbing.

"Remember to use a firm hand with my parents," the prince had said. "Today the king is the sovereign but tomorrow the sovereign will be me."

Edgar climbed the spiral staircase ahead of Falcon. Falcon was the head of his personal guard but, more than that, he was his cousin.

Sometimes, in private, the two joked about the incident of the courtier's son. At age thirteen, this boy had beaten up the prince.

"You're a weak, craven cur, Boy," his father told him afterwards, before leaving the room in disgust.

Falcon had then taken the boy to the Blue Forest, beaten him badly, and instructed him to tell the world that this was the doing of the prince.

The king had never called Edgar 'Boy' again, and from that day, Edgar viewed Falcon as his older brother.

The staircase was dark and musty. At the top of each flight was a long narrow window, through which light illuminated dancing motes of dust. After five flights, they reached the top floor.

Outside an oak door stood Bloodhound, second in command of Edgar's men. The soldier stood to attention at the sight of his prince.

"Your Royal Highness," he said.

"For now, Bloodhound. For now."

The hint of a smile formed on Bloodhound's face, but he suppressed it.

"Everything is in order, Soldier?" Prince Edgar inquired, bringing his face close to Bloodhound's.

"Everything is in order, your Royal Highness," he replied, staring into the distance.

"Excellent!" Edgar declared. "Now, let us visit the k... my father."

Bloodhound turned the oversized key and pushed the door open. Following a guiding gesture, the prince walked inside.

The large circular room was dark, a sensation accentuated by the black stone walls and matching floor. Meagre light entered the room through the sole window to Edgar's left. On the far side, huddled on the ground, in a black cloak, was the shape of King Harald, the Broad Head, Ruler of the Four Kingdoms.

"Hello my son."

Edgar could not make out his father's face in the form.

"Hello Father."

"Edgar, put a stop to this now! Your time will come but that time is not now. Release me. And the queen. And we will put this unfortunate episode behind us."

The form stood slowly. As he approached Edgar, a chain clanked on the stone floor. Coming into the light from the window, Edgar could now see his father's face. It bore a weak, almost fearful expression, causing Edgar's heartbeat to quicken.

"Really Father? You would overlook my transgression? Did you not always tell me the importance, the primacy, the absolute imperative of the firm hand?"

"Yes, my son, I did, but in this case, I must forgive you. Because you are my son."

"What is this word 'forgive'?"

The king looked puzzled.

"Why to forgive is to... ignore a transgression, to move past such a thing, to – "

He stopped, noting the smirk on the prince's face. His son was making the point that he had never before spoken of forgiveness. Harald's expression changed to a more familiar one of sternness.

"Edgar! End this nonsense now and the consequences to you will be limited. But if you persist in this – "

A loud knock came on the door.

"Enter!" the prince commanded.

The door opened and Falcon stepped inside, bearing a tray of food.

"The meal, your Highness," he said, offering the tray, which Edgar took.

Falcon bowed and exited, pulling the door behind him. Within seconds, the room became infused with the scent of roast fowl.

"Roast quail in cranberry sauce, sweet potatoes and roasted vegetables," Edgar said. "Your favourite, Father, I believe." He placed the tray on the ground and pushed it, with his foot, to an arms-length from the king.

"And what is this? A dinner at breakfast time?"

"Yes Father. I had the kitchen prepare it for you." He walked towards the door, then turned. "I suggest you enjoy it."

He waited for a reply, but none came. Edgar had organised the flourish of a final meal in the hope that his father would beg for his life, perhaps even break down in tears. Instead, the king stared at him with unwavering defiance. Did he imagine it, or was there even a hint of a smile in his father's eyes? It was Edgar who turned away.

He walked to the door and made to open it, but it did not budge. He pulled again to the same result. The door was locked, but why? He banged on it and waited for a response, but none came. He banged again, harder this time.

"Falcon!" he roared. "Falcon, open the door!"

Silence.

"Bloodhound! Bloodhound! Open this door! Open this door now, I command you!" Again, no reply came.

A sense of dread crept into Edgar's heart. His men just outside the door were wilfully ignoring him. They had locked the door preventing his egress. He was alone in a room with the king, but the king could not harm him, shackled as he was. Behind him, he heard the loud clang of metal on stone, the sound of a heavy chain being cast aside.

Edgar continued to face the door, delaying the moment when he would have to turn around, as if the reality would only manifest itself when he did so. In desperation, he tried the door one last time, but it remained steadfast, as he knew it would.

Finally, he turned.

His father now stood in the centre of the chamber, bathed in the light of the morning sun. Standing to his full height of nineteen hands, he somehow seemed even taller. Behind him lay the chain. The shackle that Edgar had thought clasped to his father's ankle lay open on the floor.

Harald raised his arms to the ceiling, causing the black cloak to fall away, like an unwanted skin, revealing him in full military dress. At his side hung the Sword of the Four Kingdoms. When the king unsheathed the sword, a reflection from the blade blinded Edgar momentarily. With this sword, the king had ended the lives of both noblemen and common soldiers on the battlefield.

Edgar put his hand to his side and grasped the handle of his dagger.

"Put it on the floor, Boy." His father had not called him that since the incident of the courier's son, but now, he was 'Boy' again.

Edgar took the knife from its sheath. He contemplated running at his father, but sense returned. He would be cut down the moment he got within the length of the king's sword. He placed the knife on the floor.

Obeying a nod of the head, Edgar moved to the far side of the room. The king circled to the door, holding his sword before him. Still facing Edgar, he banged on the door with his fist.

"Falcon!"

Quickly came the sound of the turning key. The door opened and Falcon stepped inside.

"Your Majesty," he said. "I see you have everything in hand."

"That I have, Falcon. That I have."

"Falcon!" Edgar shouted. "Take him prisoner! Now, Goddammit!!"

The knight smiled at Edgar.

"I'm sorry, Your *Highness*." He said the title with irony. "But I guard the king now."

In that moment, Falcon, who Edgar viewed as a brother, seemed nothing more to him than a stranger. Bloodhound entered the room, followed by Wolfsmane. There stood three of Edgar's personal guard. Bloodhound and Wolfsmane walked over and stood before him. Edgar knew he must make his play to Falcon; his men would follow wherever he led.

"Falcon," he implored, "I swore you a royal promise of two chests of gold and the lands from the White River to the sea and the castle located thereon. And your choice of wife. And your pick of the maidens of the kingdom as your concubines. Why have you... betrayed me?"

These last words hung heavy, given that Falcon and his men had first betrayed the king.

"Because, young Edgar, His Majesty promised me all of this and something else besides."

"Something else? How many castles can you live in? How much gold can you spend? How many maidens can you bed?"

It was the king who replied.

"Edgar, you should pay homage to his Royal Highness Prince Friedrich, heir to the Throne of the Four Kingdoms."

"Heir to the throne?!" Edgar gasped. "But I am the heir!"

The king seemed to consider this.

"Aye, that you are, boy. That you are. For the next few minutes at least."

"What do you mean?" Edgar exclaimed. All at once the king's intent became clear. "No, you cannot," he shouted, his eyes expanding in their sockets, his body seized with spasms. "I am your son. I am the royal blood. None of your blood runs through Falcon's veins."

The king smirked and replied, "Are you so sure of that, young Edgar?"

What could he mean? Edgar looked at his father and Falcon standing side by side. Falcon was nineteen hands high, just like the king and had a large head with a significant brow just like the king.

They both had full beards; Falcon's was flaming red, just as the king's had been before it turned grey. More than once, he had overheard courtiers whisper of the physical similarity between the two.

"Your aunt was the most handsome woman in the kingdom, Edgar, more beautiful even than your mother. Earlier, when Falcon came to me here, I revealed his true lineage to him, and made him my heir, as is his birthright as my oldest son. That he was born beyond the castle walls is of no import."

Edgar's head spun with a whirlwind of competing emotions and realisations. He had just learnt that his cousin and friend since childhood was, in fact, his brother. In the same moment, he had learnt that his new-found brother had betrayed him. The anger he felt at this was displaced in a moment by terror. His blood chilled as he realised that the king truly intended to remove his head.

King Harald turned to Falcon and demanded, "The Queen?"

"Back in her bed, in the royal quarters, Your Majesty. Recovering from her ordeal and awaiting your return."

"And Hawksclaw?" He was referring to the fourth of the prince's personal guard, the man who had struck the queen.

"In the North Turret, Your Majesty. And again, I offer my sincerest apologies for his unforgivable action. To strike Her Majesty was – "

The king raised his hand.

"You told him to expect my visit?"

"Yes, Your Majesty. We will move him to the basement where you will have every known instrument of pain to hand. He is expecting your visit with... intense anticipation. When I left him, he was experiencing a severe case of slack bowel."

The king smiled. Seeing two soldiers waiting outside the door he beckoned them, and they entered. One carried a basket, the other, a chopping block.

They bowed to the king giving him his title, laid the items on the floor and exited.

"Now then," Harald said. "Let's get this done."

Edgar began to yell. "No, you can't do this! I am heir to the throne.

He kicked and writhed as Bloodhound and Wolfsmane dragged him towards the block.

"Wolfsmane," he said, trying in vain to make eye-contact, "I beg of you. In the name of all that is holy – "

"Silence him!" the king commanded.

Bloodhound punched Edgar in the face, breaking his nose. Blood streamed from his nostrils onto his tunic, turning the garment from white to claret.

At the king's signal, they dragged him, writhing and screaming, to the block, forcing his neck into the cradle. Bloodhound took a rope from the basket and tied Edgar's arms behind him. He then placed his full weight on the prince's upper back preventing all movement.

"Would you like me to do this, Your Majesty?" Falcon enquired.

"No," the king replied. "I lead by example."

He rested the blade of his sword on the nape of Edgar's neck, then raised it overhead.

"Any final thoughts to share, Boy?"

Edgar said nothing. Was this a small final act of defiance or was he simply too terrified to speak?

The king swung the Sword of the Four Kingdoms and Edgar's head toppled into the basket, landing face up. His eyes were wide in terror or perhaps disbelief. Blood spurted from his neck to the beat of his dying heart, splattering his face and, beyond that, Falcon's boots.

For some moments, there was silence.

"Well, what's wrong with all of you?" the king enquired.

"Have you never seen a beheading before?"

There were murmurs in the affirmative from Bloodhound and Wolfsmane.

"Your Majesty," Falcon enquired. "What would you like done with the body of… the prince?"

"Place the head on a spike above the city gates. And the torso, strip it and hang it in the clock tower in the town square. It should provide nourishment for the carrion as autumn cedes to winter. It will also serve to remind my subjects of the consequences of dissent each time they check the time."

"It shall be done, Your Majesty," Falcon said. "Now, would you like to return to the royal quarters?"

"Yes indeed, except…"

"Your Majesty?"

The king's eyes were trained on the tray of food that was to have been his last meal.

"… except I'm hungry. I would like to eat."

He walked to the tray, stepping over the torso, which was now slumped on the floor, the neck still in the block's cradle. He picked up the tray, sat in the recess of the window and began eating.

At Falcon's instruction, Wolfsmane took the basket containing the head and left the room. Falcon looked at the torso and the sizeable pool of blood in the centre of the room which was yet expanding. He looked to the king who was enthusiastic with his meal, oblivious to the crimson pool edging towards his feet.

"Your Majesty. Would you like us to wait until you have finished your meal before we remove the body?"

A leg of quail in his hand, his mouth full of food, the king shook his head.

"No, no, carry on," he said, before adding, "This is so good! Roasted quail with sweet potatoes, roasted vegetables and cranberry sauce. My favourite, Falcon. My absolute favourite!"

Caoilfhionn Duggan

Caoilfhionn has spent the past year becoming even more herself. With her handwriting deteriorating, her poetry is becoming more mysterious even to herself, which didn't dissuade The Morning Journal from publishing her poems this year. She writes to capture those moments that feel timeless and untamed, even when those occasions seem to be getting the better of her.

Turning now from gothic and fantasy, we steer into more modern crises of conscience. These four poems share a sense of revelation: confronting the unspoken truths of a personal medical history (Heart's History)*, the quiet resilience found in being overlooked* (The Bumblebee Beggar)*, the fierce reclamation of one's unvarnished self* (Cyanide)*, and the way small healing rituals bring fantasies into the realm of the real* (Reashore)*.*

Heart's History

"I am so sore," she said, "in the heart."
Where the clot caught,
Palpitations squatted.
Underneath cysts
And close to infection scars,
There is a child's thing,
Covered by an adult's health insurance.

"I am so sore," she said, "for the heart of my yesterday."
Where turning small,
Your years can be derailed.
There is a station where a train departs and departs.
It only ever departs,
From where everything feels
Expensive being educated.

"I am so sore," she said to the heart of it.
Sore is where a story rests.
And like bread,
What rests rises.
Don't define this pain as privilege,
You are not lucky to have hurt in this special, expensive way.
It could have been worse.
And it could have cost less.

In the Emergency Department,
A doctor wearing jeans explains that things are different now.
The dress code has softened,
Your premium has risen,
Your little heart has hardened.
They talk in doctor speak.
"Good thing you listened to your heart,
It could always have been worse."

"I am so sore in the heart."
"Don't worry,
You are covered for the overnight stay,
And we have medicine for that."
Blood thinner
Breadwinner.

The Bumblebee Beggar

I know some things we should not say
But some flowers are just ugly
And not in a good alien way
But ugly as in small, tired, lacklustre.

But, Lord above love him,
The bumblebee beggar visits anyway.
With his staggered little flight
And the optimism of stripes
He asks what his belly cannot carry.

His brittle little wings,
Opaque outlines and glassy planes.
They defy the politics of science
And cry out the one refrain,
Hold not back for me.

Not even pretty flowers have ears,
And the ugly ones neither.
But their petals moved.
They reach the lifegiving sky
And the hungry, bumbling bee?
Off that beggar will try.

Caoilfhionn Duggan

Cyanide

Peel the royal skin from a cherry,
And mash the clotted contents to pulpy paste.
That is what I pass for a woman.

Syruped cherries, a toxic red-pink,
Those sweetened, brightened, teeth-rotting sweet things?
That is what you pass me for.

There is a pit in me that would break the mightiest of teeth,
Crackle destruction down to the jaw.
You show only those surgically deseeded.

I am nothing of that.
The core in me might be small, wretched and poisonous.
But by an almighty toothache, it is mine.

Reashore

With our quest for perfect rocks,
I am perched on the biggest one.
While a tide is changing in me,
The waves are reassuring
In their woosh and clitter clatter.

The wind doesn't cut through me
But the thought does:
That on that shore,
Gathering penguin love rituals,
The absence of a nestling is rising in me.

Cold is leaching up into my bum,
And my frigid heart is softening,
And questioning why white horses
Holidaying shows me my brittle bridle home,
From which I could be smoothed anew.

The cliffs seem further away,
Truth stumbling behind my lips.
My pockets grow heavy with gifts.
So I change up my stooping down
And pick apart our stones, our stories.

“Nothing less than perfect,”
And nothing more than this.
The questioning cage is suddenly sunlit.
The bird in me is flightless, smothered and unsure.
But, together, picking up stones by the shore?
It is set free.

Ciara Campbell

Ciara is a dedicated novelist and short story writer, long-standing group contributor, and overall lover of words in any form – literature, legislation, languages. Her comprehensive style spans from the endlessly experimental to the succinctly conventional. She has been published in New Isles Press and The Martello Journal, and was the winner of the PentoPrint Award 2020.

Following this collection's shift to literal questions of perception and reality, her story 'Daltonist?' is an experimental tragedy depicting a tense conversation between a colour-blind man and a morally dubious doctor. In 'The Harpist of Grafton Street,' she offers a lyrical portrayal of the perfect memory of youth and the lost magic of a song's fleeting beauty.

Daltonist?

One table, two chairs.

What do you see?

A *frisbee; hidden.* A *notebook; pen.* A *sandwich; foil.*

Red.

The colour is green.

Okay.

You're very passive about this.
Do you actually agree with me?

Autumn; leaves fall to the ground.
It is happening outside this room.

I don't actually believe you,
but I don't feel the need to say that out loud,
I try to be respectful.

Do you actually respect me,
or do you just give me the image of respect?

A *rustle of nervous shifting around.*
A *person touches the inside of their wrist.*

You're the ones funding me right now.
That's the deal with the funders,
the ones supporting my lifestyle;

the other side is that I suck it up.
I sit here and smile and nod
and tell you everything you want to hear.
You're the best and I agree completely with your point of view!
I can learn so much from you!

That's not the point – I'm here to learn from you.

But you're not very responsive when I tell you my view of the world.

Well.
Your view of the world isn't normal,
which is why we want to learn more about you.

I don't think we have a common language.
My definition of red and green is
fundamentally different to yours.
We say the same word,
but it means something different.
We can't understand each other
and we can't communicate.
Our basis of the world is completely different.

Blazer, shirt, trousers, shiny shoes.
Jacket, emblazoned t-shirt, jeans, ragged trainers.
A silver car waiting outside; a pink bus, late as usual.

What colour would you say the world is?

Do you want me to recite
the exact number of the colour?

Daltonist?

Or shade it in greyscale to show off the light and dark?
We can agree on the shadows, surely.

I think you have a fundamental lack of respect.

Straightening up in the chair, hands clenched.

I think I'm just reflecting back
the lack of respect that I've been shown.
My whole life!
The way I see the world isn't
the exact same
that the rest of society sees the world,
but why isn't it valid?
Why do I have to conform?

Walls are light and textured with dated paper.
Floor carpeted and stale-smelling.

How do I not know that you're all a simulation?
How do I not know that I'm the only real person in the world, and if I admit and believe in your point of view, everything in my world will fall apart?
I will no longer be who I am.

To engage in a conversation,
we have to understand
the history of words
and how they have been used.

Slumping back down.

Can we change the meaning
of the words associated with colours,
can they be flexible enough to accommodate my views?

A clipboard is flipped to a printed page.
A pen is paused above the paper.

We've researched into how colour is perceived differently across cultures.
Another culture is another meaning.
Were you influenced by the differing values of your ancestry,
of your inherited religion?
To live in a society is to adhere to a common held view of the world.
Without it, societal cohesion breaks down.
This is why we have invested state resources into this research.
The state needs to convince you.
The state needs you to believe.

Sliding a glossy page across the singular table.

Let's reset. What does a colour make you feel?

Don't you mean "how"?

No,
I don't mean the methods,
I mean the evocation of emotions.
Is an emotion a solid object within the body?
Or is it a process that can be explained by neurochemicals?

A head tilted.

Daltonist?

Can we talk about how
the way I talk
is influenced by the languages
that my ancestors spoke?
Can we come back to that.
If we can't have a common ground for colours,
how can we have a common ground for emotions?
Do I know that you feel the same way that I feel?

An attempt at connection; denied.

Civilisation is
having a discussion and
coming to a conclusion.
How can we even have a discussion
without a definition of common terms?
How can you be part of a democratic debate?

Plants: stem, leaf, soil.
A room with no lock or key.
A castle no one can escape from.

I think you place us all in a box.

What can you be loyal to?
If you don't have the same definitions as your leader.
What about your history?
Do you know the same history that I do?
Do I have the same voice as you do?

Pacing. No *eye contact.*

I could have merged myself into the wall.
Fine. You got me.
I don't have respect inside myself,
I do feel disdainful towards you.
The way you know nothing,
The way that you try to project your own narrative and history
onto my story.
So I don't bring it up.
I hate the backlash.
I hate the annoying repetitive conversations.
I hate the arrogant tone of the way you speak to me.
You don't think about my voice, so I won't think about yours.
How do you feel about that?
I bet no one has ever challenged your view the way that I have.
But it's just treating you the way you treat me.

A hand warm on a phone.

Do you ever think that a conversation can be an act of violence?
A person who fears violence as a result of their view self-censors;
Therefore they cannot be part of the democratic debate,
Therefore they lack all the rights of a citizen.
Open up and tell me about yourself.

Circling back around, a raised hand, a low voice.

I refuse to sell myself,
my identity,
my history,
my trauma,
to you.

Daltonist?

You do not have a right to know my emotions,
my thoughts,
my viewpoints – because I know
you want to control and exploit them for your own benefit.
I do not exist for you.

Not every voice has equal weight.
Maturity and experience
means that you should be able to speak first.

At the end of the day,
I'm still colour-blind in a world of defined colours.

A door opens.
A door closes.
Each person has their conformities.

The Harpist of Grafton Street

Until the day she heard that song, she had no will to live. Anyone who has to pass down Grafton Street twice a day, three hundred odd days of the year, will tell you the truth: all the songs are terrible. The musicians only know one or two songs and they repeat them all day. Pop songs a decade old, tourist-trap nostalgia about a world that never existed. Áine glanced at them, wondering: what drive they have! Why are they so eager to go out onto Grafton Street and make their fortune? Are they trapped in a by-gone era where that was possible? Or maybe they just have that resilient personality dreamers do have: a disregard for the rules of possibility.

Until that day: past the midpoint of summer, the sky threatening to burst rain even though the sun was shining moments ago, Áine dragging herself down Grafton Street, uniform draped over her arm. Her to-do list has *go to work 8am-6pm* scratched out on it and *make dinner* and *try to write one poem* left clear. In a fight between the domestic and divine, the former wins every time. She's tilting her head back up, looking at the fading light, thinking: oh God, the season is changing already? Why do the years turn faster with every passing one? What did I even accomplish this year?

There's a blockade of people clustered right at the turn between Grafton Street and Wicklow Street. Áine tries to push through. No luck. She blinks weary eyes. Then her attention focuses and she hears. She stands there, just like the rest of the people, struck-still by the sheer beauty of this moment. She will spend decades trying to recapture this moment in poetry and fail every time. The silence of the collective crowd; the sparkle of the drizzle in sunlight; the harpist in her blood-red velvet dress, eyes closed, playing on, singing. Despite the weather, ignoring the audience, despite all the cruelty of the world. Only the musician and her art.

If a person is in the right time and place, the mundane transforms. The world itself softens. A person can stand, transfixed, unable to move their body, unable to break out of this moment, caught in a narrative grander than their individual worries. When Áine fell in love, it was the same. She had seen her future wife's drawn face, dark brown eyes so intent, and thought: oh. Yes, I know you, it's like I've always known you. Where else could I be but here?

Then the sky breaks and the rain descends, lashing down like tiny strikes. The crowd scatters. Áine too rushes to the nearest shop, pulling her uniform over her head. By the time she peeks her head out again, Grafton Street is as deserted as it can be. No harpist. Only laughing tourists and bazaarists. When Áine reaches home, out of breath and drenched, she tells her roommates about it, and they ask her: was it real? Did you imagine it?

The next day during her shift, when the panic spikes in her bloodstream, Áine closes her eyes and plays that memory of that song again in her mind. An echo of that peace. The next week stepping in the door of the GP's surgery she does the same. The next winter when she is submitting a job application. Countless other times, she relies on this memory.

Time slips away, a decade has passed, a life transformed. She wears a suit to her office job and a gold ring on her left hand. She still doesn't own a house, of course. It's only when she's going to the GP again about confusion and memory issues that she stops in the middle of Grafton Street, snowflakes on her coat, and thinks: what happens if I can no longer remember that song?

When she gets home, her wife makes her dinner, while Áine types various searches onto the Internet. Harpist Grafton Street. Harpist Dublin specify by year. Beautiful Harpist Dublin Rain. No results from search engines, video archives or music streaming services. She stares. Did I hallucinate that moment? It's that initial denial that spurs her on. There has to be some record of her!

Again and again, she finds nothing. She listens to obscure harp songs only listed with numbers on dated music streaming sites, she downloads sketchy audio files, watches hundreds of tourist's vlogs of Grafton Street. Nothing. She stays up late, gains circles underneath her eyes. Her wife hovers in the doorway, tilting her head.

On a forum unknown to the masses, Áine pours out her heart, describing every inch of memory and feeling. One commenter leaves just a PNG of a picture of a paper flyer pinned to a library community noticeboard. Áine calls the number listed. Despite her expectation that the number would be discontinued, the owner picks up.

There she is, on a bus to Belfast, with an address for a music teacher living in the leafy city-south. The journey is long on the bus, with empty space and time for her to wonder if she's doing the right thing. "You're mad," her wife had said as she left, half-laughing. When the bus dumps her out on a dirty city street, there's no time for last-minute fear. Áine is navigating an unfamiliar map.

As she is standing in front of the door, shivering and pulling her coat-sleeves further over her gloves, a realisation strikes her: does she even remember the person's face? Were they a woman? Were they old or young?

When the harpist opens the door, they are a woman with a many-lined face and fragile skin, silver hair pulled into a bun. She welcomes her in, offers her tea and a traybake. Áine explains the situation, halting and then brave. She's come too far to be embarrassed now about being weird.

The woman is quiet for a while, looking down into her empty flower-patterned ceramic cup. Then she looks up and nods.

"Maybe you made the memory your own," says the harpist, "and no one else will ever remember it the way that you did."

The harpist sits down on her stool. The harp is arranged in front of her. She raises her hands to the strings, takes in air to sing. Áine holds her breath. She drinks it all in, trying to memorise it all over again, despite the phone in her hands to record this moment forever for posterity.

The song is not the same. No less beautiful, but it is different. The harp and the singer's voice have both aged. The past cannot be returned to. Áine cannot re-experience that moment. The memory of it may disappear from her mind. The memory will certainly die with her. Who else would or could treasure this memory?

She loses herself to the moment and listens. Time slips away, the colours of the wall and furniture melting together, the air over-sweet like her granny's bedroom, the taste of caramel in her mouth the same as the ice-cream she had shared on her first date with her future wife, the ridges on her thighs like war trophies, the experience just as vivid as the memory she had recounted, the overlapping accumulations of recollection and desire.

Neil O'Dwyer

Neil is a debut voice whose non-fiction memoirs move with the rhythm of a seasoned orator. He is a maths teacher who has moonlighted as a spoken word storyteller in Ireland, England and Australia, including events like Seanchoíche and The Dublin Story Slam. We're proud to welcome him to his first publication.

'Town Frau, Country Frau' balances rural warmth against urban gloss, with a new angle on competing intimacy and indecision. This modern reimagining of Aesop's fable 'The Town Mouse and the Country Mouse' transforms the tidy moral into one about the pull between dedication and the allure of different worlds.

Town Frau, Country Frau

Judith owned a huge two-bedroom apartment in Berlin with high ceilings and flowing net curtains that opened out onto decent sized balconies. She had just got back from Greece that morning and when she answered the door she looked sun-kissed and fresh in a faded denim dress; barefoot, braless and radiant. Meanwhile, I was in blacks and greens and browns and dirt; a stain against her white walls, stinking up the place after living in filth for five days. Driving away from the festival in Poland was like escaping the scene of an apocalypse. I awkwardly stuffed my bags and boots in as neat a bundle as possible by the door and when I stood up straight to meet her eyes, I realised how unattractive I was then.

We had a light hug so as not to smudge her and she pointed me in the direction of her bathroom. Everything was untouched glass and stainless steel and she had a rain shower bearing down from the ceiling above. I sat under it and gradually came back to life and when I re-emerged, she was making risotto from a bag. This time we hugged properly and as her dress moved up her thigh I wondered if I was that hungry after all, but I sat patiently until she took me by the hand and into her room. For the rest of the day, she worked while I lay in bed in the heat and the breeze, drifting in and out of consciousness, waiting for her breaks when she slipped out of her dress and got back in beside me. It was by far the most wholesome afternoon of an uneventful year.

I got up later and joined her on the balcony. It was pretty. She had set the table with shiny white plates and matching cutlery and we ate politely before the sun forced us back inside. It was a nice evening but any time we were fully dressed things were too quiet and civil between us and the conversation definitely didn't flow as easily as it did over that drink in Dublin.

Judith: Thanks for making dinner, that's so nice.

Me: Sure.

Judith: The salmon is really great.

Me: Boy that sun is strong.

After dinner we went back to bed and while she slept at a distance because of the heat, I lay awake contemplating my decisions. I kept thinking about the drive away from the festival when Hatim turned to me in a moment of silence and said: come to Serbia with us. The other two travellers in the back seat chimed in and with this feeling of being wanted, albeit partly for the petrol money, I could see my summer opening up and taking me in exciting and uncertain directions. The best holidays are unplanned, he said, come, and he smiled and rubbed his hand along the steering wheel and waited while I looked out the window at the trees and prostitutes zooming by. Serbia was never on my radar but now it was front and centre, and who knew where it would lead.

Unfortunately though, I wasn't quite ready to jump into the unknown and felt obliged to follow through on my promises to visit Judith and Freya in Germany. It had been four months since seeing Judith and nearly a year since seeing Freya so I got off in Berlin before they went cold on me.

After two nights with Judith, I got the bus down to see Freya in Leipzig. She was excited to hear from me when we spoke on the phone, but at the station she didn't give me a massive hug or express much affection really. Something was up. I started blabbing about my plans for Austria or Slovenia but I could see she was struggling to focus. At one point we were walking so slowly across the road trying to understand each other that a frustrated driver shouted out his window:

Man kann wirklich schneller gehen!

Ah, fuck you! Freya called after him.

What did he say?

Something like: one can go faster.

One can go faster? I laughed. That's a very polite thing to shout at someone.

As soon as we got to her apartment, she had us straight out the door and over to the lake for my first ever skinny dip. It felt freeing to swim without shorts but once I was back on the beach, I just wanted to get dressed without giving her any ideas to do the same. It was uncomfortably hot too, and even the trees seemed to be wilting in the heat. Some had started to shed their leaves a couple of months ahead of schedule and others were completely bare. I picked up a handful and looked at Freya. Nature is falling apart, she said sadly, and continued to watch the water. Just then an adorable little toddler came over and stood between us and played with Freya's earrings while her family stood at a distance and looked uneasy. I started to cover up.

Back at the apartment, Freya suggested we put on face masks before bed but I wasn't keen. All day I tried my best to appear nonchalant about us but eventually I had to ask if we were still doing the couple thing every time we saw each other or what.

No. Not now, she replied after a slow exhale. She turned onto her back and looked at the ceiling.

Your mind is on that guy you met in Sicily, right?

Yes. Adrien.

Are you two a couple then?

Yes. So, this time nothing is going to happen.

But doesn't he live in Iceland?

I'm going again in September I think, but I haven't decided yet.

You must really like him if you can wait so long to see him.

You know he's the first guy who has ever said no to having sex with me. Seriously, it drove me so crazy.

Are you sure I should be coming to your mom's house?

Yes, of course. She wants to see you. You know, you're like some funny attraction in our family.

Like at an amusement park?

Yes.

She turned the lights off and I forced myself to move to the foot of the bed, using the morning sun in the window as my excuse. A minute later she got her pillow and joined me. We looked at each other and I wondered if I should be travelling a good two hundred kilometres in the wrong direction for more frustration, and then I replayed alternative answers I might have said to Hatim in the van. Sure, I'll go to Serbia Hatim, let's do it. Sign me up. Back-to-back festivals are just what I need.

The sun nudged me awake early and we instinctively wrapped ourselves up into each other but then she jumped out of bed and started making breakfast. While she was pottering around, I thought she didn't look the same as she did in September, or maybe I was seeing things. How perfect she was then. An hour later on the coach to Hannover, I wasn't sure what to think about us anymore but then we got to talking about relationships and it felt better to be open. I went first:

Remember you told me back in September that I shouldn't miss out on the next girl because I think there's still a chance for us?

Yes. Maybe we would be great, but you shouldn't wait for me, she said, and turned in her seat to look at me and send the point home.

Yeah, I thought about it, but you were still on my mind. You're a hard one to forget.

Do you know what is really special?

What?

That I told you that nothing is going to happen this time but you still like me. After saying this she finally gave me a proper hug.

Yeah of course I still want to be around you. I'll always want to see you.

Adrien says I say the word love too much but I don't think so. I love you, and the other boyfriends I've had.

That's nice you still think that.

I think you are perfect. Just not for me or just not for right now. You know, he didn't want to get into a relationship with me because he had a bad breakup before and I thought maybe it wasn't a good idea with such a distance but I think the pain of breaking up is so worth it for the feeling of invincibility I had when I was so in love with him those days.

Maybe I need to give it another go.

September, one year earlier:

After four years of thinking about it I finally booked a flight and went to Leipzig to see Freya. It was surreal. Her voice sounded strange without her Dublin twang and she seemed smaller too, and like she was from the future with her rusty hair and 1820's boots with red laces that could come apart at any minute. I couldn't stop looking at her and smiling internally and wanting to talk to her.

On the Saturday, we went to the canoe club to rent a boat and the guy who gave us the oars was very friendly to Freya and they talked for ages. If we were still a couple they could have been planning to meet up for sex and I'd have been none the wiser. We bought some food afterwards and sat on a blanket in the park with our bikes against the tree and a nice orange glow reflecting on the water.

I told her how we could maybe do house sitting next summer and pretend to be a couple because it's easier to get accepted that way and she said that we are a couple, but then she continued to say: when we're on holidays. We stood up and hugged and she said she feels safe with me. Her back is so trim and straight, unlike my boney bendy piece of shit, and she is hot and sound and funny but it wasn't there anymore whatever it was. That ship has sailed.

At her apartment she put on her Lumineers CD and took off all her tops while I wrote down on her note pad that we deserve to see each other more often, and how do we do it? She sat on my knee then and we scribbled some ideas and agreed that once every four years is a load of shit.

When the song 'Submarines' started playing she stood up and rubbed her boobs in my face. Submarine, she laughed, that's what we call it in German. Remember that long haired eejit downstairs in Woolwich? He was always playing it.

Yeah, it's coming back to me now actually.

I was listening to it on the bus on the way to uni then I'd hear it at home through the floor. The whole album makes me think of those last few weeks in London.

She started sniffling a little so I got up and hugged and kissed her and held her face for a bit.

We deserved more time together, I said, and she nodded and turned and backed into me. I wrapped my arms around her then and she slid her hand into my front pocket.

Did you make them?

Yeah, big pockets, aren't they?

You can scratch your balls and everything and no one will know.

Her mom collected us from Hannover and let Freya take the car for the afternoon. It was cool seeing her behind the wheel for the first time and she brought me around her neighbourhood and for coffee and cake in the village. When we eventually got to her mom's house, I felt all dizzy and in need of a nap before any more talking.

Of course, Freya said, and showed me to her room. It's good that you know what you need to fix yourself. When I feel like crap,

I don't know what to do. She was still crying after getting a message from Adrien which initially made her concerned mother flap and worry in a hilarious way because she speaks English in stops and starts but the situation called for hasty words.

We sat on her bed and Freya got a pen and paper and tried to write down what she wanted to say to Adrien, but she got so frustrated that she threw her phone across the room.

Maybe I shouldn't have come to visit, I said.

No, if he has problems trusting me then it's best to find out sooner than later because I am friends with other guys too. If someone says they won't be my boyfriend as long as I'm friends with Neilo then it's better to end it now.

She was in better form in the evening and we had some beers with her mom outside in the garden. Then Freya and I went to her old bed and got a bit close before she jumped up and paced the floor.

What's wrong?

I need to get better at not giving in every time I get a boner.

A boner? I said, suddenly confused.

Ah! Turned on, you know what I mean.

When she got back into bed, I turned over to sleep. Yeah, turn over, she said. That's what you used to do when we were in Woolwich. Come on!

We're not a couple anymore and you have the light on blinding me. I'll turn back when you turn it off.

She turned it off.

The next morning Freya's sister and brother Elsa and Alex arrived. Elsa is darker than Freya and a bit of a hippie and wears a lot of random jewellery. And she never stops smiling and laughs a lot at nothing which makes me laugh. She said good morning and laughed when she saw me and instantly put me in a good mood.

Her brother Alex is the most grounded of them all which he proved by showing up with a wife and a young son in tow, and in an effort to entertain me and the child Freya's mom planned to bring us all to the otter sanctuary for the day. This was seemingly the only thing to do in town and not really something I was too pushed about. I quietly told Freya I didn't want them making a fuss over me but she snapped and said I was the guest so I had better get used to it.

So, we filed in behind the other families to see the animals getting fed. Freya was being a bit distant on the way around so I started talking to Elsa about hitchhiking and she filled me in on her journey from France. Before long though, Freya pulled me away and suddenly got very affectionate with me for the first time. She apologised for snapping at me earlier and kissed me on the cheek and wrapped right into me and she was holding my hand by the time we got to the pine martens. They had an old-fashioned car in their cage with the bonnet open and plenty of places to climb and hide, and when Freya saw that I was interested in them she read the information out to me.

Apparently, pine martens love to chew on the wires in cars, she said. So, you need a whistle to make a high-pitched sound that only they can hear. Yes OK, but it says it works but then usually they come back in two weeks.

They come back with headphones on, I joked, and Freya laughed and told Elsa and they laughed together.

Then Freya came back and told me that she told Elsa what I said and she thought that it was funny too. She made an affectionate sigh and hugged my arm and kissed my shoulder and looked at the side of my face and laughed again while I thought about that time she said she always forgets that I'm funny.

When we got back to the house Freya declared that she was having a nap and looked me in the eye before walking down the hallway. I felt like a nap too and this time we held onto each other properly and looked into each other's eyes, and with our faces practically touching she whispered:

They probably think we're having sex.

Did you not tell them we're not having sex? I hissed, and rolled myself out of bed.

This was me trying to pretend I had no hopes or expectations and that it didn't matter if we didn't sleep together as I respected that she had a boyfriend. If only she'd give me the chance to be the second guy to refuse to have sex with her. I wouldn't hesitate.

She got straight up after me and we went outside for a run down a long empty road as the sun was setting over the fields. It felt nice and natural running together again without needing to say anything and reminded me of when we used to run away from our dump hole apartment and out into the Green Chain, leaving our London troubles behind. This was my first bit of exercise in weeks and I could feel the tensions and frustrations that come with being in cities and bars and around beautiful women start to fade away. For now, I was just happy being close to her as we turned and smiled at each other and made old reliable jokes, explored the long grass and fallen trees, and developed a rosy glow on our cheeks.

Back at home, her family were in the front room entertaining Alex's son and I felt properly at ease for the first time – the run having done its job. Freya said I could have a shower first and walked down the corridor but when I turned to close the bathroom door she was on my heels and slid in stealthily behind me.

What are you doing?

I want to watch you shower, she mumbled, and looked down at the floor.

OK, I said sceptically and took off my clothes and waited for the water to heat up. I tested the temperature with my hand, looked at her, shrugged my shoulders, and acknowledged my nakedness. I had to say something.

You know pine martens love peanut butter sandwiches?

Why are you waiting so long?

Does it not get hot? I said, but I couldn't take the silence any longer so I got in and closed the door.

Soon the glass started to steam up and I couldn't wipe it off or she'd know I was looking at her. I could still see her outline pacing around the same few spots on the floor though, and her head down. Didn't she say she wanted to watch me shower? But what did I think she meant by that though – her face pressed against the glass? Maybe I should have left the door open. But then the floor would get all wet. My breath was short now and her movements were more and more urgent, and with all of those distractions it was bloody hard to try to translate the writing on the shower-gel bottles and pick the right one. I opened the door.

She undressed and shimmied in and I reached past her and rattled the door closed. Then she bent her knees sideways to pick up a shower-gel bottle and we washed each other like before, and she looked up at me with her hair slicked back and spat water on me like she used to. Then she kissed me and everything sped up. She had one arm wrapped around my neck and started frantically trying to climb somewhere but there was nowhere she could put her foot unless she stood on my wet thigh, so her leg kept sliding down against the glass. Out of my left eye, I saw her grab the top of the shower door to pull herself up, but it was trembling under her grip so I quickly got my arm underneath her and tried to give her a boost. Her family were just a few yards away and for all they knew I was in the shower on my own shaking the door like a lunatic.

Eventually she started to run out of steam and gave up on whatever it was she was trying to do and went down on me instead and suddenly everything was fine and my head was clear of all the potential missed opportunities and regrets I'd been carrying around about Serbia and wherever else. Maybe me and Freya had our time and would never be a couple again and that's OK. We did enough. It was great seeing her and it wasn't a bad idea and I enjoyed the wholesome experience and that I have a connection with her family. So what if Berlin had more to see and a reliable girl that wanted to sleep with me and better things to do than an otter sanctuary because there's a lot to be said for getting out to the countryside, enjoying the simple things, and being in nature, and...

After dinner, we went to bed early and picked up where we'd left off, but in the morning, Elsa knocked on the door to wake us up and just like that me and Freya were back to being friends. I reached out to give her one last hug before we left, and found her feet.

We all said our goodbyes after lunch and then Freya's mom dropped her to the station to get the coach back to Leipzig. I planned to hitchhike to Dresden so we drove around afterwards until she found me a good spot. Then a car pulled up and I jumped in the back seat. In the rear-view mirror I could see myself and Freya all excited with ourselves hitchhiking around Ireland again five years earlier.

The driver pulled off and looked at me in the mirror.

Looks like you're happy to be picked up? he said.

Yeah, it's always a great feeling.

Unfortunately, we will not be driving all the way to Dresden but I can take you to Leipzig and you can catch a bus from there if it's not too late. How does that sound?

Sometimes the best detours are unplanned, I said, and looked in my bag for my headphones. Dresden could wait. Or Serbia, or wherever. At least for one day.

H.G. Nolan

Our faithful remote contributor H.G. Nolan is an Asian-American writer raised in New Hampshire and currently living in Ireland. Her fiction traces themes of cultural identity and belonging; often rooted in lived experience. Her work has appeared in Swerve Magazine and Scrimshaw Journal. Find her at hgnolan.com.

From underlying notes of indecision and reclamation, 'When We Were Girls' furthers the thread of a moral awakening and helps process the weight of the world. Instilled with empowerment and femininity, it reminds the reader how even a small, almost invisible act can leave a lasting impression.

When We Were Girls

It was just by chance that I noticed the boy putting up the poster. I had glanced up from my book and over at my brother. His head was down, hair falling forward over his brows. He had the tip of his pen to his lips and I could tell he was reading to himself from the open notebook as he mouthed the words ever so slightly. That's when the door opened. I looked towards it and the boy came in, nodding at the barista as he pulled the rolled-up poster from the limp pile draped over his shoulder. Delicately, but deliberately, he pulled the backing off with his teeth and, with his free hand, pressed the sticky side against the wall. That was it. And just as fast, he was gone, back outside to the overcrowded footpaths drenched in a heavy heat.

I saw, from across the cafe, an older woman had noticed too. She was sitting upright on the edge of her seat as if startled awake. She stared at the poster and the air felt tense. She just stared at it, and I stared at her. Her jaw was tight, her hands curled into fists. Then, she turned towards me and our eyes met. The way her body softened when she saw me – it was like she started to melt. Suddenly, she stood, walked to the poster, and tore it down in one swift movement. I think that was when my brother looked up, or maybe it was when the man stood, but by the time the man made his way to stand in front of her, everyone was watching.

"Put it back," he said to her. There was no anger in his voice, not the way he said it – like he was telling a puppy to drop a ball. He knew she would obey.

And I swear, she looked past the man and back at me and I could tell she wanted to cry. Her eyes were huge and watery. But she didn't put it back. She threw it to the ground, spat on it and walked out the door.

The man was calm as he bent down to scoop up the half-crinkled poster, torn where the woman had pulled it. He smoothed it out against the wall, wiped a hand across his chest and stood for a moment facing all the eyes. I looked over at my brother and he rolled his eyes and smirked, then went back to his studies. But things had shifted. The sun was still shining in through the stained glass windows, making kaleidoscope shapes along the wall as it moved across the sky. But something had changed. I couldn't focus on my book. I kept holding my breath like we were running out of air. And the barista seemed distracted. She was staring off into nothing, rubbing the same spot on the counter over and over. I realised that the women – and there were many of them, mostly unaccompanied – slowly began to leave. One by one, quietly packing up their things, cleaning the crumbs off their tables, stacking empty coffee cups and then floating out, until it was just us and the barista.

Finally my brother let out a big sigh and asked if I was ready to go home. I nodded and waited for him to gather his papers and books, and followed close behind him the entire way back to his apartment.

Lucy was there, setting out a spread of cheeses and fresh vegetables on the table. I was delighted to see it, as I hadn't realised my slow-growing hunger.

"First day in the city!" She said with a giddy smile as we walked in.

"She didn't get to see much of it." My brother responded for me.

"I don't mind," I said, my focus on the long crusty bread Lucy was slicing.

She nodded at me, so I picked up a piece and tore it in half, then started to eat it from the inside out. My brother laughed and said, "Sorry, sis, I guess I forgot to feed you today."

He stretched his arms up, reaching his fingers out, then brought them to the top of his head and gave his hair a tug. He looked like a kid when he did this, his shirt lifting up slightly and showing a bit of his belly.

We sat at the table and pulled apart the bread, layering it with cheese. We ate happily, quietly. And once I was full, Lucy looked at me and said, "It's too bad you can't stay a bit longer. We could have shown you more than the four walls of the Daily Grind."

"I don't mind," I said again, this time with a big smile so she knew it was true."Anyways, loads of the city came to us."

I said it without really thinking.

My brother scoffed, "Yeah, well, I guess you wouldn't see a lot of that back home".

Lucy looked confused.

"Unaccompanied girls." He said it under his breath, almost in a whisper. Lucy went a bit pink across her cheeks.

"It's very safe here," She said to me. It came out rushed, loud.

My brother crossed his arms and leaned back. "It is and it isn't," He said.

"For an adult, it's fine." She slowed herself and lowered her voice, "But, yeah, for a girl I guess it's better to be safe." She smiled at me.

My brother stood up then and started talking fast and loud. I thought he sounded like Dad – not like a boy, but a father. He was pacing up and down, telling Lucy about the woman who had torn down the poster and spat on it.

"Unbelievable!" he was saying. "Completely unprovoked. In public, with young girls there." He used both hands to point to me as he said this.

I wanted to tell her I had seen the boy put up the poster, and that the woman had looked at me with tear-filled eyes. But I stayed quiet – I let him tell the story. We both let him go on until he seemed to run out of interest and again started talking about his paper, pulling at his hair in that boyish way again. Eventually he told us he needed to finish something and gathered up his books, retreating to his room.

Lucy made a bed for me on the couch, and she was sitting there when I came out of the bathroom in my nightclothes. I sat next to her and pulled the covers up over my knees. Her expression was vacant and she stared off into nothing. I knew her thoughts must be far away.

"Dinner was lovely," I said to her. She smiled, then looked over at me. Eyes wide. I could tell she wanted to say something, but I didn't know what.

"I had a nice time today." I tried to reassure her, but her smile faded a little.

"You know...," She glanced at the bedroom door and lowered her voice. "Growing up in the city, it's a bit different. The women here, when we were girls... we didn't need supervision". She looked down at her hands, folded them together and started twisting the ring on her pointer finger.

"Back home I go to the shop on my own."

This caught her, and she looked at me with those big eyes again.

"The one Mrs. Malloy owns, just to pick up bits". I worried I might have said the wrong thing, so I tried to explain but I started talking really fast. "I know I shouldn't, but it's just when Mum has too much to do, and she doesn't want to annoy Dad with errands. I ride my bike with my big jacket on and the hood up and just go there and come right back, and it's only ever Mrs. Malloy who sees me because you know her husband died and she never had any children".

And what I thought would've reassured her only made it all worse, and she started to cry. She made no sound, just big tears rolling down her cheeks, and I didn't know what to do, so I started apologising and telling her that I wouldn't do it anymore and to please not tell my brother because he wouldn't like it at all.

But then she scooted herself over and hugged me. I could feel the tears making my cheek wet, but I hugged her back because it felt so nice to be close to her.

Before she pulled away, she whispered, "It shouldn't be this way". Then she stroked my hair gently and said, "I won't ever tell". She tucked me in then and turned out the lights before disappearing into the bathroom.

I wake to the sound of Lucy and my brother talking in hushed, angry voices.

"You're taking this too seriously, Lucy," My brother is saying to her.

"You said she was unprovoked, but you can't believe that?" She responds.

"You weren't even there. I said what I said because it's the truth. I can't change the facts, Lucy."

I hear her scoff, then my brother comes out, sheepish, his shoulders held high to his ears. He has that little boy look again, and I can't see a trace of Dad in him.

"C'mon, get your things. It's time to go," he says to me. My eyes are closed, so I flutter them open hoping he thinks I was sleeping. My brother doesn't notice, he's too busy gathering his books. We walk in silence to the Daily Grind.

I can't focus on my book. I stare at the page, but Lucy's words are playing over and over in my head. And I can't imagine her saying those words the way she said them to my brother. The anger, the strength. Instead, I imagine her saying them to me, and I imagine hugging her the way she hugged me last night. A long, tight hug. I thought that would calm her the way it had calmed me.

Before I know it, it's time for us to head to the train. My brother packs in a fury, and rushes me to do the same. As we head towards the doors of the cafe, I can't stop staring at the poster. It's just hanging there. As my brother steps outside, I stand in front of it to block it from anyone else's view and then, with one hard pull, I tug it down. It comes free easily. I scrunch it up and tuck it into my coat pocket. I know to keep it a secret. I know taking it down was wrong. I hold it tight until I get home, close the door to my room, then lay it flat on my bed.

THE FUTURE IS BORN, NOT ENGINEERED

It's written in block letters with a stamp – the same emblem Dad wears to work: three leaves connecting together in a stem with thorns, and 'Natural Order' written beneath. I don't want to be caught with the poster, so I memorise the words. Then, I tear it into pieces.

I keep the shreds of paper in my jacket pocket. Finally, after a few days, when Dad goes away for work and Mum asks me to get milk from Mrs Malloy's shop, I tuck my hair into my hood and pedal as hard as I can. I reach into my pocket, take out the pieces of paper and let them off into the wind.

Chris Tiernan

Chris is a developing talent who writes both short fiction and non-fiction. His work follows ordinary lives in tragedy with a cultural significance, reflecting his influences from Raymond Carver and Joan Didion. He attended Creative Writing at Inchicore College of Further Education and is now studying Creative Writing and English Literature at UCD.

Deepening the moralities of formulative years, this story wades into adolescent trauma, drug-fueled escapism, and the struggles of young masculinity. In 'Taking Inventory,' one transformative day lays bare the disorientation and grief of a fragile domestic life.

Taking Inventory

The dream is always at its most vivid before I wake up to an event of terrible circumstance. When I look back at certain moments in my life, I think, *And that was the morning I had the dream, the one I remember like a scene from a film.* It is always picturesque and comforting. But dreams can be suffocating. And sometimes they can be warning signs. What would it take for you to wish for a nightmare instead of a dream?

I find myself in a forest. I hear the pitter-patter of rain. Trees tower over us, and the sky is a white sheet of paper. She has her arms around me. I can't see her face but her hair is an animated extension of the amber leaves that surround us. She's whispering something to me, but the words are indecipherable. I've been here before. In my heart, I know who she is, but I don't want to know. I don't want to see her. I just want her to keep holding me. Whether it's fragments of memory or hidden desires, I refuse to listen. Everything starts to vanish as things begin to seem real.

I wake to the sound of knocking on our front door. I'm drenched in sweat and my head is throbbing. The clock says 6:43 AM. The front door opens, and I hear low voices. Then comes the shouting. I crawl to my window and pull back the curtain. Several men and women dressed in black stand outside our house. If it weren't for the naked faces, I'd swear we were being targeted by a small militia. Two men – ex-bouncers, surely – drag my shirtless father into the garden. He screams, "Nineteen years. Nineteen years I've lived here" I let the curtain fall back into place.

I turn around and see my mother standing in the doorway. Our expressions are identical. Any life in this room, in this house – it's gone. Her eyes drift to the ashtray beside my bed.

"Sorry," I say.

"Well, I don't imagine you'll be quitting anytime soon now," she says.

"I will."

She smiles and I look away.

"This is about the bank," I say. "From yesterday?"

"We don't need to talk about that now." She starts picking clothes off the floor like it's any other day

"Sweetheart," she says, "start packing some things. Essentials only. We'll come back for the rest later."

"What are we going to do?"

"And you'll need to shower. You won't get another chance today."

"Mom."

"I don't know," she says. "Just cooperate. Please".

She leaves the room with a bundle of clothes. I look around the room. Cleaner – but emptier. I think about what to take and what to forget.

I get changed and open the curtains. A man in a navy suit is talking to him now. I can't hear anything, but my father refuses to look at him, only gazing at the crowd of goons standing in our garden. Finally, he looks up at my window. I turn away.

I search for something to smoke. I find some leftovers from the night before. Yesterday morning – I heard him arguing on the phone. At the time, I dismissed it as business as usual. He was screaming at them and defiantly throwing out threats like frisbees.

This is something I've always admired about my father. He was relentless in the face of bureaucracy.

"For fuck sake." I have no doubt she hears me and immediately assesses the situation. A mother always has that kind of mystical power. One word of profanity – and more of the fog starts to clear. They understand their child a little better.

Now I hear them inside. Shuffling boots, zippers opening sharply, cupboards being slammed. In this moment of displacement, everything becomes louder. I hear heavy steps on the stairs. A burly skinhead comes up to greet us. He says nothing, but his face softens from authoritative to apologetic. We stand like deer in the headlights. She holds my hand. If it weren't for the warmth of her touch, I would burst out. Downstairs I hear laughter. I go back to my room and sit on the side of the bed. I light another half-smoked cigarette and watch the flames eat away at the skin. It falls from my fingers and worms itself into a crack in the floor. I put my hands on my face, and when I take them away, she's in front of me again.

"What are we going to do?" I try to stop my voice from cracking, but everything feels like an exercise in futility. She sits beside me and pulls my head onto her shoulder.

"I think we'll stay at my sister's. That's where we're going now."

"Do you think we'll get our house back?"

"I don't know," she says. "I really don't know. But don't tell your father I said that."

I look around the room for the last time. I stare at the wall, at my poster of 1977's *Lust for Life*, and as Iggy Pop stares back, I think about the hole hidden behind the grin. Somewhere during my descent into adolescence, I began a ritual of stopping myself from crying. In its place came swinging fists and shattered electronics. I got angrier as I got older. I rationalise this by blaming the Christian Brothers school where everyone played rugby and any sign of vulnerability gets you left in the hallway. The remnants of the crash still lingered, and men's mental health was rendered inconsequential. Ireland, will you ever change?

It's all coming undone. I feel white pain in my chest and tears dancing around my pupils. Am I supposed to feel weak? Or am I supposed to feel liberated? Everything was here once. You never realise how much structure a childhood bedroom can give you until it doesn't belong to you anymore. I don't know what I'm supposed to be. But now my mother tells me how she really feels, and I know I'll be thankful for it.

I sit forward and stare. I wonder what colour the walls will be a year from now. Suddenly, crimson doesn't look so appealing. I struggle to believe I lived with it for so long. It never really bothered me before. Only now does it make sense. *Surely this is karma.* I've been a difficult son. Neurological or learned, I can't be certain. Nevertheless, I feel as if my parents are paying for it. Now I understand why the walls are red. I am this room.

Downstairs, there are people writing things down in their clipboards, they're murmuring and 'Taking inventory'. My mother and I move through the crowd like a pair of stray cats. They rummage through the contents of our life, what little we couldn't fit into our Toyota Yaris.

The car is packed. All three of us sit in silence in the driveway. My father looks in the rearview mirror but my eyes refuse to meet him. A dozen of them swarm the house. We drive away. I watch my neighbourhood shrink and fade from view.

We arrive at my aunt's house and there is this wonderful return to normality. We make breakfast. Drink coffee. I play with the kids and try to explain things to the eldest. She's my first cousin, but I consider her a little sister. She is wise beyond her age and her maturity moves me. I was there on the day of her birth, and now she's there for me on the day of my new life. She understands me, nodding while I explain the events of the morning.

"I won't tell Adam for now," she says. "He's too young. But I think he'll be happy to have you here more often."

Adam is her younger brother and I can't say I like him too much. Too unruly. Too many tantrums. I don't like seeing myself in him. It's like I could grab my younger self by the shoulders and scream, *It only gets worse if you carry on like this.* I wonder how long before the trap of modern Irish masculinity swallows him whole. God help him if he goes to a school where Religion is mandatory.

In the kitchen, I hear my mother break down while her sister tries to comfort her. My father walks around the garden with his arms around his back. He is a man lost in thought. A million different routes to save his family but none of them seem plausible. The weight of the world is on his shoulders, and not even the lilacs or fresh tomatoes can clear his mind.

I call out to them, "I'm going out."

"Will you call me later?"

I close the front door without answering.

I open up my phone and put in my earbuds. A flash of excitement comes over me. I had completely forgotten. Today is the release of Queens of the Stone Age's latest record *Villains*. Why does it feel like the world is trying to throw me a bone? Is this some kind of sick joke?

So far, most of the songs feel dancy but with a lingering sense of classic punk. Though it's been a year since his death, Bowie is very much alive in these songs. It's not until I get to track number four that I start to have a profound sense of inevitability, like this day was preordained.

The song is called *Fortress*. Josh Homme begins with a familiar tone of compassion. It doesn't even feel like he's singing. He talks to me about bottled-up feelings. He asks me if it makes me feel safe. And when we get to the chorus, he implores that despite my world disintegrating, nothing is final. But not without sentimentality; if ever our fortress caves, we're always safe in his.

I think to myself *What the fuck?* No, *this is almost farcical. This is too cliche. This is not some bullshit movie about redemption.* I am moved and the tears are rising up again, and my love for this band is reinforced, but today, everything is overwhelming to the point of suffocation.

I need to breathe. I think about who to call. Who would be in my corner? Who in my contacts list is real? Who can I call a friend more than just a mere acquaintance? There is no one in my life right now who has the capacity for such an ordeal to be dropped on their front door on a Saturday morning.

I dial the only number I can. His name is Felix and I ask him if I can come over to buy some weed.

He lives in the rural outskirts of Bray. It is a long bus journey and I'm forced to pass by my old neighborhood again. It's been about 3 hours and yet it already feels like a past life. When I get there, His reaction is as expected – entirely indifferent. "My parents aren't going to stay with me," I say. "They'll find a place to rent. I'll stay at my aunt's. That's all we know. But I don't think we're ever going back there."

"That's fucked up, man," he says. Felix is a scrawny guy with dirty blonde ramen curls that remind me of Justin Timberlake's more unsavoury days as a member of NSYNC. His house is large and luxurious and yet his room looks no different than my ransacked three-storey residence.

I hand him a fresh fifty-euro note, and he hands me a small baggie. He turns on his large bookshelf speakers and *Desolation Row* plays. He knows I like Bob Dylan. He turns up the volume. Is this an effort on his part, or is it a way to avoid talking about it? I start to think about how I've perceived him and his friends. Maybe he just doesn't have the lexicon for consolation. He is my drug dealer after all. But this is exactly why I came here. If support and comfort were going to be foreign to me, I would succumb to stubbornness and opt for a day without sobriety.

"Here man. Take a hit off this," he says.

He hands me his water bong. It is a tall blue piece made of silicone.

The smoke immobilizes me. Sitting across from me on his dirty coffee-brown armchair, he goes through the usual routine of telling me where it came from and what strain it is and ends on the classic "but yeah, it's good shit. Straight from 'the dam'. He doomscrolls and I sit on the couch staring up at his popcorn ceiling. I start to laugh.

"What?" he says.

"Holy shit," I say. "I completely forgot. McGregor fights Mayweather tonight." What a day. I have accepted it as the beginning of my real life. Anything before has been rendered irrelevant. Suddenly all the little insecurities and anxieties of a teenager's life seem minuscule. *Oh, what if they think I'm annoying? Oh, do they like me? Oh, does she like me? Oh I wonder how pizza-faced I look this morning.* The question isn't even who gives a fuck? It's *why*. Why give a fuck.

Life will drop a boulder on your head and then carry you into bed. This is my only rationale. I decide not to question it any further. We have lost our home, and it will be a long time before my parents and I are reunited under the same roof. And I am thankful for the good things that have happened today; the new album, this opportunity for intoxication, and one of the biggest sports spectacles of the decade, but I know no one will be in my corner from here on out. I will have to quietly endure this second chapter in my life. I have my own fight to focus on. Part of me wishes for the easy way out. I believe this is a habitual line of reasoning for young men today. The prospect of modern life in the largest tech hubs of Europe is exhausting. Vulture funds will destroy this country. Tired men in a flat city; what else is there?

But then I think about my mother quietly cooking dinner. I picture my father sitting at the table with his elbows on the table and his hands clasped together. I think of my cousin and her brother playing PlayStation in the living room, and I think of the years I will be spending under the same roof. Anchors I can't ignore. But right now, I choose to escape. I roll myself a joint and I sit back and watch the circus.

"Yeah, some of the lads are coming over. I bought it on Sky Box Office." Felix says.

People start arriving. Some faces appear familiar and others intimidate me, I receive cold glances and I watch their eyes dart back to Felix. *Who's the first year?* they seem to say. Men in tracksuits come over with crates of Heineken. A scraggy Macaulay Culkin impersonator sits down beside me and offers me some tobacco for a cigarette. I remain silent for most of the night. I observe and listen to stories of travel and gossip. A tall woman with bangs arrives. She looks out of place. Too clean, too healthy. She wears a black leather blazer and Doc Martens. Her name is Giselle. "Happy Crimbo," she says with a smirk. She gives Felix a bottle of Woodford Reserve. "I'll get some glasses," he says.

She gives me a look of curiosity. "Want some?" I say. The words blurt from me as I reach across the messy table with a joint between my fingers. She leans forward and rubbery creaks escape the folds of her jacket. "Want some whiskey?" she says.

I nod and feel myself smiling. She smiles back at me. "How do you take it?"

"I like ice and 7-up."

She calls out Felix. He comes back with glasses and a bucket of ice. He winks at me. 'Here you go mate. Get that into you'. I'm not sure if it's the drugs, or if it's the anticipation of an absurd sports event, but there is a bright vibration travelling throughout my bones.

When the fight commences, it gets rowdier and I start to feel more inebriated. I receive a text from my mother. She tells me that they will stay with me for a couple of weeks but then they will find a place of their own until we get a house; whenever that will be. I have no idea when we will be living under the same roof again, if ever. I take a gulp from my glass and try to focus on the TV.

Floyd's initial strategy is one of low-output defense. The first four rounds see Floyd attempting to burn out Conor's cardio via subtle head movement and footwork, luring him into leading the exchanges. Conor starts to believe he is in control of the distance. He is an athlete built for short-bursts and early success, though his success in enemy territory is minimal. Everything goes according to plan. Floyd changes his rhythm, beginning to close distance and walking his opponent down. Forced to fight on the backfoot, Conor's famous straight-left is smothered by Floyd's close-range pressure, and now he starts to swing wildly, a classic sign of frustration and a depleting gas tank. His defense is mediocre and his fight-IQ is inferior. Floyd starts to land body shots and right-hand's with precision in favour of power.

This is his world. Any suspicions of an MMA sniper coming to disrupt his world gradually evaporate. The fact that he is forty is irrelevant. Floyd doesn't have knockout power, but the shots are still hard and when they land, they make Conor's eyes roll back. Floyd's intention: humiliation, not execution. A slow-burn performance that leaves his opponent believing there is something there to grab, but it's an illusion, and now he has nothing left to show. When he goes back to his corner, Conor looks up at John Kavanagh like a newborn baby. He doesn't know where he is.

Nine rounds in, the result of the fight is evident. I take another drink and the events of the morning start to replay in my head. I can't shake them out. What leaves a stinging wound is the sound of my father. The transition from a blissful dream to a nightmarish reality is jarring. I can't stop hearing his dejected voice as they pull him out to the front garden. I think about the state of the house and how we left it. Everything is upside down and nothing is where it's supposed to be.

I recall leaving a large portion of paperbacks scattered around my bedroom. The contents of my soul are annotated in those books and for all I know, they could be in the hands of a government agent.

My heartbeat feels icy and I think I might vomit. Giselle is staring at me. "What's with you?" she says. The volume of the room lowers and I see Felix run his eyes around the room.

"I bet on Mcgregor," I say, running my hands through my hair and taking a long drag of my joint. She doesn't say anything. She continues to look at me as she drinks from her glass.

I lay my head on the backrest of the couch and slowly close my eyes. My decision is reinforced; I'm not going to tell anyone anymore, and I hope to god I don't have another dream about my red-headed mystery woman. I know now that I was supposed to listen to her.

Lee Bristow

Lee lends a grounding variety to our group with his non-fiction work about business and technology. He has begun experimenting with poetry and his voice has quickly developed in resonance and character through the encouragement of our established poets. Known primarily as the 'AI ethics guy,' we believe he's at the promising start to a new side-hustle.

His four poems illuminate raw themes of social conditioning, defiance, and men's mental health. They move from the emotional suffocation of social media's deceiving hooks (Bait), *to a hopeful yet melancholy performance of romance* (Green and Blue), *to a defiant protest against our puppeteering leaders* (Empty Words), *and finally, to an open appeal urging the 'gentle man' to turn from harmful criticism* (Man's Superpower).

Bait

Coming home with my empty pain.
Numbing my sorrows with blame.
Remove my face from my brain.
Upload my daily dose of Insta fame.

Project my perfect love.
My Perfect Life.
Perfect, inspiring beauty.

Caption the curated time to make me feel a little less.
Letting my compassion echo between imaginary keys, hitting the apocalyptic relationship beat.

Turning to my partner.
Gagging on the real that is my life.
Carefully applying the Joker's smile, sculpting it into a beautifully cruel contoured scar.

Now, hook my eyes to my lies.
It is my time to cast contemptuous lines.

Real in my bounty.
Land my love in a sea of shame, where the rotting dreams scream for release.

My poem slides off slumped, tattered, and torn pages.
No games of joy.
No comedy of laughter.
No sage of clarity.
Just passing hope's time.

My prayers arrested.
Extinguishing the love of my dearest heart.
Release. Catch and release! Leave enough fight.

Green and Blue

The jester looks out across the joyful room. Thick with memories and rings of loving commitment.

Setting the stage for the next love story.

A glimmer of hope in green swirls past into sugar push. With each step, a secret glance is shared from behind beautiful blue orbs of shimmering attraction.

Restraints and logic buckle and splinter.

The forever court jester stands and delivers a pitch-perfect landing of vulnerable, hopelessly bound in the siren's sight.

The only defence for a couple of star-struck, lonely heart lovers caught in the fever of this night's magic.

From lofty stage, they act out the narrative of coy attraction. A lifetime of happily alone ever after. Playing vinyl singles, they struggle, turning in beautiful harmonies, going round and round, keeping the dream alive.

Just for tonight.

Willing witnesses share the special moment, first dance, first kiss. But few care or mourn the truth between peaks of loneliness in the nights that follow.

Of course, this is the best part: hope rises, anticipation builds, and a breathless moment passes, moves as one, and spirits shine in the shades between green and blue.

Empty Words

I proudly wear the suit of a dignified puppet. It's a real job. Yet, I am tired of having a hand shoved up my butt that fills my mouth with words that are not my own.

This needs to be corrected.

My thoughts are not my own; they are provided in an orchestrated script that discombobulates daily.

This needs to be corrected!

My ventriloquist speaks from both sides of his mouth, telling me one thing, then doing something different. He says it's necessary. Saying one but behaving another conveys a third, subtle, unsaid meaning. He also calls it 'comedy, politics, or showbiz.'

THIS NEEDS TO BE CORRECTED!!

The audience applauds at my shame.

Does this need to be corrected?

Has master no empathy for me, my feelings or identity?

This NEEDS *to be corrected!?*

He says it's funny, what the people want. Is this what people really want, to see my puppet master make me look so stupid, lifeless, no respect, or thoughts of my own?

This needs to be corrected!

Without his breath, do I have a life?

This needs to be corrected!

Is there an option outside of death? Is there meaning in the defiance of not caring for a life of meaning or purpose?

This needs to be corrected!

Pushed to do enough shameful things, and you won't recognise yourself or the box you call home.

Don't believe me?!

Look at your sad, sorry face in the mirror and tell me what vapid ideas tripped out of your vacant mind today?

This, too, needs to be corrected!

Man's Superpower

It is never Enough,
You are never Enough,
This is never Enough,
On repeat.

These words are just emotional hexes,
My gentle man.

Pay no heed,
And do not plead.

Make a truth sandwich and put your mind at ease.

Place those hexes between slices of "I feel" and "right now",
For
Contrast
And clarifying relief.

Reality will dawn, and you will both still be in Eden!
Any other reaction could never be forgiven!

Ignorance is no longer a defence,
My gentle man.

This story is as old as time!

So become a master of making a truth sandwich,
And draw your line –
This time.

My gentle man.

Gary O'Connor

Gary once again offers his stark and cinematic style to our collection. His work focuses on gritty crime and political thrillers with an eye for moral compromise amidst harsh injustice. Grounded in his values as a dedicated family man, he channels loyalty and social advocacy into narratives that are both gripping and emotionally charged.

'Dissonance' *follows a married couple grappling with the aftermath of a life-changing home break-in, revealing how trauma can distort relationships and ignite consequences that ripple far beyond their own lives.*

Dissonance

Geoff and Jill silently walked as they left Dublin's Criminal Court. The late-autumn afternoon was cold; the sky hung low and grey, and the wind cut through them as they got into the car. To steady his nerves, Geoff lit a cigarette and started the engine.

"You shouldn't," Jill said quietly.

"I need to," Geoff muttered, stealing a glance at Jill. She looked distant, lost in thought. His own mind was excessively ruminating and he couldn't collect his thoughts. He smoked in silence, shifting aggressively through the gears as he drove on.

"One year. That's all!" he finally said. "Did he rob a Christmas tree? And his mate – what did he say? 'Nice one, Crotty – you'll be out in six months.' Fecking delighted, he was."

"Calm down! You're running every red light!" Jill cried.

"And what if I do?" snapped Geoff. "What would they give me – more than Crotty, I bet. And Judge Dawson! 'If I see you back here, Mr. Crotty, it'll be a lot more than one year.' Like Crotty's some naughty schoolboy. 'If I see you back here...'" Geoff repeated bitterly. "He's already been to court thirty fecking times, according to our barrister."

"Take it easy, Geoff – relax."

"I can't." He dropped down a gear, his driving steadier. "You haven't been the same since the attack – all because of Crotty."

"Come on, Geoff," said Jill, letting her head fall back against the headrest. "You've never been easy to live with."

"I know." He exhaled. "But I haven't changed, have I? Neurosis is who I am – it's in my DNA."

"But that hasn't been easy for me, has it?" she said, weary.

She had left the house feeling strong, determined – but now she was deliberately avoiding the wing mirror.

She failed.

She looked.

She saw herself.

Her face was drawn and pale. The long blonde hair she once wore loose was now sharply cut above the ear, barely grazing her collar. A black trench coat clung tightly to her thin frame, worn over a navy trouser suit.

A fine sweep of eyeliner framed her eyes, lifting softly toward the brows – not for beauty, but for strength. Her war paint.

She had gone in fighting.

And she had lost.

Seeing Crotty again had made her feel sick. Her hands were still moist with sweat.

She remembered every detail – the look in his eyes, his tightly curled black hair, the thick goatee, his wiry frame. She promised herself she wouldn't look at him – but she had, perversely hoping for a trace of compassion. There was none. Crotty eyed her up and down with a deliberate smirk that sent a shiver through her body. The terror came flooding back.

She glanced at Geoff, still ranting, and then turned her eyes away. She couldn't absorb a word. She had tried to understand his OCD, but it exhausted her now. He worried and overthought everything; he needed constant reassurance.

Whilst holding down her own job, she had supported him as he built a successful car dealership. But the empathy, or rather the compassion, she had for him was gone. For Jill, empathy had become a hollow word – often spoken, rarely acted upon. People said it like it mattered, but their concern faded faster than steam from a kettle. She knew real empathy meant staying present, paying attention, even when it was hard. But her own trauma had eroded the patience and focus she once gave to Geoff.

Fear, once a stranger, had become an unwanted companion. She shuddered at the sight of every man with a goatee. The solitude she once cherished had vanished. The car had stopped, and she felt bitterly cold.

They had arrived at Canty's, a pub on Dublin's Northside that Geoff had frequented since he was old enough to drink.

He looked at her. Her deep blue eyes brimmed with tears.

"I'm sorry," Geoff said softly, taking her hand.

Jill said nothing. She let go of his hand and stepped out. Geoff watched her walk around to the driver's side.

She looked so beautiful, he thought. He loved her so much; his heart sank. He knew the day had brought no resolution. It had been a disaster. When Crotty wasn't laughing with his mates in court, he was texting on his phone. Geoff wanted to punch Crotty there and then.

"Is Derek meeting you here?" Jill asked, holding out her hand for the keys.

"Yes," Geoff replied, but before he could say more, she was gone.

"Fuck," he muttered, striding towards Canty's Bar.

Derek was already at the bar when Geoff arrived. A pint of Guinness was waiting. Geoff and Derek had been friends since they were kids.

They were the odd couple - Geoff, tall and slim, clean - shaven with a mop of black hair, while Derek was short, round, and balding with a thick brown beard. Whenever they got the chance, they played golf together and shared a love of football - especially Manchester United. Geoff took off his suit jacket, loosened his tie, and sat down. The two men clinked glasses. He waved to Philip, the barman.

"It didn't go well," said Derek.

"It was a disaster," Geoff replied, with a weary shrug. "That piece of dirt, Crotty, got one year for terrifying my wife. He'll be out in six months."

Geoff took a gulp of his pint, exhaling as he gathered his thoughts.

"Jill has changed," he said. "Our marriage has changed. She found that scumbag in our bedroom, going through our drawers. He pushed her hard onto the bed – grabbed her by the throat. He had a screwdriver in his hand. She thought he was going to rape her. Maybe he would have, if something hadn't spooked him."

Geoff finished his pint and gestured to Philip for another round. He continued.

"Before all this, our relationship was natural. Fun. It was like walking – one foot in front of the other. Now? Every night, she locks every door in the house. During the day, she is different. The Bank has just promoted her to senior risk manager. But she doesn't take the train anymore – now she drives everywhere."

Derek, a quiet and reticent man, shifted uncomfortably. He felt a wave of compassion for Jill. Only now did he grasp the seriousness of what she'd been through.

He looked Geoff in the eyes. "Has she seen a therapist?"

"She's seeing a therapist," Geoff replied. "It's helping her. She's talking through everything – working through the attack, but also things that go deeper. And I'm tangled up in all of it. I'm part of what she needs to deal with. For the first time in my life, I feel alone."

Geoff paused, his thoughts turning inward. His fingers tapped lightly on the table.

"I think and worry too much about irrational fears, and I don't worry enough about what really matters. But Jill and I, we have always been good."

Derek ran a hand through his beard, searching for the right words, but none of them felt adequate.

The evening passed quickly. The bar got busier, the music louder.

Geoff returned from the bar with a double gin and tonic for each of them. They'd been drinking for hours and were now well past tipsy.

"See the big fella by the pool table?" Derek asked, covering his mouth.

"What about him?" shouted Geoff.

"Shush! That's Jack Dennis – local crime boss. Drinks here on weekends with his cronies. Big United fans. Philip says they're always doing coke in the toilets, but there's nothing he can do."

Geoff glanced over. Jack was a tall, powerfully built man – well over six foot – with hulking arms and a close-cropped haircut. His navy jumper had the sleeves rolled up, revealing tattoos on each arm. Geoff thought he looked vaguely familiar.

"Fuck him and his cronies," Geoff muttered, finishing his gin and ordering another.

The bar began to thin near closing time. Philip came over, clearing glasses.

"Lads, do you have any homes to go to?" he joked.

"I'll call you a cab," said Derek.

"No – you go ahead. I'll get one out on the road," Geoff replied, giving his friend a warm hug. "I'll be in better form next time, I promise."

"You just look after yourself," replied Derek

Geoff made his way to the gents, moving gingerly. As he entered, he saw Jack Dennis at the urinal. Geoff stared.

"You alright?" Jack asked.

"No, I'm not," Geoff replied.

"Well, fuck off and stop staring," Jack snapped.

"Do you know Rayo Crotty?" Geoff asked, slurring slightly.

"Rayo Crotty?" Jack's eyes narrowed as he turned to consider Geoff. He smiled mockingly. "Who the fuck are you?"

"My wife was beaten by him. And you – being a crime boss – you probably know him."

Jack's face twisted as he stepped in, pressing his forehead against Geoff's.

"You alright, boss?" Two of Jack's men had entered.

"No. This clown's asking if I know Crotty."

They burst out laughing. "Is he serious?"

Geoff sobered up fast. He knew he'd made a mistake.

"What if I do know Crotty?" Jack's voice dropped, low and dangerous. He shoved Geoff hard against the wall, twisting his arm.

"Come on, Jack," Geoff pleaded. "You know me. I've been drinking here for years."

For a moment, the two tall men stood in silence, facing each other. Jack felt unsure – there was something familiar about Geoff, and he loosened his grip slightly. Geoff let out a slow breath, a flicker of relief passing through his eyes.

But another gang member agitatedly interrupted. "What does he want to know about Crotty? If he knows about him – what does he know about us?"

Jack's face reddened. He twisted Geoff's arm again – until it snapped.

Geoff screamed, but Jack clamped a hand over his mouth.

"Is he a copper?" one of them asked.

"No," Jack replied. "Take him outside."

They dragged Geoff out behind the pub. One of the men forced him to the ground and pushed his tie into his mouth. The other stepped forward and brought his boot down hard on Geoff's leg. The crack of bone was sharp and immediate.

It was a cold, icy night. Jack and his pals stood in silence, cigarettes glowing in the dark. Geoff lay unconscious at their feet.

"Are you going to tell Crotty he was asking for him?" one of them muttered.

"No. And don't mention Crotty again," Jack growled. "Put this fella in the park."

Then, without a flicker of emotion, Jack turned and strolled back into Canty's. He found Philip wiping down the counter.

"The cameras out the back aren't working," Jack said casually. "They need replacing."

Philip barely looked up. "I'll get it sorted. Immediately."

Geoff was eventually found by Jill and Derek. He was lying amongst fallen yellow leaves under a birch tree. He stirred, disoriented, through the haze, he saw Jill. He could see a look of shock on her face. Jill wrapped her woollen coat tighter to her breast, a wave of nausea rising in her. She could barely look at Geoff. The last thing she wanted or needed was more violence. Her hands shook as she pulled her mobile from her pocket.

"Don't call the Guards," he said.

She ignored him.

Derek knelt beside him, "What the fuck happened?"

"You don't want to know," Geoff whispered back.

Through the fog of pain, one thing became clear: he wasn't saying a word. Not to anyone. Geoff looked up at Jill. Her blonde hair caught the moonlight – then everything went black again.

He spent three weeks in the hospital, then another three recovering at home. Slowly, painfully, he resumed running his car dealership. He blamed himself for the attack and was more embarrassed than anything else.

He slipped into routine: work until one, then lunch watching the news. That day, the broadcast cut to the face of Judge Dawson. A reporter was discussing public fury over yet another lenient sentence in a brutal assault case.

"Jill!" Geoff called out, "Jill!"

He raised his voice, "Jill!"

She burst into the kitchen, flushed and breathless from exercising on the treadmill. Her eyes landed on the TV – and froze. A look of pain swept over her face. Without a word, she snatched the remote, turned off the screen, and walked out.

Geoff grabbed his walking stick and hobbled after her.

"That's him," he panted. "That's the judge. The one who gave Crotty a slap on the wrist. And now he's done it again."

Jill pressed her palms to her forehead; sweat lay like bubbles on her skin. "I don't want to think about Judge Dawson. Or Crotty."

"But you do," Geoff snapped. "You do think about them. What if he keeps letting scumbags like Crotty off?"

She grabbed a towel and started drying herself.

"Maybe he has no choice," she said.

"No choice? What are you talking about?"

"I don't know. Maybe he's limited by the law. Sentencing rules, prison space. Something."

"But if someone does wrong, they need to pay for it," argued Geoff.

"Maybe it's not that simple," replied Jill

"But if there is no prison space, why don't they speak up? If they can't do their job and put people away, then they should let the public know."

"They just can't, Geoff!" she shouted.

"So, what's going to change in Judge Dawson's life?" demanded Geoff. "Nothing! And judges like him will hide behind politicians, and politicians will hide behind judges. Round and round."

He stared at her. "Why are you shutting me down? Why can't we talk about it?"

She stormed over and ripped the walking stick from his hand. He stumbled and hit the floor hard.

"You have a business to run, and I don't want to hear about Judge Dawson or Crotty," she shouted, her voice trembling.

Jill ran upstairs to their bedroom, undressed, and stepped into the shower. She cried helplessly as she let the water drown her tears. She felt colder and she hated herself for it.

But Geoff did want to talk about Judge Dawson. He listened as Jill stormed up the stairs, then dialled Derek's number.

"Geoff, what's up?" said Derek.

"I want to go to Canty's tomorrow night."

"You're joking, right?"

"No, I'm not."

"But you know Manchester United are playing – and Jack Dennis will be there – and you seriously expect to hobble in with your arm in a sling and a walking stick?"

"Yes. And I'm going to whack Dennis with it."

Derek laughed.

The following evening, they arrived at Canty's. The bar was already buzzing. They found a seat in the corner, and Derek went to the bar to get two pints of Guinness.

Geoff felt a knot in his stomach. He hadn't been in Canty's since the attack. He knew Jack Dennis would show up soon, but for now, it was his OCD that had him on edge. Three half-finished pints sat abandoned on the table, surrounded by soggy beer mats. He checked under the table – chewing gum plastered everywhere. On other tables empty crisp and peanut packets were stuffed into empty pint glasses.

His anxiety climbed fast. At the next table sat four men and a woman – all in United jerseys – laughing, shouting, roaring.

Geoff had always been his own warrior and he needed to be. He'd built everything he had in business despite his illness. In some ways, his was an absurd, tortured existence – where the illogical part of his brain thrived like weeds in a garden. His mind was under constant siege. One fear would fade, only for another to take root.

Reclaim your brain, he whispered to himself – his private mantra. But the truth was, his brain was far from reclaimed. His mind always took him down roads he did not want to go. He edged his chair slightly further away from the noisy table.

"Two pints of Guinness," said Derek, placing them down. "And... your friend's here."

"Where?"

"In the snug, to the left of the bar."

"Is there room for us?"

Derek looked at Geoff. Geoff looked over at the ever-expanding table beside them. They both laughed.

By halftime, United were winning. The table next to them had given Geoff and Derek an unsolicited, boisterous commentary throughout the entire first half.

When Derek went to the toilet, Geoff waved at Philip.

"What's up?" Philip asked, as he approached.

"I want you to give this to Jack Dennis," said Geoff, handing him an envelope.

"No fucking way, Geoff."

"Listen, Philip. I've been good, haven't I? I haven't said a word to anyone about the attack."

"I suppose you haven't," Philip muttered, reluctantly taking the envelope.

When Derek returned, he caught sight of Philip walking away, shaking his head.

"What were you two arguing about?"

"Oh, just the match," said Geoff, draining his pint. "Philip hates United – you know that."

Geoff glanced toward the snug. Jack Dennis was standing, envelope in hand, fixing him with a cold stare.

In the days that followed, Geoff worked and waited anxiously for Jack Dennis to call. At last, he did.

"Jack, thanks for calling," whispered Geoff as he grabbed his walking stick and stepped into the back garden.

"What do you want?" Jack snapped,

"Jack," Geoff began, barely able to hear his own voice. "I want you to hear me out."

"Okay," Jack replied.

"I want you to go to a judge's house and turn it upside down. Smash the furniture. Gloss-paint the walls and floors – wreck everything. But take nothing. Hurt no one."

"I'll pay you a hundred grand to do the job."

"Take nothing," said Jack

"No, nothing," replied Geoff.

"I'll do it," Jack said after a short pause. "But I swear, Geoff – if you're playing games – if this has anything to do with what happened in Canty's, I'll kill you."

"I don't want you to kill anybody, Jack."

Geoff turned off his phone, his heart pounded steadily as the weight of his words settled in.

Weeks passed. Geoff kept working, but his thoughts never strayed far from Judge Dawson. When he wasn't occupied with work, he was digging into anything he could find about the judge.

Judge Dawson was married, with three children. Ambitious, he was already being tipped for the Supreme Court. His name popped up in article after article. In many cases, victims, and reporters alike expressed outrage at his lenient sentences.

Judges were suppose to be the last line of defence for the victim. Not Judge Dawson, thought Geoff.

Jill realised she'd come to a crossroads in her life. She was trying to fill the emptiness inside her, but she no longer found what she needed in Geoff. She had to find it on her own. Purposely, she began cutting out social media and the news – anything that stirred up the noise in her mind or brought Crotty back into view. The constant stream of outrage and drama, the way it all fed on fear – she couldn't let it in anymore. Bit by bit, she reclaimed her space. And with that came strength. For the first time in a long while, she felt something close to freedom. She didn't know how long Crotty would linger in the background of her life – but at least now, she was doing what she could to protect herself.

She was preparing scrambled eggs for breakfast. From the window, she could see the wind buffeting the trees and ripping the leaves off them. The hot weather had gone, she longed for its return – it had made her skin tingle and feel alive again. It thrilled her to see the flowers bloom. She loathed now to see the trees naked and stripped of life.

Her thoughts turned to Geoff. The harder he tried to help her, the less she wanted him. She couldn't explain it – of course, she didn't blame him for anything – but the less she desired him, the more strained their relationship had become.

They were watching Sky News when breaking news interrupted the broadcast and cut to Dublin. The reporter stood outside a hospital explaining that Judge Ben Dawson's house had been broken into and his wife had been seriously injured. Before Geoff and Jill could say anything, the coverage cut to the Taoiseach speaking at Leinster House.

"This is not just an attack on Patricia Dawson," the Taoiseach said as he looked deep into the camera. "This is an attack on every citizen of this country."

Jill turned to her husband.

"No fucking way, Geoff! You couldn't have..."

A look of anguish crossed her face. Geoff said nothing – he was in shock. A shiver ran through his body as he stared at the Taoiseach in disbelief.

"No, no," Geoff pleaded. "Come on, Jill."

Jill picked up her plate of scrambled eggs and hurled it against the wall, smashing it.

"I know you," she yelled. "And I know you're behind this. You and your grudge against Judge Dawson. That poor woman. She probably has kids, and now she is fighting for her life. What have you done Geoff, didn't you think?!"

Jill sank to the floor, buried her face in her hands and took a series of deep breaths. A hush settled between them before she finally stood up and moved to the window. Rain now lashed against the glass.

She moved closer to Geoff, looking up and gently cupped his face in her hands.

"I'm leaving you, Geoff. I was going to – even before all this. I do love you – but I can't keep holding everything together. I need more love than you are able to give me, and now you've done something really terrible."

Geoff's voice cracked. "I never wanted any of this to happen."

Her eyes welled with tears as her fingers brushed through his hair. "But it did, Geoff. You didn't stop to think. You made it happen!"

Her hand slipped from his hair and came to rest gently on his cheek. She stared into Geoff's eyes. Suddenly, images of happier times flashed through her, and she began to tremble, as if her mind were urging her to stay and help. Tears streamed down her face.

She drew a breath, steadying herself. Her voice was calm, but there was a tightness at the corners of her mouth. "This is a tragedy in the making, and I can't stay to watch it unfold."

She looked away for a moment. "I'm going to Margo's in Galway for two weeks."

Then she leaned in and gave him one last kiss.

When she stepped back, her voice was firmer. "You'd better be gone when I get back."

By the following evening Geoff's head was still spinning - Patricia Dawson, Jill, Judge Dawson, Crotty, Jack, his business - round and round, never stopping. He was used to his mind racing. Guilt had always been part of that but this was different. His mind was looping. He hadn't slept a minute the night before as he was glued to Sky News, hoping for some positive update on Patricia Dawson.

Although he alone was a prisoner of his own mind, he had never been on his own. He was now truly desperate - with no one to talk to but Jack Dennis.

Geoff waited at the 15-bus shelter in Templeogue, pulling his coat tighter against the cold relentless drizzle. The streets of Dublin were soaked. He took his second-to-last cigarette from the pack he'd bought that morning, lit it with shaking hands, and unfolded the newspaper.

His breath caught.

There on the front page was Patricia Dawson. She stood beside her nineteen-year-old son, proudly holding up a tennis trophy.

The headline hit him hard:

Judge Dawson's wife, Patricia, fights for her life after being hospitalized in a critical condition.

Geoff felt a wave of nausea rise.

The sudden screech of tires jolted him.

A car pulled up sharply just a few feet away.

The passenger door swung open. AC/DC blared out onto the street. Without a word, Geoff climbed in.

"Need a towel?" Jack Dennis asked, with a crooked grin whilst turning down the volume.

Geoff gave a shake of his head as he ran his hands through his wet hair.

It had been months since they'd last seen each other, and Geoff was struck again by how massive Jack Dennis was even bigger than he remembered. The rolled-up sleeves of his navy jumper hugged his thick arms. Geoff could see the tattoos on his forearms - one of Phil Lynott, the other of Bon Scott from AC/DC. A fresh, nasty cut sliced across Phil Lynott.

"Well?" Jack said, eyes flicking toward Geoff.

"Well, you tell me," Geoff snapped, throwing the newspaper into Jack's lap.

Jack started the engine, glanced at the headline, and sighed. "It was an accident."

"There wasn't supposed to be an accident, Jack!" Geoff's voice broke. "No one was supposed to get hurt. You fucked it up. It's on every TV station." Jack's face darkened. Without warning, he slammed his Phil Lynott-tattooed arm hard against Geoff's throat and held it there, pinning him to the headrest.

"I said it was an accident," Jack growled. "The lads were turning the house over. She ran upstairs. It was me that followed. She tripped at the top. Hit her head. I was just telling her to stop running."

Geoff's mind raced, panic flooding his chest. The cut across Phil Lynott's arm was so close, just inches from his mouth. Geoff stared at the cut, panic rising in his chest. The pain in his neck no longer mattered. He clawed at the car door, gasping but Jack's grip only tightened. He watched in horror as the cut on Jack's arm started to seep blood and got closer to his mouth.

Suddenly the car skidded, tires squealing. Jack took his arm off of Geoff's throat to regain control, yanking the steering wheel with both hands.

Geoff slumped forward coughing but relieved. He trembled as he fumbled for his last cigarette.

"Mind if I...?" His voice was a rasp.

Jack pulled out his own pack, "Go ahead."

The two men sat in tense silence, smoke curling in the car as rain pattered on the roof. Finally, Jack turned into a service station car park and cut the engine.

"I'm sorry, Jack," Geoff murmured, voice shaky. "But... what do we do now?"

Jack rubbed his face, sighing heavily. "I'm no big-time crook – I'm small-time. But right now, the Gardaí are going ballistic. They're questioning everyone – even the big drug cartels. And now the cartels are pissed. There's too much heat. Those guys want to find us more than the cops do – and I'm more scared of them."

Geoff swallowed hard, "Do you think she'll live?"

Jack was quiet for a moment. "I don't know. It didn't look good. She was alive when I left. I called an ambulance. There was a lot of blood. I stayed with her a few minutes longer than I should've. But it was an accident."

Jack pulled out two more cigarettes, handed one to Geoff.

"It's not your fault," Jack said, exhaling slowly. "It's the judge's."

Geoff frowned. "The judge's?"

Jack's expression hardened. "Yeah. Judge Dawson's yellow to the core. "I've known so many people, in and out of court, over and over again but Crotty, he is a ruthless, dangerous bastard with no scruples. There's no way he should be walking free in six months."

"In a way, Geoff," Jack continued grimly, "your wife was lucky. Crotty wouldn't have hesitated to rape her. And he sure won't hesitate to come back to your house and try again."

"I'm a criminal, yeah – but Crotty? He's a psychopath. And that judge? If he was worth a damn, he'd have known that. How many times has Crotty appeared before a judge?"

"Thirty," Geoff whispered.

"Thirty we know about," Jack scoffed.

"Add another five hundred break-ins, beatings – whatever you like. That man's been a psycho his whole life."

Without a word, Geoff reached into his jacket and pulled out two thick envelopes. He tossed them onto the back seat.

"There's a hundred grand in there," he said quietly. "A deal's a deal. Even if it all went wrong."

Jack gave a slow nod. "Thanks, Geoff. That'll buy a good lawyer."

"If we don't get caught... what'll you do with the money?" Geoff asked.

"Well," Jack said, "first off, you need to stay strong. You need to hold your nerve. If you start falling apart, if you get scared, you call me."

He handed Geoff a small card and a burner phone.

"That's a new number. No one else has it. Use it if you need me."

Geoff turned the card over in his hand, heart pounding.

"And if... we stay free?" he asked again.

A faint smile tugged at the corner of Jack's mouth. "I've got a bit stashed away. With your money, maybe I'll open a legitimate business."

He gave Geoff a knowing look. "After all, we went to the same school."

"Did we?" replied Geoff.

"I was two years behind you." Jack chuckled softly. "Yeah, I realised that – just before I broke your arm."

Geoff let out a laugh.

"It would've been nice if you hadn't," he said, glancing at Jack.

Jack didn't smile. "Will you help me?"

"With what?" Geoff asked.

"The business," Jack said.

Geoff looked at him. Jack's face was serious – steady, unblinking. For a moment, Geoff didn't know whether to laugh or cry. He took a long drag of his cigarette, then scratched at his fledgling beard. He glanced back at Jack – still deadly serious – and felt a strange mix of surprise and reluctant affection.

"Yeah," he said at last, "why not, Jack?"

Orlaith Geaney

Orlaith is a breakout new addition who hails from Cork and has spent most of her life writing contemporary literature and slice of life realism. She'll admit she wavers through varying levels of productivity, but the result seems to be some thoughtful unconventional takes on anything from psychological fiction to the occasionally morbid comedy.

She ties back the themes of memory, rituals, and agonising time in our closing stories with 'Old Pains,' a chilling missing person's case told through a unique lens. This narrative moves from the sensationalised modern 'true crime' approach and instead focuses on the hell of daily life for those left waiting for answers.

Old Pains

"We think we're after finding Marian's bones back there in a ditch!"

The words are thrown at Bridie the moment she cracks open the front door. The deliverer of the news is flustered, panicked. He can't be more than nine or ten years old, dark hair plastered to his forehead with sweat, cheeks flushed pink from running. He's barely able to get the words out through heaving breaths, holding his arm stiff by his side, ready to strike.

Bridie's slippers peek over the threshold, half-inside, almost stepping out. Her heart starts to settle, pulse calming in her neck.

Just a child. A little boy.

Alarmed by her lack of urgency, the boy repeats: "Marian! She's back over there!"

The crunch of gravel up the drive signals someone else's approach. The boy is soon joined by another, older, and Bridie recognises him; her nephew's eldest, Colin, twelve years old and in that awful, awkward stage between sixth class and first year, the spitting image of his dad with his mop of curls and short stature.

Colin's panting too, trailing to a stop a few metres away from the door, giving himself a moment to catch his breath. From the look of him, Bridie would say he's arriving with the clear hope of fetching the younger boy and not the bones.

"Sorry Bridie," Colin huffs out, the failed supervisor of their outing.

The younger is gesturing again now, over his shoulder and back up the drive. "We need to go! She's over by the crossroads! In the ditch by the turn off to Dan Brady's!"

It's nearly a mile to the crossroads, so he's not pointing at anything in particular, hoping instead to inject some life into this hapless search effort.

However, as Bridie well knows, even if it *is* Marian down there in the ditch, this is not a matter of any considerable urgency.

Things move in slow motion now. There's a system, well-oiled and beaten into her.

Marian.

She'd been gone thirty-nine years, long before these boys were born. The younger's parents might not even have any memory of it, so long ago it was.

Marian's bones.

Bridie's daughter, her own eldest for sixteen years, who disappeared on her way to see a showband in a dance hall at the edge of town, dressed in her denim jacket and smelling, as she so often did, of her mam's perfume and cigarettes.

It was a beautiful August and Marian had announced her intention to walk to the crossroads or maybe a little further and thumb a lift from there, and there was no arguing with her since it wasn't even the first time she'd done it. It was such a mundane thing, like talking about the weather or arguing over school uniforms, so run-of-the-mill that Bridie hadn't even really acknowledged it, much less objected to it. She might have hummed something about behaving or something to make her feel like a real parent, but that was that. Off she went and she was gone.

These boys at her doorstep don't know all of that, though. They know what their parents told them: that there was a girl named Marian who went missing and nobody ever found her. That her poor mam Bridie lives in the farmhouse down the end of the lane and that she misses her so very much and is so sad to have never gotten her home.

"You were right to come to me," Bridie says then, finally addressing the two at her doorstep, putting the younger one out of his misery. Her voice is hoarse and it cracks as she speaks; it's the first time she's said anything aloud in a couple of days. "I'll call my son now, and he'll be down to check."

Colin nods, embarrassed. The younger frowns but stays silent.

She walks over to the landline and, fingers sore and arthritic, dials the number for her son Brendan.

He was fifteen when it happened, a retired garda now. Calls out twice a week to take out the bins and tidy up, and diligently comes to the house every time he is summoned.

He won't be happy about this, though. He doesn't much like the mention of Marian's name unless it's Christmas or her birthday and he's had something to drink. He'll toast to her and cry and Bridie cradles his head in her stiff old arms, he'll cough out tears and straighten up a few minutes later and that'll be it for another half-year.

He was much more involved in the searches at first. He knocked on doors and handed out flyers to people leaving Mass, drafted the pleas for information that were read out on the radio. Bridie didn't know how to do that side of things and was grateful for it at the time, though nothing materialised.

He organised the renewed campaigns for the fifth anniversary. Then the tenth, twentieth. No more after that.

It's what killed Dad, Brendan mumbled right before the twenty-first. He was right, of course, to say that. Bridie's husband had dropped dead of a heart attack before that first year was even out, having been summoned to look at some remains and it wasn't Marian, it was someone else's daughter who'd been in the water for a week and he couldn't tell who it was, not even the colour of her eyes, but it wasn't Marian. That was enough to finish him off, the idea that someday, some stranger might be summoned up the country to look at Marian, that they would feel that ugly relief he had at seeing the other girl.

"*Thank God, not her.*"

"Mam?" Brendan answers after the third ring. He never says *hello, how are you* or anything like that.

Bridie explains as gently as she can the circumstances preceding the call. He waits quietly until the end, though she can almost hear the words at the tip of his tongue.

"It's some plastic I'd say, Mam, or animal bones," he interjects eventually, and though he doesn't intend it, his response makes Bridie feel like a fool. "We've been down this road before – besides, they're just kids. They don't know what human bones look like."

But *he* does, through his work. Bridie knows that well. Therein lies the problem; they have to see for themselves.

More sighs break the lull in their conversation; sad ones, pitiful ones.

"I'll be down in twenty minutes, Mam," he mumbles, resigned. "Ring Seamus too."

Her neighbour Seamus is a farmer, fit and able. Handy for beating back hedgerows and lifting old logs. He's been on these excursions with them before, the three of them performing this routine, following tips that went nowhere out to beaches and ditches and hillsides.

For a while – for a good few years, actually – whenever a tip came in or they overheard some little rumour, they'd call the Gardaí first, wait for them to come down in all their hazmat finery and examine the scene for hours of prolonged and fruitless agony. They eventually learned to carry out a cursory scope themselves first, to rule out cruel pranks or a misidentified piece of driftwood or a poorly-buried pet dog. Brendan is – *was* – a Garda himself, so knows what to look for. Not strictly by the book, but saves them some pain. A little, at least.

Seamus arrives a few minutes after he's called, ducking in the door quietly, running a dirty hand through greying hair and saluting the boys as if they were grown men. He brought with him the daily paper as he sometimes does, setting it down on the kitchen table for Bridie to read later.

Only then does she invite the boys in, making the kitchen feel busier than it has been in some time. She has nothing fizzy for them to drink so offers a cup of tea and Colin accepts, but her hands aren't great today so Seamus makes it, knowing where the sugar and mugs are. He makes Bridie one too but it sits on the table, steaming, untouched.

Minutes of silence pass, interspersed with the sound of Colin slurping on the tea and the ticking of the clock on the call, before the roar of a motorcycle turns everyone's heads towards the drive.

Bridie is the last of them to get up, her knees locking but refusing a hand. Brendan ends up parking the bike and arriving through the door before she can get out to meet him.

Brendan. Tall, broad-shouldered, balding. Looks nothing like Marian, who took after her dad.

"Lads," he greets the boys, followed by a softer, "Mam," and a nod in her direction.

No use in drawing out anything. Brendan doesn't bother taking a seat or accepting some tea; instead, they all head out to pile into Seamus' jeep, the air thick with dust and the smell of wet hay.

Bridie in front, boys in the back, tailed by Brendan's motorcycle. A strange little motorcade.

The younger boy is relishing his moment in the limelight, directing proceedings with the pomp of a grand marshal. He guides Seamus down the drive, removing his seatbelt to lean over the headrest and point, though few actual directions are needed.

He's only young, though. Not his fault for not understanding. This is probably the most exciting thing to ever happen in his life.

A couple of minutes pass before they pull into the ditch by Dan Brady's – helpfully pointed out to them, and so, again, easy to find.

Seamus insists the boys stay in the jeep, which is wise. Belts are unbuckled and protests made but none of the adults relent, not until they scope out the scene first. The younger collapses back into his seat in a huff; Colin looks humiliated again.

Bridie allows Seamus to help her out of the jeep, both of their hands unsteady. Once she's got both slippers on the road, he asks if she'll stand by to watch for oncoming cars.

Bridie's turn to protest now.

"Fighting a losing battle there, Seamie," Brendan responds before Bridie can. "If you wouldn't mind keeping an eye out yourself, then Mam can stand over there with me," he gestures at the ditch with his chin, "and I'll have a look and see. Good man."

Unlike with the boys, there are no objections on Seamus' part.

Bridie takes up her position and watches as Brendan takes a hurl from the back of the jeep, starts beating back some of the gorse.

The hedge is thick, a heaving mass of yellow flowers and branched thorns. Not a nice resting place for Marian at all, at all. She preferred clothes in blues and whites – what would now be considered a Grecian aesthetic, but it was just *Marian* back then, all denim and white linen shirts. Some people in town would tease her for trying to dress like Madonna but most silently admired her for it, or so they told Bridie afterwards. Not that Marian minded much, of course. Took pride in her own style and her own ways. Didn't mind when other people copied her; was flattered by it, kind to those who tried to emulate her.

Bridie's eyes aren't great, but she still looks on as Brendan searches. Watches as her son unleashes targeted whacks against the shrubbery and she squints, thinking that she can maybe see something. There's a flash of something pale deep in the ditch – maybe the fabled bones, an untidy pile of something calcified amongst all the greenery.

She waits to recognise something. It should hit her, a burst of recognition she's spent decades chasing. She's not sure she'd even be able to identify the feeling at this point, but tries nonetheless.

Brendan is stepping deeper into the ditch now, holding up his arm to shield himself from the thorns. He angles his head, inspects the pale pile of somethings, and stays there for longer than he has done in a while.

Bridie's heart races. She forgets the aches in her joints. In a fleeting moment of madness, she even considers stepping down into the hedge with Brendan, all muck and dirt and briars surrounding them, just to be with her, to be within touching distance.

Brendan steps back up onto the side of the road. Sets down the hurl, dusts his hands off his work trousers. Moving too slowly for this to mean anything.

"A sheep," Brendan delivers the news with dignity, no desire to rub in the fact that he was right, as he often is. "Must've gotten stuck in the hedge or got hit by a car or something. Saw the yellow ear tag over there," he points for no reason, "stuck on one of the branches; Dan Brady was probably out here looking for it a few years ago."

Not Marian.

Makes sense, Bridie thinks. Didn't feel right. Surely, as complicated as things were – *are* – surely there'd still be some flicker of a feeling deep inside her to tell her that Marian was so close by.

There's no such hope.

No, the most likely scenario is that someone saw Marian that evening, wanted her, and took her, before throwing her away somewhere far up the country, granting her less dignity than a passing motorist gave that sheep in the hedge.

Now, Bridie is left to go home again, repeating this sad ritual every year or so in perpetuity. Or maybe today's the last – she's getting old, after all. Like her husband, she dreads the twisted relief that this would bring.

Now, Bridie must turn back around, inform Seamus and disappoint the boys, smile and pat their heads and tell them they were still right to tell her.

Must scold herself for getting back in this way. A silent reprimanding when she gets home, to remind herself to ask the messenger more questions next time before calling Brendan.

She's not sure which would be worse: this happening again like it just did, or not.

Lorna Keane

Lorna writes hypnotically gloomy fiction and is the steadfast founder of Stoney Writers Group. Intrigued by themes of adolescence, identity and feminism, her writing emphasises the tension between the fleeting beauty and everyday hardships of Irishness. She studied literature and spent some of her academic life in Paris, studying her favourite French authors – and many of the pubs that inspired them.

In the spirit of changing seasons, our final stories turn from autumnal demons to midsummer muses. In 'Nell Bowen,' a local woman's death sends ripples through a small town during a peculiarly hot Irish summer, and a young girl, battling her own demons, develops a fixation that reshapes her innocence.

Nell Bowen

It was the summer Nell Bowen threw herself from the roof of her house. A stifling heat clung to us all after, as if she wouldn't let go of the island. The whole town seemed to move slower than usual, trapped in a heavy hue of airlessness; lethargic and zombie-like. The air felt dead, the sun relentless.

I knew little of her really, so I'm sure my obsession seems strange to you now. I'd bump into her at Tom's Bakery where she'd buy fresh loaves of sourdough, sometimes a plain croissant or a cinnamon roll. Other days I'd watch her go into Mahon's Butchers and come out with several small packages of meat that she'd bundle into the bottom of the buggy, one package at a time. She never seemed to be without that buggy. That summer I'd caught her once or twice down by the pier too. She'd sit on the bench closest to the water, buggy to one side, staring out to sea in trance as if somehow able to block out the deafening screams coming from the nearby amusements.

I never heard her speak, but the most I imagined she mustered was a "hello", a "thanks", or a nod of the head. Perhaps that's why people didn't think much of her. "Always in a hurry that one", Mrs Rafferty would say under muffled breath as she rushed past. I wondered why she hurried so much since she had no job and stayed home all day with the children. We didn't know how she filled her time. We knew very little in fact, except that she was beautiful.

Her long coffee-brown hair was littered with grey, matted and unruly, but that didn't matter since her face was so perfect. She had these high cheekbones that were layered in a deep pink, and a pointed chin that accentuated her rosebud mouth and full lips, big and bare. Her olive skin glowed noticeably among the milk-skinned locals. On the few occasions I glimpsed her large almond-shaped eyes, they were lined in a thick black - the kind a teenager would wear. Dark blue I think they were. Green maybe.

I envied her, and then I was haunted by her.

Talk moved fast from the insufferable heat to her suicide and for a time the little town was ensnared in a whirlpool of stories about what happened, glorified of course for dramatic effect. One story told of how she was impaled on the egg-white picket fence that lined the narrow driveway. Another we assumed to be true involved her remains being found in the perfect rockery to the front of the house – blood speckled across the carefully planted purples, blues and pinks Dr Corcoran was so proud of.

He was a physician you see. A reputable one too. So he knew how to handle her, Mam said. She'd tried to leave him once or twice, but she was what she called a dreamer, a flight risk. She mused that was why she never took the Corcoran name. It was a sickness, Mam said, and a dangerous one, to dream as much. "The grass is greener where you water it", she'd say.

"She was off her fuckin' head."

Liam was sitting with his back to the wall of the old fort, bare legs outstretched in the grass in front of him. His pale, freckled skin was almost translucent against the rich green. I had been careful to keep my distance, sitting cross-legged a few meters away, yanking my denim shorts down over my bare thighs.

We'd cycled to the highest point on the island like we had every evening that week. Reaching it by bike meant following the winding dirt path that made a slow incline all the way to the top. Sweat dripped from my face like melting ice as we mounted the steep hills, past the endless fields of green and brownish-yellow on either side. Swarms of tourists were gathered in tight pockets along the sea bed below as we zig-zagged around the large pot-holes littering the way to the old fort. It's there most of all I remember our conversations of Nell Bowen that dominated that summer as the unusual heat droned on.

"Know why it's called Kyteler's peak?" I asked, ignoring his comment.

"Wasn't it after a witch?" Seán was too close to me, lying flat on his back using his hands as a pillow. I winced as I felt the short blonde hairs on his leg brush against me.

"Yeah, Alice Kyteler." I was pulling blades of grass out of the soil and forming a neat pile between my knees. "It wasn't proven she was an actual witch. She was accused alright, and they tried to kill her. She escaped though. Ended up here."

"Oh yeah. Didn't she poison a load of husbands?"

I wished Seán would stop talking. It was Liam I wanted to speak, but he stayed silent, leaning on his bent knee as he stared out to sea.

"We're surrounded by mad women, Liam. We ought to be careful, man". He snorted loudly as I flicked a few blades of grass towards his face. "My da says the same about Bowen though. Daft as a fuckin' brush."

Seán always repeated what Liam said, as if he never had a thought of his own.

"Apparently she was normal enough when she was younger", I said sheepishly. "Like at school and stuff."

"Oh sure didn't your dad hook up with her once, Ray?" Liam had turned to look at me with a half-smile. "Lucky bastard."

They both laughed. I liked it when Liam called me Ray. There was an air of affection to it that wasn't lost on me.

"That's a load of shite, sure he thinks she was nuts too."

I wasn't sure why I felt the need to reaffirm her madness, but I did. In truth I knew little of Dad's romance with Nell Bowen. Only that they were close for a time when they were sixteen or so – not much older than we were that summer. The morning the news of her death came to our door, I heard him sob softly to himself after retreating into the conservatory with the Sunday Times under his arm. He told me that evening as he swirled a huge ice cube in his whiskey glass that he'd always known she was more than what we made her – than this island made her.

"Conformity is the jailer of freedom", he'd said.

The sun was retreating, making its way towards the vast sea that stretched out in front of us, ready to be eaten by the dark. I longed for the bright orange hues to stay a little longer as the threatening purples and pinks swarmed overhead. The few luminous blue clouds that lingered were clumped together like scrambled eggs on a clean plate. The only sounds came from the distant chatter of the townspeople below and the piercing calls of the seagulls overhead.

I wanted the conversation to shift to something other than Nell Bowen. It was enough that thoughts of her dominated my sleep. Ever since that night, shadows had crept through my room when the hour was at its darkest, hissing at me from invisible corners. They would strip me bare and rattle my insides like a lamb ready for slaughter.

They were familiar to me of course, these shadows. But I had enjoyed such a splendid pause from their visits that their return was a deeply troubling thing. I'd started running again to stave them off, rising at the crack of dawn and sprinting the long stretch of sand along the sea bed until pain coursed through my legs and blood oozed from the cracked soles of my feet. I savoured the burn that seared through me after. It was the same one I craved in the thick of night as I lay on the rug by my bed and did as many crunches as I could muster before returning to sleep satisfied – a dull ache ripping through my abdomen.

"What kind of mother would do that to her kids anyway?" Seán had a suddenly sombre expression.

"Selfish bitch."

"Jesus Seán. Calm down there, man", Liam chuckled as he threw his eyes up to the sky.

"You know what I mean like. A fuckin' mother."

I was too embarrassed to ask why it was so much worse for a mother to end her life in such a way.

"Ah she was hardly much of a mother like." It surprised me how Liam uttered the words with such certainty.

"Couldn't handle the kids", Mam said. No interest in GAA or nothin' like that."

I wondered who she bought all the cinnamon rolls for if she was such a bad mother. Then I thought of the other mothers who congregated at the school gates every morning to swap recipes and tales of poor Mary Dowling from down the road whose boys had swanned off to Australia leaving her all alone with her bad hips. Or Breda Smith, the new teacher from the mainland who'd been spotted in a car with a man who wasn't her husband. I thought of the fundraiser for the GAA club they'd held last month and the endless spread of perfect cupcakes baked from scratch in every colour. Homemade scones with blueberry and raisin; rhubarb and apple crumble, sprinkled with icing sugar.

A loud groan escaped my stomach.

"Jesus Ray, will ya eat somethin' for fuck's sake!"

My cheeks burned as the two boys erupted into frenzied laughter.

"Fuck you." My voice cracked a little and the laughter stopped. The fact that Liam had said it hurt more than I cared to admit. I wanted the long patch of grass we were sitting on to swallow me whole, like the way Mrs Lynch would swallow every chocolate from a box of Butlers, one after another without a second thought. I wondered how many grams of fat would be in each one and decided to look it up later. My mind jumped from this to breakfast the following morning and how I might switch my oats for cauliflower without Mam noticing.

"I'd say she always had a darkness in her though." Seàn sat up, pulling his knees towards him. "You could tell by the eyes."

I averted my gaze and focused my attention on the imposing cliffs across the way, filled with all the secrets of the town below. The boys seemed to relish in the mystery of her. Something wild and untamed they needed to understand or control – which, I wasn't sure.

We'd cycled past the house on the way here, stopping on the opposite side of the road mid-way up the hill to peer over the big stone wall and the steel gates. It was as dark as it had been the day the family left, leaving half their belongings behind. Only the attic window was visible from where we looked on – the one we presumed she'd used to climb onto the roof. I wondered why she chose to do it that way rather than taking pills. It seemed like an easier and cleaner way out, though less certain perhaps. We paused in silence, staring up at nothing. I pictured her standing on the edge of the roof in a long satin robe and little else, mad with power.

"Apparently she fancied herself a bit of an artist. Sure the arty ones are always nuts."

"Oh is that right Seán?" Liam sneered. "And how the fuck would you know?"

"Sure everyone knows that", Seán rebuked. "Mustn't 'a been much of an artist though. They left all her stuff behind."

A strange despair crept through me as I pictured a big empty basement with half-finished paintings strewn across the concrete floor, riddled with mouse droppings.

"Maybe she was just really sad." I felt small and pathetic as I uttered the words and immediately wanted to take them back.

"Sure what did she have to be fuckin' sad about, Ray?" Liam's eyes were fixed on me now as he spoke with a new assertiveness.

"Fine house like that. And sure he must'a made a mint. Treatin' every fucker on the island and overchargin' every single one of 'em."

"True", I nodded with a faint smile, eyes fixed to the ground. I felt more exposed than I had the night Liam kissed me in the field behind my house and shoved his hand down my jeans. Things had been different since. He'd been different. Perhaps he'd solved the mystery of me and was done, or my complications scared him off. Whatever the reason, I was thankful to Nell Bowen for plunging to her death that week and bringing us back together. The tension between us was obvious I think, though my anxious heartbeat would often tell me lies.

A blood-orange light disrupted the moment, dazzling us with its brilliance as the sun made its final descent. The entire sky lit up as if someone had set it on fire. I longed to stay there, cooking in its heat. It seemed to ease the cramps rising like giant waves in my belly, though I enjoyed pushing them back down. Moments later, the fiery sun disappeared leaving us alone in the pale blue twilight with nothing but our desperate thoughts and frail bodies.

I felt the prickly hairs on my bare arms and knew I'd soon be home, fearful of tomorrow. Mam would have left two pills on my bedside table and I'd take each one, patiently praying for sleep but knowing it wouldn't come. And I'd lie there waiting for my midnight caller and the voices telling me to move, or purge. I always felt relief after a purge, even if it meant giving in. I hated the feeling of food, haplessly devoured, sitting heavy inside me.

Before long it would be 6am and the same sun would reappear to suffocate us again and I would relive the same day. I would run the same shoreline until my body begged for mercy; I would carefully consume the same select foods and lie and cheat my way through all four meals of the day; I would push the voices down and think of little other than Nell Bowen in her final moments. A broad smile stretched across her lovely face as she leapt from the roof of her house in a gleeful surge towards freedom. And how I envied her.

"Right lads. I'm off."

Seán yanked himself up from the grass with an exaggerated sigh and headed towards his bike, leaving Liam and I alone in the eerie light that lingered. I felt naked, cold. My heart threatened to burst out of my chest. An unnatural silence strangled me and I prayed he would speak first. I wanted him to scooch closer until our legs were touching. I wanted him to lie with his head in my lap like he used to. I wanted him to apologise for his weirdness and to tell me it was simply because he liked me too much. I felt his eyes on me, and they stayed that way for a long time.

"I may head on too, sure. You ok headin' back on your own?"

The words hung heavy, like a desperate thirst. Something huge seemed to pummel me from the inside.

"Yeah, no worries."

I felt him move further from me as he walked towards the little gate, untied his bike and cycled away. I was careful not to move an inch or even breathe too loud. I stayed there until the sky turned from purple to black and stars were peppered across the night like heaps of tiny diamonds, ground up and spit out. It was here I'd be stuck – in this defining moment. On that forlorn hilltop above that wretched little town, unforgiving. Dancing untamed with the ghosts of Alice and Nell. Remnants of women gone mad before me.

Jack Kennedy

Jack is an acclaimed talent, returning with his signature style of restless narration and mordant humour. His work captures the tensions of an ordinary life pushed to the edge of the surreal. He is the winner of the Seán Ó Faoláin International Short Story Competition 2024, and has been published in Southward, The Storms and New Irish Writing. As clinical biochemist, he writes best in the staff lunch canteen, influenced by authors such as Kevin Barry, Otessa Mosfegh and Eliza Clarke.

In closing this compendium from lush harvests to barren deserts, 'Uncaring Continent' confronts the cold indifference of isolation. Along California's Central Valley, a man estranged by the loss of his parents drifts through desert highways as bleak as his sense of belonging. Comparing private grief with exploitation, it poses the question: what do we do when 'home' is lost?

Uncaring Continent

He began to think of the town as an open-air prison. Squat bungalows like cells, arranged along dimly lit streets. Chain mesh fences choking small patches of parched grass. Police cruisers circling lazily in the hot night.

No one walked anywhere. Seemingly every service was available in drive-thru form: coffee, food, drugs. An insular vehicular people, hidden behind darkened windscreens. He began wondering if there was anyone in these vehicles at all, or if they were empty and on auto pilot. Spinning around in the night for his benefit. To maintain some charade. He was willing to recognize this was not a healthy notion, but nevertheless struggled to dissuade himself from it.

He did not make inroads with the locals. He had attempted to be social in the places that passed for pubs but the people he chatted to invariably seemed reluctant to reciprocate. Their conversational reticence indicated by a flared nostril, an arched eyebrow, a swift exit. The period of his solitude had become so long as to become self-perpetuating. His loneliness terminal.

He began to wonder why he had chosen this town out of all the other towns spread like stars across the continental United States. On leaving home, he had assumed he wanted to be someplace completely different to his birthplace. His theory at the time being that it would be easier to start a new life someplace unrecognizable, a place where he would see scant reminders of his homeplace and all that came with it.

Yet this difference simply made him crave his home more. The rolling hills, the damp green fields, the windy roads that led to nowhere. The house, filled with his mother's delicate voice, his father's chortling laughter, the crackle of the fire in the grate and the wind that whooshed through the chimney. Everything outside the kitchen window black, as if the three of them were in orbit over the world rather than stuck on its surface.

Of course, home was no longer an option available to him so he would have to find a suitable substitute. He was like a speck of pollen blown into some barren wilderness in which he was incapable of taking root.

So he elected to pack up his car. His few earthly belongings (clothes, books, toiletries) arranged neatly in the boot, in plastic boxes. His bank account still in the high six digits. The car full of gas. The decision was made suddenly. He fled the town and its environs like some fugitive on the hot desert night.

The town rolled past his window. Bungalows giving way to warehouses and car dealerships and RV liquidation centres giving way to lonely prairie. Yellow grasses swayed in the breeze, dancing to the rhythm of the wind. A dun-coloured moon hung over it all, aglow with a supernatural intensity. The headlamps flaring in the eyes of an occasional startled cow. Little signs of habitation: a liminal wilderness incapable of sustaining human life.

The radio hissed static. He turned the dial, the white noise oscillating in response. Eventually, he'd tune into something: some far out country music station, a late-night talk show, or some demented insomniac evangelical, preaching hellfire and repentance and paradise. Until then, any sound was preferable to silence.

Morning found him in a dusty town identical to the one he had fled. In an iHop, he scoffed down an egg's benedict and a milky, sugary tea. Builders' tea, as his mother would call it. The sweet taste like a little cup of home.

He drove on until evening, seeing little benefit in lingering in such similar surroundings.

He took his dinner in a Carl's Junior a few hundred miles down the freeway. Cars parked outside, hidden occupants chomping their burgers and slurping their colas in the wheeled extensions of their own homes.

He didn't want to eat in his car, so instead knocked on the front door. The server unlocked it for him, visibly shocked by his desire to sit in and eat his guacamole bacon burger on the scuffed Formica. He attempted to watch the television mounted on the wall, but the TV seemed to bleed in and out of different channels at random. A snippet of the Simpsons followed by a wailing baby in some far off or nearby warzone or natural disaster followed by news footage of burning forests followed by a glimpse of what he took to be an aureole followed by searchlights swooping dramatically over the 21st Century Fox logo. With every glimpse of the Simpsons family, he was flung back the decades: for a brief moment he'd be a boy again, reclined on the leather sofa. Smell of dinner from the kitchen, the racket of pots and pans pulled from cupboards, the chatter of his parents over the RTÉ news.

Were the staff fucking with him? The lone man behind the counter seemed not to notice, instead talking incessantly into his headset rig. 'What can I get for you today... Do you want fries with that... What would you like to drink... Is there anything else I can get for you today...' Would the man see what he was seeing? Or was it just him who found the images fluttering across the screen so jumbled and incomprehensible? Was it the receiver or the viewer that was faulty? He did not know. He had wanted to ask but did not.

Night found him in a motel on the edge of nothing. The heat outside brain scrambling. The ice machine 'out of odor', according to the note duct taped to its rusty exterior. Creaking bed springs, muffled moans, stifled groans.

There were women in the motel courtyard. Idling, chatting to each other, smoking cigarettes. He felt their eyes on him as he passed, but he just stared at his ratty Reeboks. One of them called after him, a taunting, coquettish tone to her voice. He fled from them, into the privacy of his room.

Amber light seeped through the shutters, distorted by the spinning ceiling fan. Forming and dissolving and reforming on the wall. He laid on the bed, flicked on the television. He closed his eyes and hoped the newscaster's soothing voice would lull him to sleep but it did not. At length, he rose and tied his laces and left the room.

He found the vending machine. Bare shelves greeted him.

'Hola baby.' She grinned at him. Olive skin, dark hair, an insincere smile. Tight denim shorts and a loose black tank top.

He looked at the empty shelves and shook his head.

'Thirsty baby?' Her hand ran along the inside of his arm, leaving a trail of risen follicles and goosebumps. A subsequent stirring in his slacks, an impulse for something that he knew would do him no good.

'¿Cuánto cuesta?'

It didn't matter if the love he received was fake, since the only other option was the absence of love entirely. The artifice of affection preferable to the ache of its absence.

After he had finished, what had seemed desirable became merely squalid. He was acutely aware of the stuffy room, the stained bedsheets, the tang of their genital secretions. The false smile she wore on her face.

'Baby...'

After a few moments, her fingertips lightly pushed him off. His member flaccid, like a leech attached to his pelvis. She rose and began to collect her clothes.

'Where are you from?'

'Mexico baby, but you already knew that. Por supuesto.'

'What brought you here?'

She turned to face him. Her body in silhouette against the streetlight that seeped through the shutters. A presence like an absence. A person shaped void.

'Do you really want to know that?'

He could not see her expression, but the tone of her voice had changed. No longer theatrically accented and flirtatious, instead curiously flat.

'I suppose I do, yeah.'

The ceiling fan swirled above them. Beds creaked. Shrieks were silenced by sweaty palms or stained pillows. Money changed hands.

An outreach of intimacy. An attempt at achieving something real. Or simply prolonging the simulacrum.

'It's a long story baby,' she said, with a trace of her earlier coquettishness, 'it'll cost you.'

He pulled out his wallet.

She laid down beside him, her body striped in the light that bled through the shutters. Brown eyes aglint. He put his head on his chest, and she curled her arm under his chin. His legs latched onto her body. Slowly, she rubbed his cheek, and began to speak.

They snatched her from the roadside when she was 13 years old. Dressed in her school uniform, chaste in a blue dress and white shirt. A crucifix dangling from her neck.

The country was invisible from the interior of the van. The two men watched her, expressions inscrutable. She had screamed at first, but a slap had put a stop to that.

She was deposited in a house on the outskirts of a city. There were other girls, some her age and some older and some younger.

There were rooms with mattresses on the floor. There were men and women who would show her what she had to do in this new, uncertain world.

They flew her over the border. The price is better, they said. She recalled sitting in the plane, terrified as it accelerated off the runway. The void in her stomach as she watched the brown landscape below them recede; her homeland consumed by clouds.

Passing through the airport, she looked like just another child on vacation. Wearing a pretty summer dress, a crucifix on her neck, clutching a teddy bear. They hustled her through the airport, past indifferent security guards and distracted travellers.

They left her in a roadside establishment surrounded by desolate scrubland. It was uncomfortable at first, but eventually it became routine. The girls would all rise early and wash themselves and apply their make-up and pull up their stockings and squeeze into their dresses. Then, the customers would arrive, and she would do whatever was asked of her, and after a time some things that were not. Her crucifix hidden in the bedside drawer until the final client had left.

She was not supposed to accept tips, but she did after a time. All the girls did. She loosened a floorboard in her room with a man's penknife while he dozed and began to squirrel away her money. Slowly, she discovered each of her clients' peculiarities. There were ones that wanted her to moan and ones that wanted her to scream and ones that wanted her to be silent and still as a corpse. Sometimes, they would want her to pretend she was someone else, perhaps a person from their lives that they were unable to touch. It ceased to matter to her. All that mattered was the cash.

A wheezing, whiskered old man took a particular shine to her. His father was a dirt-poor farmer, who through the miracle of the American Dream and the presence of petroleum beneath his property had become a multi-millionaire overnight. The father drank himself to death, leaving a sizable inheritance to the son. Now, the son's primary occupation was being professionally wealthy, paying legions of lawyers and accountants to dodge tax and generate more wealth through shrewd investments, enabling him to live a life of excess and lechery. He was wide and dominant and nearly crushed her with his bulk.

He tipped well so she did not mind.

'How much it cost to buy her?'

He was quoted the usual price, inflated due to his obvious wealth.

'I don't mean rent, I mean buy. B-U-Y.'

'She's not for sale.'

The old man chuckled and pulled out his cheque book.

Once again, she was spirited away, though this time in a vintage cherry Mustang rather than a windowless van. Something that was not exactly freedom, but maybe closer to it than before. She looked out the window placidly, watching the oil derricks bob and penetrate the Earth for her mineral wealth, and tried not to worry about the stash of bills she had secreted away in her articles of clothing.

In his mansion, she was assigned a room. A double bed, a 45-inch plasma TV, and an ensuite, but beneath all this luxury she was just as confined. There were no windows. The door was locked.

'Welcome home darlin,' he said, as he unbuttoned his jeans.

He showered her with gifts. Lingerie. Short skirts and high heels. Schoolgirl uniforms. When she was not with him, she watched the television or was accompanied on walks around the property by the Oil Magnate's personal security force. He insisted she went outside in the sunlight. 'Wouldn't want ye lookin too wan,' he chuckled. She attempted to converse with the guards on these strolls yet was always met with monosyllabic answers or gruff silence. Clad in bulletproof vests, armed with fully automatic rifles, numbed to the banality of human suffering in whatever lurid forms it could manifest.

The days passed. The seasons swung schizophrenically, the scorching summers giving way to freezing winters. The years accumulated. Then, one morning, she got violently sick. The Oil Magnate had never bothered with protection. He got a doctor to check her out after he had acquired her, and besides he always had assumed he was too old to bear children.

She elected not to tell him of her discovery. She went about her days as before, whilst in the core of her a life slowly began to take shape.

One day, the Oil Magnate ran his hand over her belly and frowned. He stood up and left the room and did not trouble her for the rest of the night.

The next morning, she ate her breakfast. She was not brought for her daily walk. She ran her hands over the small bump in her belly and frowned. Lunch arrived. Then, dinner. Just as she slid into bed, the door opened.

'Vamos.'

They hustled her into a van and out to a doctor's surgery. Wearing a plastic gown, she was ushered onto a chair, and instructed to place her legs in the stirrups. Metal implements gleamed in the white aseptic light. The doctor twisted the valve on a canister till the hiss of gas was audible from the mouthpiece.

'Buenas sueñas Sen-'

A bedpan collided with his liver spotted head and he crumpled like autumn leaves. She dropped the bedpan and sat on his chest and held the respirator to his mouth until his feet ceased struggling for purchase and his flailing arms fell flat on the linoleum.

She fled into the hot desert night. A furnace heat smothering the dusty town. Wads of bills in her pockets. A scalpel in her hand. She did not know where she was or where she was going. She ran and ran until she came to what passed for downtown. Taxi's idled outside a stretch of neon lit bars. She approached a car and calmly entered the backseat.

'¿A dónde vas?'

'Lejos de aquí.'

In the motel room, the ceiling fan whooshed overhead. Cicadas hummed in the hot desert night. He listened to the tha-thump of her heart: stout and resolute.

'Why do you still do this?'

'What, baby?'

'This. With people like me.'

'School fees. Tutors. College when the time comes. This is just my side hustle. Mostly, I wait tables.'

'How do you cope?'

'I just do. That girl of mine is all that matters.'

'What about your home? Your family?'

'She's my family now, and if I cross that border there's no guarantee I'm getting back over it again. Sometimes you gotta let go of everything you had to try and grab what you got. Home isn't a place: it's the people you chose to spend your life with.'

His mouth opened, and he began to speak. A torrent, unstoppable once it started.

Home. His mother and father. Their slow but unstoppable decrepitude. The years spent caring for them: cooking for them and cleaning up after them and getting them their newspapers and bringing them for walks. His mother's sudden death in the night. His father's rapid decline afterward as if her absence were an untreatable abscess.

After the father went, he did not know what to do. Pictures of them everywhere, mementos of their time together, the life they shared that had come to an end. He had cared for them and minded them as they slowly crumbled to dust and after his father's funeral he sat alone in the rambling mansion and looked around at the life they had shared together and knew if he never left he would never stop wishing for it back. That the only option left open to him was to sell the house and flee.

Flee to what though? Towards what? He knew he was not really running towards anything; he was simply running. That his flight had no endpoint. Once he arrived in a simulacrum of his homeplace, it would be the same as before: he would fail to settle, fail to make a home. Instead, this place would be a prison: like the town he had left, like a room with no windows and a locked door. Like a life defined by what has happened, rather than by what will happen.

When the flood ceased, he was silent. All he heard was the tha-thump of her heart, the gentle whisper of her breath. Such was its consolation that his eyes grew heavy and-

Morning found him in a motel many miles from home.

She was gone: the only evidence of her presence was his lighter wallet, their shared secretions that stained the sheets.

Sunlight sliced through the shutters. Already, the heat was unbearable.

He sat behind the wheel of his vehicle. The road ahead of him quivered as if it were not entirely solid. He turned the key in the ignition and heard the engine rev to life and with a heavy heart set the nearest international airport as his destination. The sodden fields, rainy summers, stodgy dinners beckoned him, and for all the fear that bloomed inside him he felt a curious kick of life.

About us

Stoney Writers Group *is a Dublin neighbourhood troupe, founded by author Lorna Keane and brought to life by its sixty contributing members, Irish and international authors and poets. We carry a mission to celebrate independent writing by fostering a community of shared creativity. We believe modern literature thrives when diverse styles and identities are given a safe space to shine.*

PC Studios Publishing, *founded by publisher Paul Carreo, is an independent press dedicated to developing bold new voices for contemporary writing. PC Studios promotes emerging writers by sponsoring local art communities as inclusive centres for peer-to-peer excellence.*

For more information, look us up at meetup.com or contact the publisher at www.paulcarreo.com.

Printed in Dunstable, United Kingdom

67513784R00163